Were her eyes playing tricks on her?

Trudy re-read the name on the driver's license: Regret James. What kind of name was that? Surely a misprint.

Five foot eleven and striking green eyes. She calculated his age from the birth date given: thirty-one to her twenty-eight.

She flipped through the rest of the wallet and found three credit cards, a pilot's license, an insurance card and almost fifty dollars in cash. Under the last flap was a foil-wrapped condom. It hadn't been there long enough to crease the leather, and certainly not since he'd been a hormone-driven sixteen-year-old. *So, R.J. is a man of the world,* she mused. She thought of his strong hands brushing against hers. The foil package wasn't meant for show. For a man called Regret, it was intended for use....

Dear Reader,

The weather's hot, and here at Intimate Moments, so is the reading. Our leadoff title this month is a surefire winner: Judith Duncan's *That Same Old Feeling*. It's the second of her Wide Open Spaces trilogy, featuring the McCall family of Western Canada. It's also an American Hero title. After all, Canada is part of North America—and you'll be glad of that, once you fall in love with Chase McCall!

Our Romantic Traditions miniseries continues with *Desert Man,* by Barbara Faith, an Intimate Moments-style take on the ever-popular sheikh story line. And the rest of the month features irresistible reading from Alexandra Sellers, Kim Cates (with a sequel to *Uncertain Angels,* her first book for the line) and two new authors: Anita Meyer and Lauren Shelley.

In months to come, look for more fabulous reading from authors like Marilyn Pappano (starting a new miniseries called Southern Knights), Dallas Schulze and Kathleen Eagle—to name only a few. Whatever you do, don't miss these and all the Intimate Moments titles coming your way throughout the year.

Yours,

Leslie J. Wainger
Senior Editor and Editorial Coordinator

Please address questions and book requests to:
Silhouette Reader Service
U.S.: 3010 Walden Ave., P.O. Box 1325, Buffalo, NY 14269
Canadian: P.O. Box 609, Fort Erie, Ont. L2A 5X3

A MAN
CALLED
REGRET

Lauren
Shelley

Published by Silhouette Books

America's Publisher of Contemporary Romance

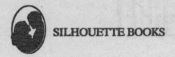 SILHOUETTE BOOKS

ISBN 0-373-07582-0

A MAN CALLED REGRET

Copyright © 1994 by Lorna Tedder

This edition published by arrangement with Harlequin Enterprises B. V.

® and TM are trademarks of Harlequin Enterprises B. V., used under license. Trademarks indicated with ® are registered in the United States Patent and Trademark Office, the Canadian Trade Marks Office and in other countries.

Printed in U.S.A.

LAUREN SHELLEY

grew up in tiny Donalsonville, Georgia, picking mayhaw berries and honeysuckle where her ancestors
walked one hundred and fifty years ago. Although
Lauren escaped small-town life to become a contract
negotiator for the Department of Defense, she could
never escape writing about the deep South, its strong
women and its hunky rabble-rousers. Lauren now lives
in Niceville, Florida—another small Southern town
with her husband and two little girls.

For my mother, Katie Tedder,
whose love of nature and generosity of spirit
were my inspiration for Trudy

Chapter 1

"*Regret!*" He could still hear his mother's exasperated screech. "*Regret James, you get down from that tree this minute! You can't fly!*"

Regret. He grimaced, fists tightening around the grooved steering bars of his little Cessna 152. No one called him that. Not anymore. Not since he'd turned eighteen. Not since thirteen years ago when he'd disappeared into the sultry Georgia night to start a new life. Why had he thought of her now—now after all these years?

He dipped the wing of the two-seater airplane to the left to get a better look at the lush countryside below. He'd never before seen the South Georgia farmland from the air. The long rectangles laced with new green of crops and brown circles cut by irrigation systems made the land below look more like a grandmother's quilt than rolling terrain. High above the two-dimensional surface, he thought he could smell the newly turned dirt below.

Ah, the Southland in the springtime. He smiled to himself. And the best time of year to make a buck.

Brushing the blond curls off the bridge of his nose, he raised his binoculars to his eyes and scanned the scattering of buildings directly ahead. This farm was different from the others he'd seen in the area. For one thing, its hues were more vivid than those of the farms around it. Fuchsia azaleas flanked the white farmhouse, and in the front yard, majestic white dogwoods dripping with purple wisteria lined the dirt drive. The house seemed sturdy, maybe recently painted, but the barns and rickety tin-roofed sheds along the perimeter of the yard had missed their prime by more than a generation. Chuckling out loud, he could almost picture that farm in a magazine—and the check that would precede publication.

The second thing he noticed was the broad strip of pine trees east of the house. One long clearing scarred the woods. As he drew closer, the clearing turned pale green in the light haze. He saw dots of lazy black cows at the far end.

Lowering his binoculars, he checked his altimeter and dropped to two hundred feet, skimming the treetops. He dumped the binoculars in his lap and picked up the telephoto camera, firing off a quick succession of shots. Again he dipped the plane to the left, focusing at a new angle and using his knees to steer.

A picture may be worth a thousand words, he thought, but it's even better if it's worth a thousand *dollars!*

The third thing he noticed was the woman. If it hadn't been for her, he probably would have taken a couple of pictures of the farm and flown right over. The Florida-Georgia state line wasn't far. He'd planned to head down to the Gulf of Mexico beaches for a few days of sunshine before he turned back toward Atlanta. He'd need to call his client in the next few hours and warn the company of what he'd seen near Johnson's Creek. He dared not radio the information to the nearest tower. If anyone else on the same frequency heard of the impending disaster, all hell would break loose across South Georgia. But they would be okay for now—as long as it didn't rain.

Again the woman caught his eye, and he forgot all about his job.

She wasn't his type. Not that he had a type. He'd never been involved with a woman long enough to develop any sort of comparison. And if he did have a type, then it was probably that oh-so-common variety of she-devil who sat—

ready to molt—in a skintight dress and leg-lengthening high heels on a bar stool, cigarette dangling from her painted lips, a strong-smelling concoction in her taloned grip.

No, this country nymph was nothing at all like the women who had seasoned his life in the past. Her dress was a floral print, loose and flowing in the breeze. Instead of a cocktail in her hand, she held a small trowel as she toyed with something in her garden. She was sitting cross-legged on the ground, her dark hair tumbling onto her face. He could tell she was barefoot. And that she was pretty.

Expectantly she jumped up, turning her face toward the skies and shielding her eyes from the sunshine with the back of her hand. For a moment, she turned back to her garden and gestured for something there to join her. Then a child, who barely reached the gathered waistline of her dress, ran to the woman's side. The two of them waved cheerfully at his airplane as Regret soared overhead.

He waved back, although he knew they couldn't see him in the cockpit. He smiled at them, the woman and child dressed alike in loose frocks, the same dark hair. But the woman who had caught his eye earlier suddenly seemed so young. As they went back to their work and play, he decided that she was probably just a teenager taking care of her baby sister.

Gunshots spattered across the tin roof of the barn.

"Dulcie? Dulcie!" Dropping her basket of spring strawberries, Trudy scrambled to her feet. Her two-year-old had been there only a moment before, running in circles in the backyard and pretending to be a tyrannosaurus rex.

"Mommy!" A thin wail rose from behind a trellis. Dulcie was crouched behind a huge, pink rosebush, staring at the sky where the airplane had been only moments before. Her bottom lip trembled.

A second round of lead pelted on the tin roof of a nearby shed, then thudded like soft rain over the shingles of the house. Another discharge of guns echoed from the edge of the woods and across the open pasture.

Trudy snatched up her daughter from the shelter of the trellis and ran for the low shed nearest the vegetable garden. Hugging Dulcie to her, she whispered urgent assurances that everything would be all right, but at the same time felt the anger redden her face.

It wasn't the first time this had happened. Not the first time that hunters had trespassed on her family's land, killing doves and deer out of season. Not the first time they had stupidly aimed their guns toward the farm, where they could hit anything—a window, a cow, Papa on his tractor, Dulcie playing in her own backyard. No, it wasn't the first time this sort of thing had happened. To be exact, it was the fifth time since her husband had died two years ago.

If Johnny were still alive, she told herself, *they'd never set foot on my land!*

"Mommy!" Dulcie was trying to be brave, trying not to cry. "Airplane's gonna get us."

Trudy kissed her daughter's cheek. "No, baby. Airplane's all gone."

More shots peppered overhead, only inches above them. Dulcie shrank against her mother. "Mommy..."

"Come on, baby." Her hand over Dulcie's face, Trudy hugged the child protectively to her. "I'm going to put a stop to this."

The little girl was almost too big to be carried, and Trudy could barely run with the thirty pounds of extra weight in her arms. Lead rained down again. She ducked under a pecan tree for shelter.

I wish Grendel had stayed home instead of following Papa to the peanut fields, Trudy thought. Grendel was a four-year-old Irish wolfhound, still a puppy when he wanted to be, but weighing more than Trudy and Dulcie together. The last four times poachers had come on her land, she'd taken Grendel with her to confront them. Each time, Grendel had merely bared his teeth, and the trespassers had stumbled over one another to climb the wire fence and get off her land as fast as they could. One of the hunters, Claude Tabor, had tripped over the electric fence and ripped his hand on the strand of barbed wire linking the fence posts. He'd left screaming and cursing, but he'd known that his injuries were minor compared with what Grendel's fangs could do.

"Stay here," Trudy ordered as she dumped Dulcie into the front seat of the old green pickup parked under the pecan tree. "Mommy will be right back," she yelled assuringly over Dulcie's whines. She dashed back toward the house.

By the time the screen door slammed behind her, Trudy had already grabbed her keys from the kitchen table and unlocked the closet door in Papa's bedroom. Her hands were shaking as she pulled out Johnny's hunting rifle. It was kept loaded in case of emergency, but it was also kept locked in Papa's room for the sake of an inquisitive toddler.

Dulcie's blue eyes widened when she saw the long cylindrical object in her mother's white-fisted grip. "You gonna shoot somebody, Mommy?" the little girl asked, her voice hardly more than a whisper.

"No, baby. Not unless I have to."

Trudy nervously laid the rifle in the space behind the seat. As she buckled Dulcie into her car seat, another round of gunshots pinged off the roof of the truck and bounced off the shed. Dulcie cringed for a moment, then stretched her neck to peer out the truck window.

"Mommy, airplane's coming." She pointed one tiny finger into the distance.

"Not now, baby."

She pulled out of her driveway and across the dirt road to a small white house. As Trudy's brakes squealed, the woman in the oval flower bed glanced up with a frown. Rubbing her arthritic hip, she stood slowly and swiped at the sweat in her gray-tinged hair.

"Trudy, you all right, hon?" Naomi Melton limped toward the truck.

"I need to leave Dulcie with you for a little while, Miss Naomi." Trudy unbuckled Dulcie and hauled her out on the driver's side of the pickup. "If that's all right with you."

"Of course it's all right." Miss Naomi pressed a playful finger to Dulcie's nose and waited for the giggle that always came. "What's wrong, Trudy? Is it your grandfather? He's not feeling puny again, is he?"

"No, no." Trudy climbed back into the truck. "Papa's fine." Gunshot spattered the open field behind her. She aimed a nervous glance over her shoulder. "It's those gun-toting lunatics again. They think they can come on my land anytime they please."

Miss Naomi patted Dulcie's head. "Stay here, Trudy. Don't go gettin' in trouble. When Horace comes home, I'll have him go back there and give them boys what-for."

Trudy shook her head. "Thanks, but it's my land. My responsibility." Dulcie and Miss Naomi waved as she whipped the truck out of the driveway and back toward the woods.

The dusty dirt road skirting the perimeter of her property was smooth with use, but Trudy instead chose a bumpier shortcut. She maneuvered the rusty old truck across the grassy pasture and headed straight for the source of gunfire at the edge of the woods. The truck seemed to hit every bump and anthill in the pasture. She braked only to creep across the dry creek that cut her property in two. Johnson's Creek was dry most of the year, but when the rains came, the swift waters were impassable and anything—or anyone—on the other side stayed there until it was safe to wade the stream. The trespassers usually came when the creek was dry.

She knew where to find the hunters. They always parked on the neighboring property, driving their trucks right up to the barbed-wire fence so they could jump off the tailgates, over the fence and onto her land. Then the three or four hunters would scatter along the little pond that was fed by the overflow from Johnson's Creek. A hundred years ago, her great-grandfather had frequented the same site to play illicit card games. Now the only wild life Trudy permitted on the land was either feathered or four-legged.

A sick feeling twisted in Trudy's stomach when she spotted two familiar trucks parked on the other side of the fence. She'd seen the same two trucks parked there four times before. One of the hunters—she could see only his tight jeans and long legs—was busily fishing something out of the cab of the red truck with the yellow fireball painted on the side. The oversize tires made the truck look like one of Dulcie's toys.

Trudy groaned. The truck belonged to Rooster Reed, but the man leaning into the cab wasn't Rooster. The local boys were hunting out of season. Again.

And that meant Rooster was already on her land.

Biting her lip, Trudy parked the truck. With or without the rifle, she would have given anything to have Grendel by her side.

The keys still in the ignition, Trudy stepped out of the truck. She decided to leave the rifle where it was, at least for the moment. She stood barefoot in the tall grass, her unsteady hand on the open door of the truck.

"You're trespassing," she called out in a voice that seemed weak even to her ears. "There's no hunting allowed on this land."

"Shut up!" a man's voice yelled back. "You're scaring the birds!"

Laughter.

"Rooster Reed, get off my land!"

"You gonna make me?" the voice countered.

The heat in Trudy's face deepened. Papa had deeded the land to her when Johnny had died, and now it was in her trust to protect and pass on to Dulcie as untarnished as when it had been passed on to her. Bad enough that she was about to lose the land to the bank, but she wouldn't let the local rednecks destroy it first. "My grandfather and I don't want any hunting on this land." She squinted at a quivering clump of bushes, but saw no one.

"Then why ain't he tellin' us to leave? Or does he always send a girl to do a man's job?"

The bushes directly in front of her shook violently, and Rooster crawled out, grinning. Bits of dry leaves littered his receding yellow hairline and splotchy red face. Resting a deer rifle against his camouflaged beer belly, he cocked his head and winked at her. Then he looked down at his feet, stomped an empty beer can and kicked it toward Trudy.

What's he doing with a deer rifle? she wondered. *Certainly not hunting birds.*

"Hey, Rooster." Claude Tabor sprang up on the other side of Trudy's pickup. "She ain't got that beast with her this time." He clenched his scarred fist at the memory of Grendel.

"Get off my land," Trudy warned quietly.

"We got a license to hunt," Claude said. He held up his .16-gauge shotgun for proof.

"Not on my land you don't."

"I'll hunt wherever I damned well please."

She followed Claude's aim to a sapphire-feathered bluebird clinging to a perimeter fence post. Uttering a curse under her breath, Trudy reached inside the truck and pounded on the horn, frightening away the bluebird as well as several dozen other birds. They fluttered into the air, then settled back into the trees.

Claude glared at her. "You damned stupid little..."

She glanced back at Rooster. His grin had faded. He and his friends knew her well enough to know how much she hated their mockery. They had treated her the same way ten years ago in high school.

Bullies never grow up, she concluded silently.

The two men stood there, defying her. Rooster twisted his lips to one side, sucking on his upper teeth. Claude coughed, then spit in the tall grass.

"Get off my land," Trudy ordered again.

"Your land? Not for long it ain't," a voice behind her said. "And if you want us off, you're gonna have to throw us off yourself."

Trudy whirled around to face Claude's younger brother, Wayne. He was carrying a shotgun and—of all things!—a metal detector. She wouldn't let them see that she was nervous, but she didn't like the fact that she was surrounded by three gun-toting rednecks. The fourth man was still hiding in Rooster's truck, most likely with more guns and more bullets.

She wouldn't get anywhere arguing with Claude or Wayne. They had always followed Rooster blindly, as blindly now as when they'd been only sixteen and seventeen years old. Trudy knew the only way she'd get them to leave was if she talked Rooster into leaving. And if he refused, then neither hell nor the high water of Johnson's

Creek would convince his cronies to go against Rooster's will.

She took a single step toward Rooster. "What gives you the right to come on my land?"

He laughed. "What gives you the right to keep me off? What gives you the right to put up fences to keep me out or to keep your birds in? Mother Nature's free to everybody, Trudy, or haven't you heard?"

She took another angry step toward him and felt something warm and soft and wet against her bare toes. Blue feathers glinted back at her in a patch of sunlight. She touched them with her toes and felt the fading life flutter out of the ruddy breast of a male bluebird riddled with shotgun lead.

Trudy couldn't breathe. All she could think of was the forty-plus birdhouses that dotted her farm in her effort to keep the bluebird from extinction. Saving the bluebird had always been her pet project, just as it had been her mother's. She hadn't been able to save her mother, but Trudy had provided shelter for countless bluebirds in the past decade, and somehow the soul of her mother seemed to live on in each cobalt fledgling that Trudy fostered. It was a respect for wildlife that she hoped to pass on to her daughter, a legacy from the grandmother Dulcie never knew. Tears filled Trudy's eyes. The bird at her feet had probably fledged from one of her hand-built birdhouses.

"Why can't you hunt on your own land?" she screamed at Rooster. "Your daddy's got more land than anybody around here!"

"Yeah, but he ain't got good huntin' woods like you do."

"You want to cut all your trees down? Fine! But leave my bird sanctuary alone!"

"Now, Trudy, don't make a face like that. Might freeze. Besides, a girl with your looks should try to look her prettiest. I told you before—you should've married me instead of Johnny Reb."

"A cold day in hell . . ."

Wayne's footfalls crunched behind her.

"Hey, Rooster! Man, you know what would be really funny?"

"What's that, Wayne?"

"Well, if Trudy cain't behave herself while we have a little fun, maybe we should teach her a lesson."

Rooster grinned and cracked his knuckles.

"No, man, I don't mean that way," Wayne protested, as
seemingly fearful of the expression in Rooster's eyes as
Trudy was. "Old man Dugan would kill you for sure if you
laid a hand on his granddaughter."

Rooster winked mischievously at Trudy. "I s'pose you got
a better idea, Wayne?"

"Well, yeah. We could put her down that hole over there.
It ain't rained in a while. Should be right dry. A little dark,
though."

Trudy's heart pounded in her chest. She backed against
the truck. The hole Wayne was talking about was a well on
the ridge between the pond and the denser woods. It had
been there for as long as Trudy could remember. Even as a
little girl, she'd been warned not to go near it. She'd heard
once that it had been built in the late 1800s when the Dugan lands had supported the booming turpentine industry.
Wells were expensive to dig in those days, but necessary to
provide water to the men working in the humid woods. The
woods had grown quiet again except for the frequent card
games. The well had never been covered over. Papa often
told a story of how he'd lost his only mule during the Great
Depression because the animal had wandered too near the
open hole.

She shuddered, and she knew they had seen her shudder.

"Well, now," Rooster said, swaggering toward Trudy,
"that ain't a bad idea. Might teach Miss Priss here to stay
out of men's affairs."

Trudy had no intention of spending one minute down that
dark shaft. Without breaking the icy glare she shot at
Rooster Reed, she reached into the space behind the truck
seat and brought out her rifle in a two-fisted grip.

"Ooooh!" Rooster crooned, pretending to cower.
"Didn't your daddy teach you not to play with guns before
he ran off with that Benton woman? Your mama wasn't
even cold on her grave when he married again and left
town."

Wayne laughed from behind her. "I bet Trudy don't even know how to use that rifle."

Pride played at the corner of her lips, twisting them into a half smile. "See that tall pine?" She pointed at a tree on the other side of the pond. "Lowest branch. Biggest pinecone. Now you see it—" she brought the rifle to her shoulder and fired "—and now you don't."

Rooster and the Tabor brothers were silent, all of them staring at the empty bit of sky where the pinecone had been. A cloud of birds fluttered back down to the trees as the echo of the shot died.

"Well, I'll be," she heard Wayne whisper behind her.

"Shut up," Rooster growled uneasily. "She ain't gonna shoot us."

Trudy tightened her grip on the gun. "Then don't give me reason to."

"Yeah, but there are four of us and only one of you," Wayne reminded her. Claude nodded in agreement.

"True. But I can make sure there are fewer of you before there are fewer of me." She prayed they wouldn't call her bluff. Shooting a man was a lot different from shooting a pinecone.

Glancing over the fence at his truck, Rooster scratched the underside of his belly along the ridge hanging over his cowhide belt. Then he looked back at Trudy. The sneer on his upper lip was slight but enough to reveal his agitation. He paused to listen to the distant buzz of a propeller and shrugged.

"You know, boys, I could sure use a cold beer right now."

"Oh, we got more in my cooler if you—" Wayne broke off when he saw the threat in Rooster's eyes.

"Come on, boys. I've had enough huntin' for today. We'll come back later when the birds ain't quite so skittish." Rooster stalked away, as much of his machismo intact as he could salvage.

The Tabor brothers followed him. Neither spoke, but Wayne risked a glance back over his shoulder at Trudy. He'd likely never seen a woman best Rooster Reed before, she realized.

She exhaled loud enough the men could probably hear it as they reached the fence. Trudy didn't realize until then that she'd been holding her breath. They couldn't possibly know how scared she was. If they had known how scared she was, they wouldn't be leaving. They were the type who, once they smelled blood, descended for the kill.

The Tabors crawled into their old blue pickup. Wayne slipped behind the wheel and raced the motor a few times to let Trudy know she didn't scare him. The fourth hunter, the one who had hidden in Rooster's truck, sat in the driver's seat. Trudy still couldn't see his face, and the baseball cap he wore hid the color of his hair.

Rooster started to lay his gun in the cab of his truck, but changed his mind. Walking around to the tailgate, he stared back at Trudy on the other side of the fence. He grabbed the raised tailgate with one plump hand and used his arm as a lever to propel his entire body into the truck bed. Landing on his feet, he let out a triumphant whoop and lifted his high-powered deer rifle.

Trudy's pulse quickened. He was aiming directly at her! After seeing him crawl over the fence, she had relaxed too much. She could never get her rifle in the air in time to shoot first—and maybe not in time to shoot back!

Trapped! A sickening sensation burned in the pit of her stomach. Trudy froze, a scream catching in her throat.

Rooster's laughter bellowed through the emptiness between them. He aimed his gun again, this time pointing it toward the sky. Whether too cowardly or too decent to shoot at a human target, he fired a shot straight up into the air in a final act of defiance.

A cloud of birds thundered into the sky.

Regret told himself it was stupid to fly over the woman's farm again, but it wasn't the first time he'd ignored the little voice in his head that usually kept him out of trouble.

As he circled the farm, he searched through his binoculars for the woman on her knees. But this time she wasn't on her knees. She was running, hugging something—the child?—to her. Curious, he watched from the cockpit as the woman left the child inside a faded old truck and sprinted across the yard to the house. A large pecan tree in the backyard hid the house temporarily, and Regret swung to the right in a futile attempt to see around the tree.

Intending to double-back, he followed the fenced boundary of the farm beyond a dry creek bed and over the thick woods that stretched across the back half of the farm. Two trucks, a blue older-model pickup and a fire-engine-red custom job, were parked close to the fence on the barren side. Regret reasoned that trees had once occupied the yellow-beige wasteland of grass that contrasted starkly with the evergreens and spring growth on the woman's farm.

He turned the plane back toward the farmhouse and the woman. The truck in the yard was gone. Beyond the house, a gray dust curled upward from a tractor that crept in the opposite direction. A small horse—no, a dog—ambled along behind the tractor.

Probably her father on the tractor, Regret decided.

Lowering the binoculars, he rubbed his eyes and scanned the dirt road below. Nothing.

Damn it, where are you?

Out of the corner of his eye, a dry dust rose, and he followed the cloud, circling just ahead of it to see its source. A pale green truck. It was her, all right. And she was moving like a bat out of hell across the pasture.

He glided away from the truck, dropping to two hundred feet over the woods ahead of her. He wondered what in those woods could be so important, so urgent. He squinted through the hot glare of sunshine. Nothing moved below except the occasional flutter of birds and the black cows in the rectangular pasture in the center of the woods. Nothing *seemed* out the ordinary. Just trees. Pines, a few oaks, low-growing hawthorns and cypresses in the swampier areas. Nothing but trees and cows and birds.

He turned the two-seater to the right, completing a backward S as he buzzed back over the woods and toward the farmhouse one more time. Casually he glanced below—and was surprised to find himself almost over the two trucks he'd seen earlier. Just beyond a sun-glistened pond, he saw the woman's truck, saw the woman, saw three men scrambling into the two trucks on the barren side of the fence.

He was too low!

At two hundred feet, he was barely clearing some of the pines. He'd maintained an altitude of a thousand feet over the farmhouse, as he was required to do over populated areas, but he hadn't expected the woods to be populated!

Grabbing the steering bars with both hands, he lurched backward in his seat. The plane pulled straight up—and with a double thud, the engine seized. His sight flickered doubtfully over the gauges for clues. The needle on the oil-pressure gauge trembled and fell, and the oil temperature gauge shot higher. The RPM needle sank. He was going nowhere but down!

He couldn't understand it. He was always so meticulous in his preflight check, and Hughie was a great mechanic. Hughie would never let him go up with even the slightest hint of a problem. Then he saw a flutter of birds, and a second later, he noticed the black feathers and a sprinkling of red flung across the plane's canopy. The problem wasn't mechanical. He'd hit a bird—maybe several—and sucked it right into the propeller, probably tearing right through the oil lines.

Frantically he searched the horizon for a place to land. The barren field would be ideal, but the strong draft along the ground pushed hard against the plane, forcing him back down toward the trees. He leaned to his right, remembering the long, rectangular pasture and the black cows at the far right angle.

It was just below him now. Every muscle in his body tensed as he sliced through the air toward the green clearing. The landing would be rough, but it wasn't impossible. If he was lucky, he could probably make it with only a few broken bones. On the other hand, he hadn't been very lucky on this flight.

For the first time since he was five years old, Regret prayed.

"Well?" Trudy screamed at Rooster, who stood gaping in the back of his truck as though it were a stage for his performance.

"Well what?" he boomed back at her.

Both of them were staring at the white airplane with the blue stripe on the side as it twisted in the air above them. The flapping of birds' wings and the hollow echo from Rooster's rifle still rang in her ears. Even the Tabor brothers were leaning out their truck windows and squinting up at the shadow hanging between the sun and them. The plane was coming down, but not directly down on top of them. The Cessna seemed to drift downward sideways, just beyond the treetops.

Oh, God! Not again!

"He needs help," Trudy insisted, turning desperately to Rooster. "Aren't you going to do something?" She barely recognized her own voice, which was at least an octave higher than usual.

Rooster stared at her blankly for a moment, then jumped over the side rail of the truck and opened the passenger door. "Yeah, I'm gonna do sumpin'. I'm gettin' the hell outta here!"

Trudy glared after them, hardly able to see the trucks through the dust that billowed up behind them as they sped away. She heard the deafening but dull thud the plane made as it hit the ground.

Oh, God, please!

She waited. No explosion, no smoke. She held her breath. *Maybe he'd made it after all.*

She hadn't heard the crackling sound of breaking trees, and she was sure he'd landed nearby. Then her ear caught the distraught lowing of cows. Not the mournful moos she usually heard when they were hungry, but the soft warning moans that something or someone had disturbed their afternoon grazing. She'd rarely heard that sound. Once when she was ten years old, a stalking bobcat had sent the cows into a frenzy of lowing and nervous stomping. Another time, a stray dog had provoked that same herd anxiety. The cows were sometimes disturbed by a stranger, but they were used to her and Papa. Even Grendel and Dulcie were familiar faces. But they weren't used to airplanes landing beside them.

He's in the clearing.

She was running already. Running for the truck.

She had to get to the pilot! She had to save him!

She slammed the truck door behind her, then fidgeted with the key waiting in the ignition. Somehow she pulled it, then dropped it. With sweaty hands, she picked it up off the dirty floorboard and crammed it back into the slot.

She had to hurry. She couldn't just let him lie there help-lessly and bleed to death the way Johnny had. Unfortu-nately the dirt road ended at the pond. There were only two ways to get to the pasture, and one was to walk.

Thirty minutes later, Trudy bounced into the pasture on her all-terrain vehicle after following a narrow trail. The four-wheeler had replaced their last horse, and Trudy and Dulcie used it at least twice a day every day unless it was raining or wintertime. About ten o'clock every morning, the two of them would set out to take Papa a fresh jug of lem-onade to help him cool off when the mornings in the field grew hot. Then, in the afternoon, they took Papa a second jug. Sometimes they combined their lemonade runs with their daily route along Trudy's bluebird trail. Trudy had even had special mommy-daughter helmets ordered to make their rides safer and a small four-by-four-foot trailer to haul small loads. The only things on the trailer today were a blanket, a first-aid kit and one of Dulcie's rag dolls.

The Cessna lay at one end of the field, less than fifty feet from lowing cows, which seemed slightly more at ease when they recognized Trudy's four-wheeler. One wing was bowed and the propeller appeared bent, but the plane was still in one piece. Not that it meant the pilot was in one piece. She knew that from experience.

Trudy revved the engine of the four-wheeler and bumped across the field. She pulled up alongside the plane, close enough for a better look but not too close in case there was trouble.

After first killing the engine, Trudy dismounted. She was glad she hadn't brought Dulcie with her this time. If she found a bloody mess in the cockpit, she didn't want the lit-tle girl there to see it.

I can't do this again. She squeezed her eyes shut. It should have been someone else—Papa, Mr. Horace, Rooster, anybody but her.

She opened her eyes. The plane was still there. A bad dream but real. A man was still inside.

But no one else was there. No one else was coming. It was just her. Just like last time. And if this pilot survived, it would be up to her.

Dread shifted in Trudy's stomach as she moved toward the cockpit. The grass felt dry, scratchy, under her bare feet. The first-aid kit weighed less than two pounds but suddenly seemed leaden in her grasp. Somehow she was reliving Johnny's death all over again. Trudy reached for the pilot's door, not knowing if she would scream when she opened it.

She didn't.

There wasn't much blood. Just one deep gash across the man's forehead. He was still strapped in, and he wasn't moving. But he was alive. She was sure of that. Dead men didn't bleed, and the gash leaked crimson droplets that ran down his cheeks. Soft blond curls soaked up most of the blood.

Tentatively she touched his chest. When she pressed harder, the man moaned. *Good,* she thought. Johnny's chest had felt like a crushed eggshell under her touch. This pilot was luckier.

Taking several deep breaths, she assured herself that she was still in control. She fumbled with the first-aid kit, pulling out cloth and gauze. If she didn't want Dulcie to see all the blood, she'd have to clean the man up a bit before taking him back to the house. Carefully, gently, she cleaned and bandaged his forehead. The blood quickly soaked through, and she felt the tremors of panic as she realized she might not be able to help this man either. Déjà vu pricked at her spine.

The pilot stirred under her touch, a soft groan piercing his lips. Without reason, he smiled a big playboy grin. His eyes fluttered open, trying and failing to focus on her face. Startled, she hesitated. At first she thought something was wrong with his eyes. Perhaps he'd been blinded in the crash.

His irises were pale green, like faded jade, and there was something alien in them that frightened her. He looked a little older than she was—maybe thirty—and with that easy grin and head of playful blond twists, he could have been an all-American boy. Except for the deadly seriousness in his eyes.

He coughed and grabbed his chest in pain.

"Shh, be still." Trudy tugged at the shoulder harness and the belt across his waist. Without the restraints, the pilot slumped out of his seat and fell against her. The solidity of his weight caught her by surprise, and she almost tripped as she stepped backward to accommodate the shift in balance. He grabbed her shoulders awkwardly and she went down, with him tumbling on top of her. He yelped in pain, nothing breaking his fall but her smaller frame.

"Are you all right?" she asked, gasping. She tried gently to shove him off her and pull herself up from the ground.

"Will be." His eyes closed momentarily and a smile crept over his face. "You're beautiful. Not a teenager."

She frowned. "Can you walk?"

"Think so."

"Good. Let's give it a try."

Hoisting the man to his feet, Trudy pretended not to notice his arms, more muscular than they looked through the white T-shirt. He draped one arm around her but couldn't hold himself steady. She caught him in her arms and pulled him upright. In the back of her mind, she heard a seventeen-year-old Rooster Reed admitting grudgingly, "You're stronger than you look."

She helped the pilot into the blanketed trailer and crumpled one corner of the blanket for a pillow.

The man strained to keep his eyes open. He was hurting, but he wouldn't admit it.

"My gear. Don't leave my gear."

"There's no time to—"

"Please." He grabbed her wrist tightly. "It's a matter of life or death."

She was about to say the same about getting him to a doctor, but living on a farm all her life, she'd nursed enough wounded animals to know that he wouldn't die of his injuries. Not if she helped him. He wasn't like Johnny. This man was coherent and strong, and already the bleeding from the head gash was slowing to a trickle. She guessed he probably had a concussion and a few broken ribs. Not enough to kill him, but enough that he'd die of thirst if she left him there. She'd treated worse injuries for Papa.

Trudy shrugged and ran back to the cockpit. The only "gear" she could find was a pair of broken binoculars, a fancy camera and several dozen rolls of film on the floor. She gathered everything in her arms, including her first-aid kit, and dumped it all in the trailer next to the pilot.

The man's eyes were closed again and his breathing was labored. She bent to whisper, "Don't worry. I'll get you to a hospital as soon as I can."

With all its fading strength, one hand grabbed the neckline of her dress and pulled her face to his. By sheer willpower, he opened his eyes again, this time focusing on hers.

"Let go!" She tried to pull back. Her heart was pounding. She was trying to help him. What was the matter with him?

Then she read the fear in the green of his eyes. Fear that would kill rather than succumb.

"No hospitals," he rasped.

"But you should see a doctor—"

"No. No hospital. No doctor."

"But you need—"

"You. You're all I need."

His eyes rolled backward in unconsciousness. The errant hand fell to his chest.

Chapter 2

Regret heard the raindrops long before he opened his eyes. They pelted softly against thin glass, and he reasoned there was a window nearby. The rain soothed him, made him long to fall over the brim of sleep again. He was dreaming he was at home in bed on a Sunday morning, that he didn't have to go to work and could lie in bed as late as he liked.

He shifted in the bed, suddenly aware of the cool, fresh-smelling sheets and the strong scent of honeysuckle a few feet away. That wasn't quite right. No, at home were wrinkled sheets ironed to the bed with his own body. No honeysuckle, either. The house he shared with Hughie had a distinct smell about it, but it was more of a cross between the musty scent of Hughie's moldering shoe collection near the back door and the empty beer bottles temporarily stored on the kitchen cabinet until they could be carried to the recycling bin. Nothing at home smelled remotely of honeysuckle.

Confused, he wondered if maybe he'd gone barhopping and had ended up in some sweet thing's bed. No. None of the women he ever met at bars were the honeysuckle type. And he was sick and tired of barhopping.

The crash! He pried open his eyes, sitting up too quickly. The pain in his head seared down his spine. Helplessly he dropped back to the thick pillow. He managed to keep his eyes open to glance around the large, high-ceilinged bedroom.

A guest room, he decided. The room was sparsely furnished in a blend of early-twentieth-century furniture. The bureau and nightstand were well cared for, both polished and draped with hand-crocheted lace doilies. On the nightstand next to the bed was a large depression-era glass vase teeming with white and yellow honeysuckle blooms.

Definitely a guest room. *But whose?*

He looked down at the crisp white sheets on the bed and the patchwork quilt at his feet. Then he frowned. He was wearing pajamas—light blue with royal-blue piping. That was strange. He never wore pajamas. Ever. He preferred to sleep in the nude. Apparently so did the owner of the pajamas. Judging by the deep creases left by tight folds, the blue pajamas were fresh out of a plastic bag, and at least two sizes too large for him. Probably an ill-chosen Christmas gift, he guessed.

A shadow moved in the doorway. A tiny shadow with dark hair. Regret couldn't take his eyes off her. She was a pretty child, somewhere between a baby and a little girl. A floppy white bow held her flowing hair out of her big blue eyes. Her white eyelet dress hung by ribbons from her tiny shoulders. Aware of his gaze, she hung close to the door.

Gradually timidity gave way to curiosity, and she tiptoed toward the bed. She hesitated. Then he smiled. She grinned back, struggling laughingly onto the bed with him. She came close then, almost too close to his face, as she examined his eyes, his nose, his brow.

To Regret, she looked like a little angel sent to minister to him. Maybe he had died in the crash. Died and gone to heaven.

The little angel reached toward his forehead, and he waited, anticipating her healing fingertips on his brow. He smiled appreciatively as she reached for him—then howled as her touch burned his flesh.

"You got an owie," she whispered in awe. She poked again at his bandage.

He tried to sit up, tried to push away from her, but the thunder inside his head racked him again. He shut his eyes against the pain.

Thunder. Rain. Johnson's Creek. *No!*

He sank into sleep once more.

Trudy watched the old man chew his fried chicken carefully. At seventy-seven, Papa was grateful he could eat solid food at all. He was even more grateful that he had a granddaughter who loved him enough to live with him, one who was willing to cook three meals a day for him. Trudy always cooked his favorites, too, and prepared his meals in such a way that even an old man with ill-fitting dentures could enjoy baked cream corn or a sweet-potato casserole. But for all his gratitude, Papa was a product of his time. He still believed a woman's place was in the kitchen, barefoot, a baby on each hip and one on the way. And since her grandmother and mother had died years ago, taking care of Papa had fallen to Trudy.

Papa sipped his iced tea and glanced disapprovingly across the supper table at Trudy. "It ain't right. People will talk."

"Baby, use your fork," Trudy reminded Dulcie, who sat between them at the head of the table. Trudy toyed with her own fork, molding the steaming buttered rice into a mound and then lifting it in her fork to her lips to blow on it. "People don't have to know," she said in a low voice.

"They'll know. And what they don't know, they'll make up."

Trudy dumped the forkful of rice back onto her plate. "Papa, he's been here two days, and nobody knows but you and me. And Dulcie."

"They'll come looking for him."

"Who?"

Papa shrugged his bony shoulders. "Maybe his folks. Maybe his friends." He reached for another piece of chicken. "Maybe the law."

"Papa!"

"You don't know a thang about him."

"Dulcie, I told you to use your fork." Trudy looked back at her grandfather. "I know he's hurt, Papa."

"Then drive him to the county hospital and let's be done with him. He ain't our kin. We ain't got no reason to keep him here against his will."

Trudy straightened her posture defensively. "I'm not keeping him against his will. All he's wanted to do is sleep and eat a little broth. He's mumbled only a few words—nothing I could make out. Except something about the rain. Papa, I don't think he'll even have a will of his own until he's stronger."

"No reason for you to nursemaid him. We got doctors in town for that."

"But he's afraid of hospitals. If you'd only seen the way he looked at me when—"

"People who are scared of hospitals have got sumpin' to hide."

Trudy narrowed her eyes at the old man. Papa was frail now, only a husk of the man he'd been forty years ago. Yet despite the hardness of the life he'd lived, he could still strike a handsome pose in a Sunday suit. He had more hair than many men half his age, but his years under a farmer's sun had left a white circle around his tanned forehead where he wore a mesh cap most of the year. When he was freshly bathed and ready for church, the white rim made Trudy think of an Easter egg that hadn't been dipped in dye long enough.

"So what have you got to hide, Papa?"

"Huh?"

"Last summer I nearly had to kidnap you to take you to the doctor to get that hand looked at."

"Humph! That's different. I thought it might be cancer like your mama and—" Papa broke off. He'd said too much already.

"No, it isn't different. Not really. You were just as afraid of going to the doctor as he is now."

"It ain't the same. I was gettin' along jes' fine without goin' to the doctor. That man's been in a mess of a plane wreck, and it's plain to see he needs a doctor. If you hadn't been there, he probably would've bled to death like—''

Papa stopped again, and for a moment an uncomfortable silence hung between them until Trudy once again urged Dulcie to use her fork.

"I jes' don't want you to make another mistake. Last thang you need's another boy with his head—and his feet—in the clouds. I'm an old man. I don't have much of a future left, but I worry about you, girl. What's gonna happen to you and your young'un when the bank forecloses?''

"So that's it, Papa. You're still blaming me for losing the farm.'' Tears welled in Trudy's eyes, but she refused to cry. "Well, I haven't lost it yet.''

"Girl, I don't blame you for losin' the land. We ain't talkin' about the land. We're talkin' 'bout that stray you took in. Trudy, you don't know where he's been or why he's here. He didn't have no identification on him when you found him. And I can feel it in my bones—he ain't flyin' over this land by accident.''

Trudy didn't say anything. She stared out the window at the darkness and the spitting rain. When Papa felt something in his bones, he was generally right. His bones could be counted on to forecast the coming rain or a cold front with more accuracy than Frank the weatherman. His bones were also credited with a talent for frighteningly correct first impressions. If he met a stranger in town, he could tell right away whether the man was honest or up to no good. And hadn't Papa told her when she was sixteen that Rooster Reed would only break her heart? Hadn't Papa told her later not to marry a man who defied the laws of nature by soaring into the sky?

"As soon as he's able to talk, I'll find out who he is and why he's here,'' Trudy promised.

"You're courtin' trouble, Trudy.'' He stopped eating and stared at his plate, frowning. "I don't like leavin' you here in the house with him. No tellin' what he might do if he took a fancy to you.''

"Really, Papa! He's so weak even Dulcie could overpower him right now.''

"He won't always be weak. Not if you keep feedin' him your grandma's chicken soup."

Trudy smiled. "Always worked for you."

"I don't like it, girl. Him bein' here, that is. He's got sumpin' to hide."

She pushed her plate aside. "Don't we all?" she said in a voice too low for the old man to hear.

Trudy's bedroom was dark except for the light of a single candle. Only there wasn't a candle. She was dreaming, but she knew she was dreaming.

She was alone in her bed, alone in the room. Yet she knew Dulcie was sleeping in her crib on the other side of the bedroom.

Trudy was wrapped in white. Sheets. No, a dress she'd worn ten years ago. Her wedding dress. Instead of a veil, she was wearing a bandage. But not gauze. A white satin bandage.

She was suddenly cold, shivering in the night heat. The sheets around her were gone. Her dress faded into nothingness.

"You should've married me instead of Johnny Reb."

She whipped her head to one side, searching for the voice. Rooster Reed stood at the foot of her bed with a machine gun in his embrace. His eyes gleamed as cold and gray as they'd been several days ago when he'd aimed his gun at her.

But this Rooster was young. Except for his eyes, this Rooster had the leaner, muscular look of the high-school senior who'd thought he could conquer the world and put Trudy's heart in cold storage while he stalked off to Atlanta. This was Rooster before he'd grown up, or at least before he'd grown older. This was Rooster before she'd married Johnny Sandlin.

"If you'd married me, you wouldn't be losin' your land."

Abruptly she realized she was naked, both in flesh and in spirit, before Rooster. She grabbed at the quilted coverlet at her feet. Her fingers grazed the fabric as the barrel of his gun lifted it up and out of her reach. Rooster's laughter echoed though her head. Before her eyes he aged, became the Rooster who routinely trespassed on her land, killing the wild things she favored over lovers. He turned harder, too, as his long and wavy hair receded on his scalp, his face reddened with the influence of alcohol, his body widened to accommodate his excesses.

Gazing beyond her, he growled, "Why would you choose him over me?"

Johnny? She turned to look beside her, expecting to see her husband's easy smile. Instead the green-eyed pilot lay sleeping next to her. His bare skin gleamed bright in the candle glow. His chest held a false firmness, for it was crushed and bleeding and dying inside.

Bolting upright, Trudy blinked into the darkness. The rush of her pulse thundered in her ears, but she was alone in bed. No nameless pilot. No Johnny. No Rooster Reed.

As her heartbeat calmed, she heard Dulcie's soft breathing from the crib in the corner of the room. Somewhere on the far side of the house, Papa's snoring rose and fell and faded into the night air. The windows in Trudy's bedroom were up, and a soft breeze stirred the curtains and held them suspended before they settled again. From way down in the woods came the familiar night call of the whippoorwill.

And from deep in the alligator swamps came the unfamiliar growl of chain saws.

Regret awoke at dawn the next morning, and for the first pale hour of daylight, he lay perfectly still in bed, listening to the chorus of birds outside his open window. For all their varied songs, he couldn't have slept even if he'd wanted to. He'd been in an aviary once, years ago with foster parents who had been fond of zoos. He smiled to himself. That was one of the few pleasant memories of his childhood.

A breeze fluttered through the lace curtains, carrying with it the scent of faraway rain. Regret lifted his head to look out the window at the distant dark clouds, but the pain throbbing through his temples brought him back down to the pillow. He wasn't sure how long he'd been asleep, dozing in and out of consciousness, awaking barely in time when the dark-haired woman had brought him a steaming bowl of delicious soup and cradled his head in her arms while she fed him. He'd been too lightheaded to sit up, too weak in the knees to stand. He'd hated his helplessness, but was glad it was a stranger who'd held him like a sleepless baby in her arms. Friends and family could only be counted on to walk away when he needed them most.

The little girl appeared in the doorway. She couldn't have been more than three feet tall, but she stood hunched over with her shoulders raised. She held her bent arms close to her chest, her hands dangling in front of her. She wore a light-blue dress that emphasized her eyes. The little girl crept on bare tiptoes toward the bed. She was grinning devilishly.

"Hi," Regret said in a weak but friendly voice. "Who are you?"

"Rawhrrrrr!" She giggled and ran to his bed. "I'm a dinosaur!"

"Uh-huh." He noted her carnivorous posture and grinned back. "So what's your name, little dinosaur?"

She leaned against the bed, stretching her neck out and eyeing him with curiosity. "Dulcie Anna Sandlin," she announced proudly with a touch of her mother's Southern drawl.

"Dulcie, I need your help." The breeze blew harder through the window, carrying with it the urgency of coming rain and the disaster at Johnson's Creek. If the stream flooded, taking with it the precious little dirt around the gas line pipes, the explosion would blow one hell of a crater in the state of Georgia. "Can you tell me where your telephone is?"

Pleased to help, Dulcie nodded enthusiastically. "You want me to bring it to you?"

Yes! His heart leapt in his chest. Finally—*finally!*—he could get to a phone. Or rather, this little girl of two or three would actually bring it to him. A cordless phone, he concluded. He could call Hughie from his bed. "Yes, Dulcie. Please bring me your telephone."

Having forgotten her imitation of a tyrannosaurus rex, the toddler loped off into another room. Regret relaxed against his pillow. There was still time.

When the child returned, his heart sank. Happily she presented him with a telephone—a pink, plastic toy telephone.

"You wanna draw your name?" she asked, holding up a handful of crayons. When he shook his head, she put a blue crayon in her mouth and pouted.

"I see you're finally awake," a warm, feminine voice noted from the doorway. "Maybe today you'll keep up your end of the conversation."

Regret glanced up at the woman holding a wicker tray. He smelled that wonderful soup again. She was wearing a blue frock that matched Dulcie's. The swell of her chest moved slightly under the loose dress and Regret felt the first stirrings of desire, just as he did on most occasions when he met a beautiful woman. A blue satin ribbon caught her thick hair at the back of her neck and held it away from her astonishingly blue eyes, which also matched Dulcie's. He wondered silently who she was and what was behind that hint of sadness in her smile. Was she the one who had discarded his T-shirt and jeans in favor of the pajamas? Was she the one who had washed his wounds and changed his bandages so often? Was she the one who had bathed him like a soiled baby? He felt himself blush at the thought of it, and he was a man who did not embarrass easily.

"Mommy!" Dulcie grinned up at the woman.

With the crayon in Dulcie's mouth, the word was barely intelligible, but enough so to make Regret wince. He liked the woman. He already appreciated her simple beauty. He'd sampled her Southern hospitality and yearned to sample the graciousness of her lips. He genuinely liked the child, too, but the thought of this angel of mercy sharing a mother-daughter bond with the child made him ill with jealousy. The parent-child bond was a special one, and one he'd never shared with either of his parents.

"Dulcie, our guest needs his rest," the woman was saying to the little girl. "You mustn't wake him up when he's sleeping."

"Okay, Mommy."

"And take that crayon out of your mouth. You're not supposed to get your crayons wet, remember?"

"Okay, Mommy. I'll go dry it." Dulcie disappeared through the passage behind her mother.

"You look a little pale," the woman said to Regret. She seemed worried. "I was hoping you'd feel up to talking today."

His lips twisted into a smirk. It wasn't talking that interested him, although he did want to know everything about her—how many strokes she brushed her lustrous hair every night, whether the muscles of her stomach were as taut as they appeared, why she preferred honeysuckle to roses.

"People don't usually care that much about what I've got to say."

"Well, I'm dying to hear a little of your conversational skills." She smiled sheepishly and sat on the bed beside him. Placing the wicker tray on the nightstand, she watched him out of the corner of her eye while she stirred his steaming soup.

Regret managed a faint smile in return. With all his injuries, he could barely sit up, yet he was daydreaming of tugging her into bed with him and peeking under those breezy skirts to see if her legs were as long as he imagined. "What's your name?"

"Trudy."

"Trudy what?"

She tucked a linen napkin under his chin and then helped him lean back against the pillows. "That's really all you need to know for now. What's your name?"

"You can call me R.J."

"R.J. what?"

He grinned. In his younger days, he'd been on a first name basis with many women. He never remembered their last names anyway. "That's all you need to know for now."

"Fair enough."

She fed him two spoonfuls of soup without looking into his eyes. He sensed that she was denying her attraction to him.

"Is there anyone I should call?" she asked finally. "Won't somebody miss you?"

She was groping for facts, he knew. She wouldn't be so blatant as to ask if he was married or if someone out there might actually care whether he was alive or dead. No, she was too reserved for that. This was her way of playing it cool, and she was bad at it. On the other hand, it was a legitimate question. "I'll call him myself."

"Him?"

So she did want to know if he was married or if someone out there cared if he was alive or dead! "Yes, *him*. My business partner."

"Oh?" She seemed to brighten. "What kind of business?"

"None of yours," he answered without thinking. He regretted it immediately. He was so used to building walls to protect himself that he'd forgotten how to answer an honest question. Seeing her frown as she persisted in offering him another spoonful of soup, he relented. "Airplane business. I'm an aerial photographer second and a damned good pilot first."

"Oh." She jerked her head up, startled, spilling the soup down his chin. She dabbed nervously at the mess with a linen napkin.

He shifted uncomfortably in the blue pajamas. The soup was hot. Her touch was scalding. "My clothes. Where are they?"

"In the wash. Again. I've tried several times to get them clean, but . . . there was some blood."

"Did you . . . change my clothes?" When was the last time a woman had disrobed him? When he'd been drunk or passed out? Probably never. It was supposed to be the other way around, wasn't it?

She didn't answer until he'd swallowed four more spoonfuls of soup. "My grandfather's been taking care of getting you changed and cleaned up." Her mouth crimped in amusement. "He doesn't think it's proper for a young lady to see a man in that state."

"What state? Georgia?" He was trying to look confused. Actually, he was flirting with her.

"No. The—" she blushed right on cue "—the naked state. Sometimes Papa forgets that I'm a grown woman who's had a husband. He forgets I've seen a man naked." She stumbled over the words.

"Where's your husband now?" Regret had the distinct impression he was treading on holy ground.

Trudy made him finish his soup with one last gulp. "Good. You've got a good appetite. Means you'll be up and around in no time at all. I'm sure you're eager to be getting back to...wherever you came from." She placed the spoon back on the wicker tray. "My husband died a couple of years ago. I live here with my daughter and my grandfather."

"Where's 'here'?"

"About ten miles north of town."

"What city?"

"Cornerstone. Cornerstone, Georgia."

He sighed and leaned back against the headboard. "Aptly named." He remembered the hodgepodge of crumbling tarpatched rooftops he'd seen from the air. Cornerstone was the last town before flying out of Georgia airspace and over either the Florida state line or the Chattahoochee River, which threaded along the Alabama border. The town was kind of like a cornerstone to the whole state.

"It's a dying little town," she told him. "Nothing but a few farms and a timber mill in the next county."

"I saw your hometown from the air. Got some great pictures of—" He sat up abruptly, then clasped his pounding temples. "My gear. Did you get it?"

"Yeah. It's over there." Inclining her head, she indicated the corner of the room.

"The camera? You got it?"

"And the film. Binoculars, too, though they're a little worse for wear."

"And my plane?"

She frowned. "I didn't get *that.*"

"No, no. How does it look?" He'd brought it down much more smoothly than he'd ever dreamed possible. "All in one piece?"

"Yeah, but a little beat up."

His headache worsened. "Damn. I'll have to have it hauled back."

She stood up and lifted the tray. "In little pieces, maybe."

"What do you mean?"

"There aren't but two ways to get your plane out of there. Either you fly it out or you have it cut up and hauled out on my four-wheeler. There aren't any roads leading into the pasture you landed in. You were pretty fortunate that I could get to you. You might've—" She swallowed hard. "You might've died if I hadn't seen you go down."

"I suppose I should thank you for that."

"I s'pose."

The pounding in his head doubled in intensity. The pain from it almost closed his eyes against his will. He tried to glimpse the distant clouds out the window near the foot of the bed. The blacker clouds seemed closer than before. "It's going to rain," he choked out.

"Hmm, probably. It's rained the past three days."

"The past three days!" Regret struggled to sit up, then to stand. Hughie wouldn't know he'd had trouble. Hughie was expecting Regret to be soaking up the Florida sun alongside some bikinied sorority girl on college break.

Trudy dropped the tray on the bureau and bent over him to help. "You need to lie down. You can't just—"

"I've been out of it for the past three days?"

"Four, but—"

"I've *got* to get to a phone!" He pushed her away, and if he'd had all his strength, he might have hurt her, instead of simply catching her off balance. She seized him by the elbow to pull him back down to the bed, but he fought harder to stand. "I've got to get to a phone!" he rasped. The throbbing pain overtook him. He collapsed in her arms.

Not long after she'd washed the dinner dishes, the telephone rang. Trudy dreaded hearing the phone ring these days. It was only a matter of time before Buck Witherspoon, the loan officer at the bank, called to tell her they were foreclosing. She answered on the second ring, before the bell could wake Dulcie from her afternoon nap.

"Hello?"

No one replied, but she could hear muffled breathing, as though someone had muted the mouthpiece. The rest of the house was eerily quiet. Soft raindrops on the roof deepened Dulcie's nap. Papa had driven into town to pay a visit to Miss Clarice Welty, who was recently widowed and, like any old-fashioned Southern belle, desperately in need of a man's companionship. Too groggy to accept his dinner, R.J. had slept since breakfast. Both the house and the phone were too silent to suit Trudy. She waited for a voice over the telephone line and, when she didn't hear one, decided to hang up. She didn't have the patience for such childish games.

"Hey, girl."

She put the phone back to her ear. "Hello?"

"Whatcha doin'?" a hoarse voice asked.

She'd heard it before, but she couldn't connect a face with the disembodied voice. "Who is this?"

"Guess."

"I will not." She slammed the receiver back into its cradle. Before she could walk away, the phone rang again. "Hello." Her voice brimmed with irritation.

"Tsk, tsk, Trudy. Where are your telephone manners?"

"Who *is* this?"

"Have you forgotten me already? Why, I remember the time when you used to sit by the phone every night waitin' for my call."

"Rooster."

"See? You do remember me after all."

She didn't even try to hide her annoyance. "What do you want?"

"Maybe you and me should git together sometime. For old times' sake."

"You should listen to your own gossip, Rooster. What is it you've said about me? Oh, yes. I don't like real men. I only go for wimpy pilots."

"Then this is your chance to prove me wrong."

"But you're right, Rooster. I don't care much for bullies who come on my property and threaten me. If that's what makes you a 'real man,' then no, I don't like real men."

"I could change your mind," he offered.

In spite of the threatening undercurrent, Trudy heard a hint of sincerity in his voice. But she wasn't certain what he was sincere about.

"I told you before, Rooster, I'm not interested. Not in you and not in anybody else."

"Pretty girl like you's too young to be an old maid."

"It's what I've chosen."

He laughed. "What? Bein' a nurse to an old man? Least your daddy had good 'nough sense to leave that farm. He lost a mate and got on with his life. Why cain't you?"

"What do you want, Rooster?" She knew Rooster Reed, all right. Men like him always wanted something, and usually something for nothing.

"Just to make sure you weren't too riled up about the other day."

"Depends on what you mean by 'too riled up.'"

"So how bad was the crash?"

Trudy's heart skipped a beat. "I couldn't get to it," she lied. Maybe Papa was right about the pilot having something to hide, but she wasn't about to betray him to the man who'd made her life miserable more than once.

"Why not?"

"Maybe I wasn't in the mood to walk that far. You know I don't have paved roads through those mayhaw swamps. What did you expect me to do? Take a boat?"

"Well, how's the pilot? Better or worse than Johnny Reb?"

"How would I know?" she snapped. "I told you I couldn't get to him. I'm not even sure he landed on my property."

"Yeah, right."

Rooster's voice was edged with accusation, but Trudy ignored it. The only way he could know she was lying was if he had been to the crash site himself.

"I need to go, Rooster. I don't like leaving Dulcie alone."

"Well, maybe I'll just drop by and see y'all sometime."

"I'll be waiting," she said quietly. "With my rifle." Rooster's laughter still echoing in her ears, she hung up the phone.

Her hands were trembling as she walked into her bedroom to check on Dulcie. She steadied them by grasping the wooden rail of the crib and studying the peacefully sleeping face below. Dulcie had fallen asleep while playing, and a whole herd of tiny dinosaurs was scattered across the bedding. Toy airplanes, the only toys that captured her affections as much as dinosaurs, were stacked in one corner of the crib next to a huge stuffed dinosaur that Aunt Louisa had given her for her second birthday.

Dulcie cooed in her sleep and rolled over. Everybody in town said she was the spit and image of her mama, but all Trudy saw was the likeness of Johnny Sandlin, especially around the eyes and in Dulcie's superb cheekbones. Johnny would've been such a proud daddy. The week before Dulcie was born, he'd bought a box of cigars with blue ribbons. He'd always wanted a son. Too often, he'd joked that if the baby was a girl, he'd have to take her back to the stork and get her exchanged. But after he'd witnessed Dulcie's birth and held her for the first time, he'd been so taken with her that he'd stayed outside the nursery until Trudy had brought her home from the hospital. Johnny hadn't bothered to hand out cigars—blue or pink—because he'd been too in love with his daughter to leave her side.

Trudy sighed at the memory and ran one fingertip the length of Dulcie's nose. The little girl wrinkled her face in a semisneeze and flopped in the other direction. Trudy reached into the crib, digging out the scattered toys, making the bedding more comfortable for the child. She heaped the dinosaurs and airplanes onto the rocking chair beside the crib. Gently she reached under Dulcie and pried out an old purse she'd given the child to play with. The brown leather purse was rectangular, with a long, thin cord. Dulcie usually liked to slip the cord over one shoulder—although the purse itself still dragged the ground behind her.

Trudy opened the purse to check its contents. Usually it contained several coins, a couple of crayons and pens and expired grocery coupons that Dulcie considered "moneys." Sometimes a comb or a tube of lipstick was pilfered from the dressing table and taken as treasure for her purse.

"Oh, no," Trudy said aloud, pulling out a cowhide wallet. Dulcie was fascinated by Papa's black wallet and the green plastic coin purse advertising the local barbershop Papa frequented. Once or twice Dulcie had stolen into Papa's room in the early morning before he was awake and had been caught playing with the coin purse he took out of his pocket at bedtime and left for safekeeping on top of the low bureau by his bed. Papa never scolded her, though. Almost always, he gave her the contents of the coin purse, instead. Naturally she kept coming back for more coins.

As Trudy removed the wallet and slipped it into her own pocket, she noticed that it was shinier, newer, than she remembered. Papa still carried the wallet Trudy's mother had given him the Christmas before she'd died, and over the years its square form had molded into a curve to fit his body. She retrieved the wallet from her pocket and examined its soft squareness.

From the moment she opened the leather flap, she knew the wallet wasn't Papa's. The Georgia driver's license confirmed her suspicion when she saw the photograph of a somber-faced pilot with faded green eyes. She fumbled with the plastic sleeve over the laminated license and held the photograph ID closer to the light. She was looking for anything the little rectangle could tell her about the brawny-armed pilot whose sleeping body had made her bite her lip in curiosity on more than one occasion.

The first thing she noticed was that his name wasn't R.J. but Regret James. No middle initial. Were her eyes playing tricks on her? She reread the name: Regret James. What kind of name was that? A misprint? A stage name, perhaps? Maybe he was a circus pilot for an aerial sideshow.

She recognized the town in his address. Newnan, Georgia. It was the same small Georgia town where she and Johnny had suffered a flat tire on their way to the mountains on their belated honeymoon. About an hour south of Atlanta, they'd pulled off the interstate at Exit 9 and found a service-station owner willing to sell them a used tire on a Sunday afternoon. She wondered if maybe she and Johnny had met Regret while they were there. She decided they hadn't. Even as much as she'd loved Johnny, she would've remembered Regret's striking green eyes.

Trudy's own eyes lingered over the statistics. His hair and eye color weren't given, but she knew those already. He was five feet eleven inches—six inches taller than Trudy—and he weighed a hundred and sixty pounds, which on a good day was forty-five pounds more than she weighed and on a bad day after a chocolate binge forty pounds more than Trudy weighed. She calculated his age from the birth date given:

thirty-one to her twenty-eight. Like hers, the license showed no vision restrictions. Unlike hers, he wasn't an organ donor. Johnny hadn't been, either. Pilots never expect to become donors.

She flipped through the rest of the wallet and found three credit cards, a pilot's license, an insurance card and almost fifty dollars in cash. Only one picture graced the plastic pages: a faded black-and-white photograph of a woman in her late teens or early twenties. She was wearing a black, off-the-shoulder gown or shawl, and she was smiling. Not the phony "say cheese" smile of a photographer's subject, but a genuine display of happiness. Her unlined face bore a faint resemblance to the pilot's face, though his features were sharper. Trudy slipped the picture out of its sleeve and read the scrawled words on the back: Geneva James, high-school graduation.

Under the last flap was a plastic-wrapped condom. It hadn't been there long enough to crease the leather, and certainly not since he'd been a hormone-driven sixteen-year-old. So, R.J.'s a man of the world, she mused. She thought of the strong hands that had brushed against hers. The foil package wasn't meant for show. For a man called Regret, it was intended for use.

Folding the wallet in her hands, Trudy took a deep breath. She wasn't quite sure what to do with it. Or, for that matter, how Dulcie had acquired it. The pilot hadn't had it in his pocket when she'd unloaded him into the guest room. Had he dropped it in the trailer behind the four-wheeler? Had Dulcie found it there?

By nightfall the rain was coming down harder, and Papa wasn't home yet. Most likely Miss Clarice had talked him into staying for supper, and Papa savored his independence enough that he wouldn't call Trudy to let her know where he was. Sometimes, she thought, he was worse than a teenager. She still worried about him being out at night, visiting his "lady friends," but she'd learned a long time ago not to ask Papa where he was going or with whom he was spending his time, because he'd let Trudy know in no uncertain terms that he was a grown man and his social life was none of her business. The only thing worse than a feisty old man was a toddler going through a bout of the "terrible twos" and semisuccessful potty training.

Watching a videotape of *Barney and Friends* for the third time, Dulcie sat entranced in front of the television while Trudy folded clothes in the laundry area behind the living room. The washing machine was churning away at a load of towels, and the drier beside it was still full but silent. Trudy preferred to have a soft breeze dry her clothes, but the modern convenience of a drier was necessary on rainy days like this when she couldn't use the clothesline.

As Trudy folded the last towel and stacked it amid the others in a white clothes basket, Dulcie waltzed into the room carrying a coloring book. "Whatcha doing, Mommy? Whatcha doing?"

"Folding clothes. I thought you wanted to watch *Barney*. Again."

"I wanna color some. Are my colors dry, Mommy?"

Trudy frowned. The last time she'd seen Dulcie's crayons was that morning in R.J.'s room when the little girl had been chewing on the end of a blue crayon. "I don't know, baby. Where did you put your colors?"

"In there." She extended one tiny finger toward the drier.

Trudy dropped the basket on the floor. "In *where?*"

"In there," Dulcie repeated slowly, as though her mother had difficulty understanding plain English.

A sick feeling rose from the pit of her stomach. Hadn't she told Dulcie to keep her crayons dry? She reached for the door of the drier and gave it a quick jerk. That morning, before she'd prepared R.J.'s breakfast, she'd washed his clothes again, still trying to brighten their dingy stains. She had awakened to the smell of rain in the air. After the washing machine had finished its cycle, she'd tossed R.J.'s jeans and T-shirt into the drier, leaving the door open until she could come back to her laundry after breakfast. Nearly an hour later, she'd remembered the damp clothes waiting in the drier and flipped the door closed, turning on the drier and forgetting about it until now.

Pulling out the T-shirt first, she was confused for a moment by its 1960s tie-dye appearance. Swirls of red, blue and green blotched the plain white shirt in a random pattern.

Then she pulled out the jeans and discovered the same splotchy colors—and a melted blue crayon encrusted in the denim.

Trudy collapsed on the floor and put her head in her hands. Ruined! R.J.'s clothes were ruined.

"Whatsa matter, Mommy? Where my colors?" Dulcie bent close with concern.

"Colors all gone." Trudy sighed. She couldn't punish Dulcie. Not for following instructions. But she'd have to tell R.J., or Regret, or whatever his name was. And she'd have to find something else for the pilot to wear when he got back on his feet.

Trudy directed the toddler back to her video and closed the door to the laundry room. The rain was coming down harder than ever. Outside, Grendel whined above the patter of the storm. The poor dog had ended up on the back doorstep again and wanted—though he knew he wouldn't get it—a dry haven inside the house. Usually he slept in the barn or under the carport, but only when Papa was safely at home. He seemed to sense when his mistress was alone. Especially at night.

R.J.'s room was dark except for the occasional flicker of lightning that lit the room. Trudy reached for the lamp, contemplating whether to wake him now for supper and tell him the fate of his clothes or let it wait until tomorrow. Lightning struck nearby, illuminating the room—and the empty bed. A rumble of thunder followed immediately, rattling the windows throughout the house.

If he's strong enough to walk...

She heard a voice down the hall and followed it in the dark. For the first time, she wondered if she'd been wise to bring a stranger into her home. Why had he been flying over her farm, not once but three times? The farm was only a few hours from the Gulf of Mexico. Maybe he was hauling marijuana. Or something worse. Maybe he was running from the law as Papa had thought. Or maybe he *was* the law. But nothing in his wallet or his conversation indicated that he was on the right side of the law.

Lightning flashed outside again as an unbidden thought struck her. Maybe Papa had never left the farm. Because of the downpour, she hadn't been outside and hadn't checked to see if Papa's car was parked in its usual spot. Maybe Papa was lying dead in his car. Maybe Papa had never made it to Miss Clarice's house in town. Maybe R.J. had killed him and slipped back into the house to wait for Trudy to bring him supper. Was she next? Was Dulcie? How naive she'd been to bring this stranger into her daughter's life and into their home!

"You're the only one I can trust," she heard a voice in the next room say. The pilot was talking to someone on the telephone, she realized.

"Tonight. Tomorrow may be too late. It's been raining for days, and you know what that means when the creek fills up. I'll get pictures to them when I can, but they've got to get there now, or we stand to lose a good chunk of South Georgia."

Trudy put her ear to the door, straining to listen.

"I know I'm four days late in calling you, but I couldn't help it... I don't know. Concussion. A few broken ribs, maybe. Feels like it. I'll make it. No, the bird's down. I'm not sure how much damage. I'll let you know... a place called Cornerstone. About ten miles north of there. Johnson's Creek flows right through this place. Yeah, I know. My life's on the line, too. Look, Hughie, I..."

R.J.'s voice trailed off, then revived. "Sorry. I feel like hell. Just do it, okay? Good. Sorry about not filing a flight plan, but you know how I hate to be restricted by anything. You could've found me four days ago if I hadn't been so damned stubborn. I've never had trouble before, though, and I was flying visual. Not a cloud in the sky, and I got some great shots of... of... great shots."

Thud...

Trudy froze. Had he found her hiding in the darkness? Her breath loud in her ears, she peeked around the corner. Her dangerous patient lay slumped on the floor, unconscious and exhausted.

She knelt next to him. Lightning flashed across the room, illuminating the phone in his hand. She picked up the receiver and held it to her ear.

"Hello? Hello?" a voice asked desperately. "R.J., are you okay, man?"

Trudy bit her lip and decided to take a chance. "Hello?"

Lightning lit the room. Then the line crackled and went dead.

Chapter 3

At noon two days later, just as Trudy was putting chicken and dumplings, cream corn, black-eyed peas and corn bread on the dinner table—all Papa's favorites—he waltzed into the kitchen with a surprise. He was freshly shaven and wearing a clean white shirt she'd ironed for him earlier in the week. Without apologies, he announced he was having dinner with Miss Clarice, since the fields he'd intended to plow were wet enough to bog a gnat and he couldn't possibly get any work done. An angry Trudy held her tongue. Papa had done the same thing to her before, and when she'd confronted him, he had contended that his special diet was no trouble at all. Of course, having never cooked a meal in his life, he couldn't possibly understand the trouble of preparing the soft foods his ill-dentured gums could tolerate. Tersely she told him goodbye, sent her love to Miss Clarice and called Dulcie for dinner.

"Mind if I join you?" asked a voice from the kitchen door.

Trudy looked up and smiled at Regret. "Sure. I've already got a plate set," Trudy said, neglecting to tell him the third plate was meant for Papa.

"Good. I was getting awfully tired of breakfast in bed. Not to mention lunch and dinner." He eased himself into a chair opposite Dulcie and wrinkled his nose at her playfully.

Trudy poured a tall glass of iced tea for him. "Well, if you're tired of my cooking, you'll get no reprieve here."

"Oh, no. The cooking's fine. But I was getting tired of eating flat on my back."

Trudy watched the green-eyed pilot devour the feast she'd prepared for Papa. He seemed too hungry to make conversation, so she accepted his appetite as appreciation for her efforts.

"I have strawberry shortcake for dessert," she declared proudly when he'd finished his second helping of chicken and dumplings. "The strawberries are fresh from the garden. Grew them myself."

His eyes shone as he looked up at her. "Do you always cook such a big lunch? Or am I special?"

"Dinner. It's dinner at noon and supper at night. There's no such thing as lunch in South Georgia. And I don't know enough about you to know if you're special, but yes, I always cook a big dinner. And if you don't eat it all, you'll see it on the table again tonight as leftovers."

"Trudy," he said, grinning at his empty plate, "I'm not planning on leaving any leftovers for tonight."

"An empty plate is the greatest compliment you can pay a cook." She nodded toward Dulcie's untouched food. "Although my daughter doesn't compliment me very often."

Regret politely asked Dulcie's age and then lapsed into the silence of a man who'd probably spent little time in the presence of children.

"Tell me about yourself," Trudy urged. Her gaze kept wandering over his clothes, the faded jeans and a short-sleeved jersey she'd taken out of storage to replace his crayon-ruined garments. They fit him well. Maybe too well.

He shrugged evasively. "What do you want to know?"

"If I knew what I wanted to know, I wouldn't have to ask."

"You don't have to get testy about it," he teased. "My name is R.J. James, and as you're already aware, I like to fly planes."

Pilots don't just like to fly planes, she thought, stabbing at a dumpling on her plate. *They love to fly planes. They live to fly planes.* She let the dumpling drop back to her plate. *And they die flying planes.*

He leaned across the table toward her. "And now a question for you. Why me?"

"What do you mean by that?" She didn't like to be teased.

"Just what I said. Why me? I remember you dragging me out of the plane. Why'd you bring me here? Why are you trying to nurse me back to health?"

Trudy shrugged, then rose and walked across the room and brought back a dessert plate of strawberry shortcake and a dessert knife. "Why you? Because you fell out of the blue. If I hadn't helped you, who else would have? If I hadn't seen you crash, nobody would've found you until the birds were circling overhead, and it would've been too late for anybody to help you then." The way it was for Johnny, she thought, but didn't say. Instead she hacked through a piece of strawberry shortcake, slapped the dessert onto a rose-painted saucer and pushed it across the table toward him.

He took one bite and chewed thoughtfully, glancing up at her and then down at his dessert. "But why did you bring me here? Why didn't you just call an ambulance or something?"

"Because you asked me not to. You *begged* me not to. Why are you so afraid of hospitals, R.J.?" she continued, whipping his name with an intentional emphasis. She'd lost her appetite. And her patience. Pilots were trouble, nothing but trouble. And pilots in trouble were even worse. "What is it you've got to hide? Are you running from somebody?"

He shook his head. "Just myself."

"Then why wouldn't you go to the hospital?"

His green eyes turned dull. "When I was a kid, I had a very bad experience in a hospital. Haven't cared much for them since."

"I don't care much for hospitals, either, but if I'd just crashed—"

"You think I meant to take a dive? Believe me, I would've been happy to keep right on flying."

"Really? Then why did you fly over my farm *three* times?" She could think of only one explanation. The bank.

Regret picked at a strawberry on his dessert. "Why did you wave at me?"

"We always wave at airplanes," she answered defensively. Somehow Dulcie always connected them with the father she didn't remember.

"Maybe I always fly over a farm three times."

"Somehow I doubt that. Out with it, R.J.—or whatever your name is! Did the bank send you? If they did, you can wait till they foreclose to come snooping around. I told Buck Witherspoon if I could just have until this fall's harvest—"

"I'm not with the bank."

"Then why were you flying over my farm?"

"Sorry. Didn't realize I was violating your airspace."

"Well, you were." Her hands had started to shake. She twisted a dishcloth between her fists. "That's exactly what you were doing. You didn't have any business flying over my farm." Or crashing on it.

"What's the big deal about flying over your farm? Are you growing pot in the woods or something?"

"You're probably the one running drugs," she retorted.

"Look," he said, shaking his head, "I'm a photographer—"

"I know you're a photographer. You told me. But I knew it from the moment I pulled you out of that cockpit."

He squinted at her. "How'd you know that?"

"Your camera. Your film. It didn't take a genius to figure it out. I may be pretty naive about inviting a stranger into my home, but I'm not a country bumpkin, you know."

"I never said—"

"You didn't have to. It was written all over your face."

Abruptly Trudy stood up, listening motionlessly like a doe caught in a hunter's sights. She put one finger to her lips, and then Regret heard it, too. A quiet but insistent rapping at the back door had caught her attention.

"Maybe it's your grandfather."

She shook her head. "Papa wouldn't have knocked.

"Stay here," she whispered. Trudy tiptoed across the kitchen to a side window and cautiously peered around the homemade curtains. A polished silver sports car had pulled up next to her truck under the pecan tree.

"Maybe it's just a salesman," Regret suggested. "You do have traveling salesmen out here in the boondocks, don't you?"

She felt the old guilt weighing down her shoulders. *She's a real salesperson, all right!* "I know who this is," Trudy said aloud. *Trouble, that's who!*

"What's wrong?" he asked. He was frowning at her, as though he suspected she was hiding something.

"Go to your room and stay there."

His face turned beet red. He rose from his chair and looked down at her. "Maybe I wanted to stay here with you."

"Do you want the whole town to know you're here?" She gave him a less-than-gentle push toward the kitchen door. "You're a pilot, R.J. The *last* kind of man I should have in my house."

Quickly rebounding, he countered, "Why? Are you ashamed of me or something?"

She stared at him. Why was he fighting her? After all, he was the one who was hiding from God-knows-what-all and scared to death of hospitals. "I'm not ashamed of you," she answered tightly. "I'm *trying* to protect you. Do you have any idea what Louisa will say if she finds out I took you in? I don't need another man in my life. Specially not a devil-may-care pilot."

He threw up his hands in resignation and stalked out of the room, muttering, "Women!"

* * *

"*Regret! Go to your room! Right now!*" He could still
hear his mother's voice echoing through his memory as he
stumbled into the guest room he'd come to know so well.

"*But, Mommy, I wasn't doing nothing—*"

"*I don't care. Go to your room. You look too much like
your father tonight.*"

With one simple demand, Trudy had brought it all back.
She was a mother, all right. Trudy had used that same maternal voice on him that he remembered from childhood, the
same one that had sent him to his room so many times and
without any reason other than his mother wanting him out
of her sight. What kind of monster had rescued him from
his downed bird? He bent over a vase of fresh honeysuckle
and snipped off a yellow bloom, bringing it to his nose for
a lingering inhalation. His anger softened.

A beautiful monster, he thought. Trudy was everything
he'd never known he wanted in a woman. Lying in bed, day
after day, with nothing pleasant to dream of and only a disaster at Johnson's Creek to feed his nightmares, he'd found
himself unable to erase her image from his mind.

Not that he was falling in love with this simple barefoot
nurse. No, sirree. Regret James didn't fall in love. Regret
James kept his liaisons brief and uncomplicated, disappearing from brokenhearted lives without a trace. Just as his
mother had broken his heart and disappeared from his life.
Behind him was a trail of women who knew only his
aliases, or if he'd trusted them enough to tell them his last
name, they'd found only an operator's announcement of an
unlisted telephone number waiting for them. Regret James
liked to think he'd covered his tracks, both with the women
in his past and with Trudy.

That's why he'd slipped his wallet into Dulcie's doll's
dress for safekeeping. He'd been much too weak to have
Trudy strip his bloodied clothes and find his wallet—his
identity, the picture of her—in his jeans pocket. Dulcie had
since shown him the "treasure" she kept in her purse. After promises of every game he could think of, Dulcie had
relinquished the wallet, now hidden between the mattress
springs of his bed.

Still, he couldn't keep his mind off Trudy's face. She wore little or no makeup and didn't really need it, although a little rose on her lips would have brought out their natural fullness. Occasionally she left her dark, tumbling hair long and loose, but during the warm days she usually kept it pulled off her face, either in a loose braid or a ribbon. By the frequent hum of her sewing machine, he concluded that most of her dresses, as well as her daughter's, were homemade, yet they looked as well sewn as any store-bought dresses he'd seen on—or off—a woman. Either she didn't have any shoes or didn't like wearing shoes, because he'd never seen a pair on her or her little girl. She didn't talk much, but she had a delicate voice well suited for the a cappella hymns he'd heard resound through the house enough times to know all the words himself. He'd overheard Dulcie's temper tantrums, potty training failures and episodes of spilled lemonade, and he knew from listening to Trudy's chats with her daughter that she could be a loving, giving, patient mommy—damn her!

He heard Trudy at the back door and then the grating laughter of another woman. Who was this Louisa he needed to be protected from? Was there any chance Trudy wanted to keep him all to herself? Maybe not, but he could hope. He slipped closer to the door, close enough to hear their conversation in the kitchen.

"Trudy, I haven't seen you all week! I tried calling, but all the phone lines are out. Storm, I guess. Jordy said they should be fixed in the next day or two. And how's my little Droolcie? Have you been a good girl?" The voice didn't wait for an answer. "Trudy, is that your ATV out there?"

"The four-wheeler? Yes, it's mine. Why?"

"Oh. I just thought maybe it belonged to somebody else."

"No, I bought it a couple of years ago when we gave Rosencrantz and Guildenstern to the Meltons. After Johnny died, it just didn't seem right riding only one horse. Besides, they were really more than I could handle."

"It's no wonder you had to give them away instead of selling them. With names like those..."

"I named them after characters in *Hamlet*," Trudy answered defensively. "I may not have gone to college like you did but—"

"Whatever," the other woman cut in. "You know, Trudy, I'm going to do you a big favor. It's a good thing I noticed your ATV out there. I'll check your policy when I get back to the office, but I'm positive you're not insured for it, and lots of accidents happen every year."

"Well, we're very careful, Louisa, and we always wear our helmets."

"Whatever. But as soon as I get back to my office, I'm going to call my headquarters and have them add ATV coverage to your policy. Don't worry, hon. It won't cost you anything. I'll make sure they throw it in free with the rest of your farm coverage."

"Louisa—"

"Oh, no need to thank me. What are sisters-in-law for?"

A sister-in-law. So that was it. Either a brother's wife, which Regret somehow doubted, or a husband's sister. She was pushy, too, but he didn't see her as a threat. Not yet, anyway.

"Dulcie and I were just having strawberry shortcake for dessert. Would you like some, Louisa?"

"Oh, no, thanks. Gotta watch my figure for Jordy. A good figure's so important to keep a man. So where's your guest?"

Regret listened closely but heard only silence. Finally, after a long while, Trudy asked, her voice wavering, "What guest? What are you talking about?"

"Your dirty dishes—oh, my! I guess I really should've called before popping in unannounced. Here I haven't given you time to finish your dinner or clean up." Then she added with a simper in her voice, "But I see you've set three plates, and they've all been dirtied."

"Papa . . ."

"Don't try to fool me, Trudy. I minored in psychology in college, remember? And anyway, I saw Papa's car at Miss Clarice's house not more than forty or fifty minutes ago. I'll bet he preferred her company to yours. Sure does look like an awful lot of food eaten today by just you and Dulcie."

"Okay, okay. You caught me. I'd already cooked for Papa, when he tore off to town to see Miss Clarice. I'm really embarrassed to admit it, Louisa, but I ate most of his share, too. You know how I eat when I get depressed."

Regret stifled a chuckle. Trudy didn't have a liar's voice.

"Oh, Trudy!" The other woman clucked her tongue. "Just because you don't have a man in your life is no reason to let yourself go."

"Thanks. I'll try to remember that. So what's Jordy up to these days?"

"Same as usual. His daddy gave him a promotion down at the police station, but I'm still making more money selling insurance than he is and that just galls him. He has such big dreams of striking it filthy rich. Nothing seems to make him happy anymore. Sure would be nice if you'd sell us a little chunk of your land. Jordy wants something with lots of trees. He'd even . . ." She hesitated, choosing her words carefully. "He'd even be happy with that old swamp down by Alligator Pond."

"Louisa, this is the tenth time we've talked about it. Like I told you before, I really couldn't part with it."

"Not even the worthless land? We were thinking you wouldn't mind getting rid of Alligator Pond. Nothing but a mosquito breeder, anyway. Or, if you're willing, we'll buy the whole farm from you. I know the money would come in real handy about now."

Trudy needs money? Regret strained to hear her response.

"I really can't sell any of this land. Not even the swamp. My ancestors have walked these woods since the early 1800s. You know how important this land is to me. I think of it as an heirloom to be passed down through the generations."

"Whatever. I'm just trying to help. You remember that. You're gonna lose it to bankruptcy, anyhow. At least if you sold it to Jordy and me, you'd be able to keep it in the family."

"I'll find a way to keep it. If the crops do well this fall, I think we'll come close to paying off the debt. If not, then I don't know what I'll do. When Papa passed it on to me, he thought it would keep me here with him after Johnny died.

And he was right. But he never dreamed all Johnny's creditors would come after the land once it was in my name."

"Just how much did Johnny owe?"

Trudy didn't answer.

"Come on, Trudy." A pause followed. "You know I have ways of finding out."

"Seventy-two thousand, one hundred eighty-nine dollars. And thirty-two cents."

"That's not too bad. I make close to that in a good year if I count the bonus trips to Hawaii for high sales." Louisa laughed. "Some years it's all I can do to spend it."

Then loan some money to Trudy! Regret wanted to yell from behind the door.

"Seventy thousand might not seem like much to you, Louisa, but if the crops don't do well this year, it might as well be a million."

"That's too bad. Didn't Johnny have anything other than the business?"

"He was your brother. You know as well as I do. He didn't have a head for business."

"Yeah, you're right about that. I was the only one in the family with a head for business. Sell us the farm, Trudy. Hell, *give* it to us. At least the bank won't get it. And we'll even let you keep the house."

"That's very generous of you, Louisa, but this land isn't mine."

"Of course it is. Mr. Lester deeded it to you."

"It's Dulcie's. I'm just holding it in trust for her."

"Whatever. Be stubborn. Lose your land. Just don't come crawling to me and Jordy."

"I don't crawl."

"Whatever."

The house was silent once more, and Regret waited.

"So, Trudy, I hear you had another airplane crash-land."

"You heard what? Who told you that nonsense?"

"Oh, I guess maybe Rooster mentioned it to Jordy."

"I— Did Rooster mention why the plane crashed?"

"Uh, no. Just that he was out with some of the guys and saw it come down on your land. So? Did you get a good look at the pilot? Was he cute? Was he *alive?*"

"I, uh, couldn't get to the crash. Too far away to go on foot. And since then, with all the rains, I sure can't get back there. The bridge over Johnson's Creek got washed out last year, remember? Jordy was going to help Papa rebuild it for me."

"Oh. So you haven't seen the pilot."

"I'm sure the authorities will be out looking for him. Pilots are supposed to file flight plans before undertaking a—"

"Yeah, yeah. I've heard all that before from Johnny. Well, I hope you're not planning on getting involved with this . . . this pilot."

"I'm not," Trudy answered too quickly. "I mean, if there were a pilot, I wouldn't get involved with him."

"Good. Spare yourself the heartache a second time. Better yet, sell us the land and get out of this podunk town. Start over somewhere new, someplace that you won't be reminded of . . . of that pile of metal you keep in the barn."

"I can't just haul it to the dump. That airplane was Johnny's dream."

"And look where it got him."

Her husband had died in a crash? Was that it? Trudy had fallen for a pilot? And now he was a dead pilot? Regret leaned his head against the door. No wonder she'd been upset by all his talk of flying.

"You know," Louisa began again, "I'd be really terrified if I were you."

"Why?"

"Here you are all alone in this big old house with your baby girl and an old man who's hard of hearing, and somewhere on the other side of Johnson's Creek is a man who's probably a drug dealer or something."

Regret groaned to himself. Scare tactics. Why did Louisa want her to leave this farm so badly? She was concerned about more than Trudy's heart. He'd bet on that.

"You're safe now, girl. But remember, those waters are gonna go down sooner or later, and then there's nothing between you and him."

Trudy laughed, and Regret was relieved to hear it. "Nothing but Grendel and my rifle."

"This is no time to be joking about—" Louisa lapsed into a paroxysm of coughing. "Trudy, I think I'll excuse myself to your bathroom. Would you please cut me a piece of that delicious-looking strawberry shortcake?"

"Sure, but I thought you had to watch your figure. Louisa?"

The coughing faded as footsteps drew closer to Regret. Quietly he retreated to his room, closed the door and sat down patiently on the bed. He was beginning to understand why Trudy hadn't wanted him to meet Louisa. She was trying to protect him from Louisa's nosiness. Even without seeing her, he knew the woman was rude and insensitive. Her only purpose in visiting seemed to be to find out whether Trudy had a houseguest. And to get her to sell the farm. Who was this Louisa to feel so superior to Trudy? He didn't like it—not one little bit—the way she belittled his savior.

The old farmhouse creaked under Louisa's footsteps, which were loud and purposeful until she reached the bathroom door and opened it. Then the footfalls fell in a different direction, stealthily toward Trudy's bedroom. The door next to his squeaked as it opened. A moment later it closed. The footsteps moved again, this time to his door. Before he could stand, his bedroom door was flung open and had banged into the wall.

They stared at each other. Neither spoke. He scanned the woman's face and body, assessing her as all flash and little substance—his kind of woman. Louisa's hair was platinum blond and straight, and it hung short at the back of her neck, falling to a longer length at her chin. She had wide-set eyes that were too violet in hue to be natural and cherry lips that had been tailored with several shadings. Her makeup had taken at least an hour of her time, he guessed, and her designer suit had certainly not been bought locally. She was the antithesis of Trudy.

Her violet eyes narrowed as she stood perfectly still in the doorway. Several seconds passed before her gold hoop earrings stopped swinging. Then her long, red fingernails drummed against the doorframe.

"Who are you?" she asked coldly.

Regret stood up but didn't close the distance between them. "I prefer to be properly introduced by my hostess."

"Proper? What would you know about proper?"

Trudy appeared and stood open-mouthed beside Louisa. "I, uh, I—"

"Don't bother explaining, Trudy. I'm sure it'll just be another lie."

Regret winced as Louisa's tone cut into her sister-in-law.

"Louisa, it's not what it looks like. He's staying in his own room. I'm not—I mean, we're not—"

"Just shut up, Trudy," the blonde hissed, shoving Trudy and little Dulcie out of her way as she stalked off. She glanced back one last time at him and then glared at Trudy. "My brother would roll over in his grave if he could see this!"

At the far end of the house, a door slammed, followed by a car door banging shut outside. Trudy slumped against the wall and rolled her eyes to Regret.

"Sorry. That was by ex-sister-in-law, Louisa Clayton."

"So I gathered." Regret tried to offer her a smile. She was trembling, and he felt sorry for her. He'd behaved so badly toward her earlier. "Why was she so upest about me being your guest? And in your guest room, no less?"

Trudy shook her head and closed her eyes. "It's not that you're a guest. Although it may be rather scandalous in these parts for a young widow-woman to offer room and board to a stranger. And it's not that you're a man. Louisa's tried to get me to date Rooster Reed for the past year."

"Then why? It's because I'm a pilot, isn't it?"

Her eyes moved over him, and he felt their longing. "And because you're wearing Johnny's clothes."

Chapter 4

Trudy brought her hammer down with every ounce of her displaced fury. The spike sank impressively into the scrap of wood. Picking up another scrap, already measured and cut, she laid it against the first two lengths and connected the third with a single blow of her hammer. At Trudy's feet and under the edge of her worktable in the backyard, Dulcie played with the remaining wooden blocks, stacking them into the form of a tower.

Having Louisa catch her in a lie was the worst thing that had happened to Trudy since Johnny's death. But what choice had she had? And why had Louisa been so intent on finding out if she had a houseguest? True, Louisa could outgossip any old busybody in town, but her mission had been one of determined fact-finding, not the usual trivial snooping. Her sister-in-law rarely concerned herself with Trudy's lack of a social life except where Louisa had motive. Most of the time, Louisa was too absorbed with her own life to bother trying to manage Trudy's.

Still, it upset Trudy that she had offended Louisa. Not only was Louisa Johnny's little sister, but she'd also been a good friend to Trudy back in high school. Louisa had been a year behind her in school, but for the year before Louisa went away to college, she was the closest thing to a sister Trudy had ever known. Louisa had graduated from the University of Georgia and had gone on to get her master's degree in business administration before returning to Cornerstone to marry the sheriff's son.

Jordy Clayton's family was well respected in Cornerstone, but with all his parents' coddling, Jordy simply wasn't destined to cut the apron strings and venture out into the world. At first he'd attended an Alabama college on a football scholarship, but since academics had never been one of his strengths, he'd dropped out after two years and come home to the safety of his family name and a guaranteed career working for the county. College hadn't really changed Jordy. He was the same vain demigod he'd been in high school. Now he was thirty years old and still reliving the glory days of his early youth when he'd had an aptitude for football and cheerleaders.

Louisa, on the other hand, had come back from college a different person. She was strong and daring—or at least Trudy thought so. Independent and worldly, Louisa was in many ways the person Trudy longed to be. She liked to think she was lucky to have Louisa Clayton for a friend as well as an insurance agent, but every now and then Louisa's tone seemed a little condescending. Louisa wore her diploma like a crown, as though it somehow made her better than the townspeople she'd left behind.

Maybe Trudy should have trusted Louisa with her secret. The thought had crossed her mind several times since she'd found the pilot in the crumpled Cessna. Louisa had been there when she'd buried Johnny. If anybody understood why she had to save Regret, Louisa would.

Once again she dismissed the urge to tell Louisa. She told herself to trust her own instincts. Louisa might be the best friend she had, but Louisa also had a big mouth. When she'd found out she was pregnant with Dulcie, hadn't she and Johnny told Louisa right away and sworn her to secrecy? And hadn't Louisa confessed to Jordy, later defending herself with a sharp tongue, "You don't expect me to keep secrets from my husband, do you?" No, she'd done the right thing by not confiding in her sister-in-law. And then she'd done the wrong thing by not hiding the truth better.

"I hope you're not thinking of me."

Trudy spun around, hammer in hand. Dressed in Johnny's clothes, Regret stood a few feet away, grinning that sexy playboy grin at her. Slowly she laid the hammer on the worktable. "No, I wasn't thinking of you."

"Good. Judging by the look on your face, I'd say you're building a whole bunch of little coffins before you murder someone with that hammer."

"Don't be silly." Trudy pursed her lips to keep him from realizing how much she appreciated the sentiment. "I'm building bluebird houses."

"Oh."

His gaze flicked over the row of finished boxes on her table and then over her body. She felt the heat of his appraisal and leaned backward against the table's edge.

"Why bother? Let them fend for themselves like the other birds."

Trudy shook her head in mock disgust. Secretly she was pleased to be in the presence of a novice. It was so hard to get Papa and Louisa excited about her hobby when they'd heard about it a thousand times before.

"When I was a little girl, I couldn't walk outside in the springtime without seeing a bluebird. Now they're struggling against extinction."

He laughed. "And you're single-handedly going to save them all?"

"If it takes it, yes. My daughter deserves to grow up with the same wonders of nature I did as a child. There's a saying about the Earth being inherited by our children...."

Regret shrugged. "Yeah, I think I read that on a bumper sticker somewhere."

"Well, it's true. You see those fields over there?" She pointed to the neighboring property to the south. Regret nodded. "And those over there?" She pointed this time to the open land to the west and north. "All that used to be forest. Less than ten years ago."

"Your land?"

"No. If it were my land, there'd still be trees there. My neighbors allowed their timber to be cut. They never replanted it."

"So? That's their land, their business."

Trudy smiled to herself. If only Rooster Reed could recognize that her land was her business! "The trees are theirs to cut down. I won't argue with that. But bluebirds don't build nests on tree limbs like other birds. They seek out hollow trees."

"And when the forests are cleared, your bluebirds get kicked out of their natural environment?"

"Right. I've kept my trees, and I've put out forty-eight birdhouses on my land. So far. That's why I've got such a nice little bird sanctuary here." She frowned and wiped at the thin mist on her forehead. "And that's why all the local hunters like to trespass on my property."

The man with the serious green eyes nodded. "To hunt your bluebirds."

Trudy winced at the memory of the dying bluebird at her feet and Rooster Reed at the far end of her rifle. "For sport. Not for food. I can't tell you how often I've found doves shot down, left, wasted in the woods. The same with deer, rabbits, squirrels. Nothing's safe from those bastards."

For a moment, he looked stunned. "Sorry," she muttered. "I don't usually use profanity. Only if I feel strongly about the subject. All those helpless little rabbits and squirrels and—"

He laughed abruptly. She glared at him.

"No, Trudy." He stepped back defensively. "I wasn't laughing about your poor little animals. I was remembering this scene out of a storybook I had when I was a kid. In fact, it's the only storybook I remember at all. It belonged to one of my foster sisters. *Sleeping Beauty,* I think, was the name of it. She was sitting in the forest with all her animal friends. Rabbits, squirrels, bluebirds. It reminded me of you."

Trudy smiled. She knew the storybook. It was one of Dulcie's favorites.

"Well, look, Trudy, I want to thank you for everything you've done for me. Getting me back on my feet and all. But

I've been in your hair long enough, and after causing all that trouble with your sister-in-law, I'd better go ahead and find me a hotel room in town while I make arrangements to get my plane back in the air." He rammed his hands into his pockets. "But I'll be close by if you, um, need me."

She ran her fingertips along the raw edge of the table. It was a poor excuse for looking away from him, but she couldn't let him see how much she'd miss his company if he left. She'd forgotten how much she enjoyed having a man—a young man—around the house. And she especially missed blond-haired pilots

"I...won't need you."

"What about the hunters? What if they come back?"

"I'll manage."

They stood in silence.

"Maybe you could recommend a hotel. One not so far from here. In case you change your mind about needing me."

"There aren't any hotels in town," she said simply.

Frowning, Regret cocked his head. "There's got to be something. There's a four-lane highway just south of town. I saw it from the air."

"Highway 84. It carries all the major traffic between Alabama and Florida. The Department of Transportation wanted to improve the highway through Cornerstone several years ago. Widen it from two to four lanes. At first all the merchants pitched a fit. They didn't want all that traffic coming through town. There were town meetings and church meetings and editorials in the newspaper. Sheriff Clayton talked about how we'd have to triple law enforcement to handle all the dope peddlers and speeders who were sure to come through our fair city. The school principal worried about how the bigger highway would affect the kids walking home from school. Some of the businesses would have to give up parking spaces to make room for the expanded right-of-way. Unfortunately the Department of Transportation listened to their complaints and decided to bypass Cornerstone. Almost as soon as the bypass was open to traffic, the stores and restaurants in town began drying up. The motels couldn't keep their doors open after the first year. Nobody talks about it much. People here don't like to admit it when they're wrong, especially when lack of foresight turns your hometown into a ghost town.''

"So Cornerstone, Georgia, really faded off the map. That's a damned shame. I was really hoping to find a room in town. I really don't want to be too far away from . . . my plane."

Trudy looked at him and then glanced quickly away as she nodded. She tried to make her invitation seem as casual as Southern hospitality. "Unless you know someone else in town, you can stay here until you're able to leave."

"Okay." He accepted readily. Too readily. "I won't be bothering you for too much longer. I need to take a look at my plane, assess the damage. Then I'll call my buddy, and we'll have it hauled back home. I won't be bothering you but a day or two more than I already have."

"I don't think it'll be quite that easy," she said with a sheepish grin.

He looked confused. "My leaving you?"

Her pulse quickened at his suggestion. "Your leaving. Period." At the puzzled expression on his face, she added, "You don't remember much about when I pulled you out of the plane, do you?" He shook his head. "We talked about this before, but I guess you weren't feeling too well at the time. You landed in an enclosed pasture. There aren't any roads big enough to get a truck through, much less an airplane. The only way you're going to get your plane out of there is either fly it out or chop it up and haul it out on foot."

Regret stared at her. "I have to get it out of there," he said urgently. "But I'll have to see it to tell how bad the damage is."

"Can you fix it yourself?"

He shook his head. "My buddy—the one I mentioned earlier—he's a certified mechanic. He'll have to do the work, but I can look at it and get a rough idea of how much babying it'll need."

"It'll be a while before you can take a look at it."

"I can do it today."

"Too far for you to walk."

"Could I take your truck?"

She shook her head. "There's only a path through the woods. You could take my four-wheeler, but you'd never get it across Johnson's Creek. The water's still too high."

A flicker of concern crossed his brow. For a moment he seemed to be thinking of something far more serious than getting to his airplane. "Then I'll have to walk."

She sighed audibly, then ran her fingers through her long hair. "I have an idea."

"Great. Let's do it."

"You'll have to stay here with Dulcie for a few minutes. I have to run over to the Meltons' place."

"Why?" He didn't seem comfortable with the idea of staying with a child.

"Sometimes Mrs. Melton—Miss Naomi—watches Dulcie for me. They're not home, so we'll have to take Dulcie with us." She noticed his frown and added, "But don't worry. She'll ride on my horse."

"Horse?"

Regret thought as he sat on the back doorsteps that he'd figured out Trudy's appeal. Unlike all the other women he'd been attracted to, whose faces had blended and whose names he'd long since forgotten, Trudy Sandlin possessed two rare traits: mystery and generosity. Although he'd been careful not to let her catch his stolen glances at her face, he'd seen the secret hell that burned in her blue eyes. He wondered who'd put it there. Why her sense of duty to her crotchety, never-to-be-pleased grandfather? Why the saintly tolerance of her flashy, condescending sister-in-law? Why the depthless patience with a toddling girl who wanted to do everything herself? Why the commitment to nature's kingdom and her tireless effort to save its creatures? Why the willingness to pull a bleeding stranger from twisted wreckage and apply her healing touch? Why the sadness, the loneliness that never left her beautiful cobalt blue eyes?

She was such a tiny thing, he thought, to have such strength, and he envied her. With all the struggles plaguing her life—raising a child alone, sparring with good ol' boy hunters, losing her husband young in life—why wasn't she a trembling flower? Instead she seemed to have sprouted firm roots in the dry ground; she took the brunt of the sun and gave shade to everyone else.

He had to find a way to stay close to her, a way to put laughter back in her eyes. He owed her that much. He really didn't have to wait until his broken bird was back in the air. As a matter of fact, he could get back on the road for Atlanta and hire someone to bring the Cessna home.

Fine. Let her think that was his reason for staying. To get his plane fixed. She didn't have to know the real reason he couldn't leave her yet. She took care of everybody but herself. And until those bullies started leaving her alone and everybody else started treating her with more respect, taking care of Trudy was going to be his job.

He bent his head forward, studying the grass at his feet and running his hands through his wavy hair. The grass needed to be cut, a result of several days of heavy rain. He wondered how much it had rained, how high the waters of Johnson's Creek had risen, whether Hughie had made the phone call in time. Trudy's farm was still sitting on solid ground and he hadn't heard any explosions, so he guessed Hughie had successfully relayed the message about the erosion north of the farm.

A tiny presence snuggled up beside him on the steps. He looked down into Dulcie's tiny face, staring up at him with her mother's curious eyes. Self-consciously he smiled at her. He'd spent his adult life staying far away from women with children, from women who wanted children and—worst of all—from women who wanted his children. He'd made certain that he'd never be faced with the curse of parenthood, that he would never put a child through the misery his parents had put him through. Cruelty could be hereditary, he'd reasoned. And what could be crueler than shuffling an unwanted child through twenty-one foster homes in thirteen years? Now he looked at Trudy's child and didn't know what to say.

She said something too shyly to be heard, so he bent closer for her to repeat it.

"Are you my daddy?"

His mouth went dry. A second later, his eyes stung. Of course she didn't know her daddy! If Trudy's husband had died two years ago, then Dulcie had been only a few months old. His heart twisted inside his chest. She, like him, would grow up without a daddy. Regret brought a nervous hand to the child's head and stroked her dark hair. Had she seen so few men in her mother's house? "What makes you think I'm your daddy?"

"You fly airplanes," she answered matter-of-factly.

He looked up in relief as Trudy appeared at the corner of the house. Regal in her saddle, she was riding a sleek horse with a reddish brown coat and leading a darker brown horse behind her. She smiled at him.

He smiled back with tears in his eyes.

At first Trudy thought she saw tears in the pilot's eyes, but then she concluded that the sun had caught their sparkle. After all, she told herself, the idea of this man crying was ridiculous. He looked as if he'd never cried in his life. Or had reason to cry.

He met her at the edge of the grass with Dulcie in his arms. "I thought you got rid of your horses."

She realized by his comment that he'd been eavesdropping on her conversation with Louisa. What else had he heard? "I gave them to my neighbors after Johnny died and I bought the four-wheeler. The Meltons don't mind if I take the horses out every now and then for old times' sake."

She took Dulcie from him and arranged the little girl on the saddle in front of her, between the vee of her thighs. The man watched, mesmerized. "Do you know anything about horses?" she asked him.

"Nothing."

"Well, put your left foot in that stirrup and swing your right leg over. Hold on to the saddle horn to help pull yourself up."

He made it on the third try, with a considerably pained expression and several "Oomphs."

"You didn't tell me it was going to hurt," he gasped.

"Usually it doesn't, but you've probably got a couple of broken ribs." Seeing the glimmer of worry in his eyes, she added, "Don't fret about it, R.J. They'll heal by them-

selves. Eventually. Now all you need to know about that
horse is to pull back on the reins to stop. But whatever you
do, don't kick him in the sides. If you do, he'll take off like
a bolt of lightning. If you've got broken ribs, you'll want
your horse to walk.''

"What's my horse's name?" he asked.

He was holding on to the reins too tightly, and Trudy
motioned for him to relax as they started slowly across the
pasture.

"I've got Rosie and you've got Guildy. Or, if you want to
be formal about introductions, Rosencrantz and Guildenstern."

"Named for the characters in *Hamlet,* no doubt," Regret noted authoritatively.

Trudy chuckled to herself, wondering if he was as well
read as he pretended or if he was simply repeating the earlier conversation she'd had with Louisa. She suspected the
latter. He didn't seem the literary type. Trudy put her fingers to her mouth and whistled shrilly, loud enough to star-
tle Regret out of his newfound relaxation. The huge Irish
wolfhound bounced up to them, swaying playfully from side
to side and barking.

"Of course you know who Grendel was named for." She
grinned, baiting him.

Regret glanced at her uneasily. "Of course."

"Liar." She kept a straight face, but inside she was
laughing. She was amused that he had wanted to impress her
but amazed he'd known what would impress her. Even if he
didn't know the right answers.

Defeated, Regret slumped in his saddle. "Okay. I
haven't the foggiest idea why you named that—that dog
what you did."

Holding Rosie's reins with one hand, her other arm
around Dulcie, Trudy moved gracefully in the saddle, as
though she were connected to the horse, feeling its stride,
making its gait her own. "I never went to college," she told
him. "But I read a lot. I always believed that you shouldn't
let your mind stagnate, no matter who you are. If I'd gone
to college, I would've been required to read *Beowulf* in
freshman literature, so I read it anyway. Not going to col-

lege wasn't an excuse for not knowing those things. Being lazy would've been an excuse for not learning. So I read *Beowulf.* In it there's this monster who breaks—" She interrupted herself, remembering Dulcie's open ears and inquisitive mind. No need in giving a toddler any more nightmares. "In *Beowulf,* this creature named Grendel is reputed to rend grown men limb from limb. When I found out what kind of dog my puppy was, I looked him up in the encyclopedia, and I saw how absolutely gigantic this dog could become. He was huge and shaggy, with a long nose and a fierceness that could do Beowulf's monster justice. That's why I named my puppy Grendel. He's everything I wanted in a watchdog—a faithful protector, a loving companion, and he'd kill anybody who'd hurt me or Dulcie."

"Sounds like the ideal husband."

Trudy didn't respond, and in icy silence they reached the murky, tumbling waters of Johnson's Creek. Grendel swam across the heavy current with some difficulty and waited on the other bank.

"I scared, Mommy," Dulcie whined as they stood on the grassy bank. Trudy tightened her arms around the child and felt Dulcie stiffen.

"Shh. There's nothing to be afraid of. Mommy won't let anything hurt you." Trudy glanced over at Regret's face, which was frozen with apprehension. She knew he'd be too weak to swim if he couldn't stay on his horse. She freed one hand from Dulcie and reached to touch his hand, white knuckled on the reins. "Hold on to the saddle and don't let go for anything," she ordered with as much confidence as her voice could command. "Wait for me to cross. Your horse will follow." He nodded without looking away from the swirling water.

Reluctantly her horse stepped into the stream. Trudy urged him on, prodding him as the water rose higher, washing over Trudy's bare feet and moving quickly up to her knees. The water was deeper than she'd thought. She felt the horse under her struggling to touch bottom, pushing against the swift current, straining toward the opposite bank. Dulcie was starting to whine again, and Trudy herself could not let go of the breath she'd taken when the cold water had first touched her feet. With relief, she felt the horse heave onto the muddy solidity of the bank and pull them dripping from the creek.

Regret's horse struggled onto the bank beside them. His face was ashen.

"Are you okay?" She touched him again with her gentle maternal hand, and he nodded. "Aren't you glad I didn't let you walk?"

As he managed a smile, his gaze wandered down her wet calves, which were beaded with water. "Don't you have shoes?" he asked abruptly.

She frowned. "Of course I have shoes!"

"I never see you wearing them."

She laughed as the horses entered the shade of the woods. They were following a wide trail that sometimes was covered in standing water and at other times was dark with mud that clapped against the horses' hooves. "I have shoes, R.J. I just don't like to wear them."

He looked down at his soggy boots. "Why not?"

Trudy shrugged. "I like to feel the earth under my feet. The grass. The sand. I like the sensation of nature. It makes me feel I'm a part of this vast universe."

"That's how I feel when I'm flying. Like I'm part of this vast universe. I guess that's what bothers me about the crash. Flying's the one thing I've always been good at. I should've noticed the birds before I got that close."

"You couldn't have known that rifle shot would scare the birds."

He narrowed his eyes at her. "What do you mean?"

She clamped her mouth shut. She'd figured he knew what had brought him down.

Regret was close enough to seize her wrist and stop her. He reached for her and drew back quickly at the growl of the dog that now trailed them. "You didn't shoot at me, did you?"

"Of course not." She bit her lip. "The hunters on my land. One of them fired a shot into the air. Just showing off, proving he could defy me. We saw birds go everywhere, right up into your plane. Your engine died right after."

"They shot at me?" His voice changed in volume and depth as he spoke.

"Well, not on purpose. Rooster was just shooting up in the air. As a warning to me, I suppose. And then we saw you coming down beyond the trees."

Regret rode in astounded silence, taking in everything she had told him. At last he said, "I guess I know who didn't come to my rescue. Your friends would've let me—"

"They're not my friends," she interrupted with a tightness in her voice. "They threatened me. But they could've killed you."

"Oh. And I just happened to be in the wrong place at the wrong time?"

The horses stopped at a clearing, and Trudy turned to Regret. "Yeah, that about sums it up. If you hadn't decided to buzz my farm three times, you never would've met me."

"I don't like it, Trudy. I don't like the idea of leaving you here with these rednecks when I'm gone. I thought they were dangerous before, but now you tell me they willingly left me for dead? Good grief, woman! What's going to stop them from leaving you for dead next time?"

She turned back and pointed to the far side of the pasture. "There's your plane."

"My God!" he exclaimed as the horses drew nearer to it. Trudy was staring, too. Something was wrong. Something was different.

"Mommy?"

"Not now, Dulcie."

"But, Mommy—"

"Not now."

"Mommy, I saw a man in the woods over there."

"Later, Dulcie."

Trudy and her daughter stayed in the saddle while Regret dismounted and hobbled to his Cessna. Nearly tripping over the torn-away door, he ran his fingers over the smashed glass. He walked around to the other side and returned, shaking his head.

"This couldn't have happened in the crash."

"R.J.?" Trudy's voice was shaking. "It wasn't this bad. I don't remember it being this bad. I don't understand."

Their eyes met as he swallowed hard. "This isn't crash damage. This is vandalism."

Chapter 5

The little town of Cornerstone, Georgia, seemed even smaller on the ground than it had from the air. The land lay open and flat for several miles after he had passed the sign proclaiming the city limits and the population, spray painted in black. After the driver of the fifth vehicle he'd met poked up an index finger in salute, Regret realized that it was a South Georgia tradition to greet other cars and trucks in that manner, regardless of whether they recognized the driver. He responded in kind when he met the sixth vehicle.

Driving down a two-lane blacktop in Trudy's truck, Regret passed several abandoned storefronts. The glass wasn't broken and the parking lots weren't littered, yet the buildings had the desolate faces of years of emptiness. The truck rattled over railroad tracks no longer used and onto a wide, paved Main Street riddled with potholes.

So this is where Trudy grew up.

He couldn't stop thinking of her. More than anything, he wanted a monogamous relationship. Fulfillment from one woman. He just didn't trust it. It was just too damned likely that she'd walk out on him, too, or simply wake up one day robbed of all her passion.

How could anybody with any sense of passion live here?
Regret wondered as he drove down the streets a second time.
There's nothing to do. For a midmorning Saturday, few cars
were parked on the streets and even fewer customers walked
the sidewalks. He imagined Main Street as it must have been
fifty or sixty years ago with bustling shoppers and large
families and country square dances in the evenings. He'd
overheard Trudy's grandfather speaking of those days, of
their reprieve from the depression and World War II, of the
sense of community that had faded with the appearance of
television and the self-imposed isolation of the American
family.

Still, if one liked being alone—and Regret liked being
alone—a sense of lazy tranquillity blew through the wide
streets. He liked the idea of traveling for miles without seeing another human being. The solitude was closest to what
he felt in his airplane, hanging alone in the wild blue, soaking up the visual finery around and beneath his wings. Out
here in the country he was merely another of God's creatures—unbothered, alone, just a breathing spirit on a living planet.

Hughie would like this, he thought, smiling to himself.
Hughie would fit in here.

With Regret out of town, Hughie had been twice as busy
as usual, but most important of all, Hughie had managed
to relay the message to the gas company about the erosion
around Johnson's Creek. At least Regret didn't have to
worry about an explosion.

After checking the damage to the Cessna, Regret had
called and told him about the local yokels—and, of course,
about Trudy. Hughie had agreed that someone was either
threatening Trudy or trying to keep Regret on the ground.
Maybe both.

All the more reason not to leave Trudy. Not yet. Hughie
wouldn't be able to order parts for the wrecked plane until
he'd seen it for himself, and he couldn't drive down from
Newnan until Wednesday morning. A perfect excuse to hang
around a few more days.

On his third ride through town, Regret saw the repair
shop Trudy had told him about and parked diagonally in

front. The two large windows had been tinted to reduce the noon sun's glare, but now the black tinting was peeling at the corners and where the sun had been hottest. The block wall and wood-framed door had been painted a bright emerald several times without the previous coats of paint having been removed. The green now resembled a thick layer of plastic. Regret walked into the dim, open room. The tarnished cowbell on the door clanged behind him.

He blinked and his eyes slowly adjusted from the bright outdoors to the wavering fluorescent bulbs that seemed to absorb the pale-green interior. Along the walls were several television sets and radios, in various states of decay and depths of dust. At least a dozen cameras were tagged and waiting on a glass countertop. A shadow moved in the back room, coming to life as it passed in front of a black-and-white television screen.

"Can I help you?" The woman came as close as the glass counter but stayed cautiously behind it. Did she have a pistol within easy reach? Her face faded into the transparency of the pale greenness, but Regret could distinguish the teased white hair and passionless eyes above her puckered, cold pink mouth. She was somebody's grandmother, he decided, and she was more than a little hesitant of strangers.

"I certainly hope so." Regret had hoped his broad smile would reassure the woman, but she took a step backward.

"Harry's not in yet. He'll be here in an hour if you want to come back." She watched him expectantly, wishing he'd leave.

"Oh, I don't need anything repaired. I just wanted to order some equipment."

Her eyes narrowed. "What kind of equipment?"

Slowly he handed her a white envelope with a list scribbled on the back. When she didn't offer to take it from him, he laid it on the glass counter and stepped away, giving her plenty of room. Watching him carefully, she picked up the envelope.

"Pans, chemicals, red lights." He couldn't be sure she would recognize the list, even though Trudy had told him she and her husband sold camera supplies. "Photography equipment," he explained. "I develop my own pictures."

Reading the list, the woman nodded, then flipped the envelope over. Her lips moved as she silently read Trudy's grandfather's name and address on the envelope. "Where did you git this?"

Fear shone in her eyes. Did she think he'd stolen it from the Dugan farm?

"I'm a guest at Mr. Dugan's house."

"Really?" Her shoulders relaxed. "You must be a relative."

"No, ma'am." Regret shuddered, surprised at how fast he'd picked up the rural twang. "I had a tad of an accident, and Mr. Dugan had been generous enough to let me stay in his guest room while I get my, uh, vehicle repaired."

She smiled at him, though still unsure. "Lester must've really taken a shine to you to give you a place to stay even for one night. Specially with such a pretty granddaughter under the same roof."

"Trudy? Yes, such a lovely girl." For Trudy's sake, he forced himself not to laugh at his deceit. He wouldn't leave an impression of impropriety. Trudy deserved better than that. "But unluckily for me, she's still mourning her husband too much to pay any attention to the likes of me."

"Oh, dear." The woman nodded knowingly. "I don't think she'll ever git over his death. Or finding him that way."

What way? Regret wanted to ask. He hadn't dared to interrogate Trudy on her past, and certainly not on the delicate subject of her husband's demise.

"Yes, ma'am. I'm sure these things take time. More time than I'll be in town."

"Then you probably don't want to order your camera supplies here. I won't be able to git them here for a week or more. Mail's so slow, you know."

"How about overnight mail?"

She blinked at him. "I guess so. I've never used it before. It'll cost more."

"I'll pay it." He slapped a credit card down on the counter and watched her eyes widen.

"I'll want your credit card number for the rest of it, too. Just in case."

He nodded. "Great. I'll pick it up Tuesday morning."

No longer stiff and uncomfortable in his presence, the woman chattered absentmindedly about the warm weather and the game show on television while she prepared his credit card slip and then busily filled in the individual prices of the supplies on his list, probably at a considerable markup. As Regret signed the charge slip, he wondered if the size of his purchase was proportionate to her sudden friendliness. He pocketed his card and turned to leave.

"Mornin', Miss Myrtle."

Regret sidestepped the tan-uniformed deputy in the doorway. The deputy matched the movement, blocking his exit. He was taller than Regret, with rich black hair and eyes hidden behind mirrored sunglasses. His upper arms were adorned with the type of muscles that came only from weight lifting.

"Mornin', Jordy," the clerk said from behind the counter.

"Is this man botherin' you, Miss Myrtle?"

"Heavens, no, Jordy. He—"

Regret forced a thin smile at the larger man. "Excuse me," he said politely, and tried again to step around Jordy. The deputy caught Regret by the elbow, gracefully hooking the cold steel bracelet of handcuffs over Regret's left wrist. The motion took him by surprise, and Regret winced as the man twisted him around to join the other hand in the manacle. Regret might have fought back if his cracked ribs hadn't protested so sharply.

"But—but—Jordy!" the woman stammered. "What'd he do? What's wrong?" She clutched his credit-card receipt tightly, as though she were about to discover that it was a forgery.

One corner of the deputy's mouth curled upward in a smile. "Stole a truck, Miss Myrtle. I saw him drivin' 'round town in Trudy Sandlin's old pickup. I jes' hope to God Trudy's all right."

"I didn't steal anything," Regret shot back, struggling against the pain to focus on Jordy's face. "Trudy let me borrow her—"

Wham!

The room turned from dim green to sparkling gray as the deputy shoved Regret against the wall. For a moment, he couldn't breathe. Trudy had been right about venturing out so soon after a week's stay in bed.

"You ain't from 'round here, are you, boy?" the deputy asked, his hot breath close in Regret's ear. The smell of breakfast bacon lingered at Jordy's mouth. "We don't care much for outsiders comin' in here, takin' advantage of our women."

"I'm a guest of Mr. Lester's," Regret choked out. The room slowly came back into focus.

"See? Now I know that's a lie! Everybody 'round here knows that ol' man Dugan don't like company. I 'spect I'd better escort you right on across the street to the county jail. Till I can decide what to do with you, at least."

"You can't arrest me. I haven't done anything."

"Oh, yeah? I bet if I checked around under the seat of Trudy's truck, I might even find a couple of bags of marijuani under there. Sure couldn't be Trudy's, so it must be yours. Up to you, boy, how hard I look for it."

Regret twisted away. He'd had a brush with the law before, years ago when he'd been eighteen and stupid. He was past all that now, and except for the job applications that asked about his arrest record, few things reminded him of those miserable nights in a county jail. Ironically, if this bully cared to look, he'd find out very quickly that a man called Regret James had once been arrested—for car theft.

"You won't find anything in that truck," Regret said tensely, "that you didn't plant there."

"Oh, yeah? And who do you think the people of this here town are gonna believe? The sheriff's son? Or some punk fly-by-night fly-boy?"

Regret's chest tightened with anxiety. This run-in with the deputy was no coincidence. This deputy knew who he was and that he was a pilot. There were only two ways he could've known about his plane crash: either Louisa had told Jordy about her confrontation at Trudy's house or Jordy had been among the hunters who'd put a bullet in the air and brought him down like a broken bird. This Jordy was the most dangerous of the redneck species—he wore a uniform.

"Come on, fly-boy."

Jordy opened the door and shoved him toward it. Regret caught the frame with his shoulder and planted his feet. Jordy jerked him away from the door frame and shoved Regret out onto the sun-bright sidewalk.

"You wanna add resistin' arrest to that?"

"How can I be under arrest? I haven't done anything wrong, and you haven't even read me my rights."

"Stop wastin' my time, mister."

Jordy gave him another shove, and Regret stumbled, almost losing his balance. The previously deserted streets were now peopled with gawking shoppers.

"You hear me, fly-boy? I said, are you gonna come along quietly? Or do you want me to add resistin' arrest to car theft?"

Regret turned and glared back angrily. Instead of challenging the deputy's eyes, he saw only his own reddened face mirrored in the silver lenses of the man's sunglasses. "No!"

"No what?"

Regret stared at him.

"No, *sir*. Let me hear you say it."

"Go to hell," Regret said through clenched jaws.

"Looks like you got your hands full, Clayton." A red-faced man, thirtyish with a receding blond hairline, slapped a hand across the deputy's back.

"Nothin' I cain't handle, Rooster. This here's the guy who's been shackin' up with Trudy. Thought you might want a shot at him."

"You already took a shot at me," Regret mumbled. They didn't hear.

"Real bastard, too." Jordy continued. "Stole her truck."

"Well, well." Rooster bent uncomfortably close to Regret's face. "Taken a likin' to my ex-girlfriend, have you? I know it cain't be the other way around."

Regret didn't say anything. This was the man who'd watched him fall out of the sky and left him for dead. If it hadn't been for Trudy's intervention, he might not have had the pleasure of meeting his would-be assassin.

"You got nothin' to say for yourself?" Rooster asked, grinning. He turned back to Jordy. "So whatcha gonna do with him? Throw him in jail and teach him a lesson, or do you think he's got sense enough to git out of town while the gittin's good?"

"Oh, I don't think he's got no sense at all. Else he wouldn't have come into town in a stolen truck."

A dozen townspeople had gathered on the sidewalk by the time Jordy pushed Regret across the street toward the local jail. As had so often happened in his life, Regret was a stranger in a strange place, the wrong place at the wrong time. His destiny was built on clichés.

"When do I get my one phone call?" he growled as the deputy shoved him through the door. Maybe he could get through to Hughie. Maybe Hughie could come down and get him out of this hellhole. He knew better than to call Trudy, even though she could clear up this misunderstanding right away. He would never ask a woman for help. He knew the real possibility that Trudy, like all the other women in his life, would abandon him when he needed her most.

Jordy laughed. "A phone call? You don't git nothin', fly-boy."

The sheriff's office was at least twenty degrees cooler than the temperature on the street and quiet except for the straining hum of two large window air conditioners. Regret counted three desks, evenly spaced across the roomy office, each one littered with papers, soft drink cans and black rotary telephones. Without releasing his grip on Regret's elbow, Jordy picked up an aluminum can off the nearest desk and drained it. Regret noticed the eight-by-ten photograph featured prominently on the corner of Jordy's desk and recognized the face: it was Trudy's sister-in-law, Louisa.

Jordy jerked him back from the desk. "You oglin' my wife? Well, you can put that idea out of your head right now. If you ain't gittin' nowhere with Trudy, you sure ain't gittin' nowhere with Weezer."

Again Regret said nothing. It didn't seem wise to him to add fuel to the fire that Jordy and Rooster were stoking. He wondered if they were trying to provoke him into a fight. Him, a man handcuffed, not yet recovered from a concussion and broken ribs, against two able-bodied hometown boys with guns and night sticks at their disposal. At the moment, Regret felt more alone than he'd ever felt before—more than he'd felt as a five-year-old strapped to his hospital bed and screaming for his mother.

The deputy shoved him toward an open doorway. The man still hadn't removed his sunglasses. Regret wanted desperately to look into those hidden eyes and see if they were made of steel or if there were telltale signs that the deputy was soft without the authority of his uniform.

Down a long, narrow hallway, Jordy walked behind his prisoner. Every few feet he gave Regret a hard shove forward. Except for two men sleeping off the previous night's drunken celebration, the other cells were unoccupied. They stopped at the last vacant cell, where Jordy used his booted foot to force Regret through the open gate.

"Make yourself at home now." Jordy's lips curved into a mischievous smirk as he slammed the door shut and locked it.

Regret stood there watching his jailer stalk back down the hall to the office. His blood was pumping too hard for him to sit down. He glanced around the tiny cell. A stained toilet occupied one corner, though with his hands cuffed behind him, it was only a reminder of his helplessness. He noted a hard bunk in the other corner of the cell, but he knew he wouldn't sit down. To sit down would be to accept this abomination of justice.

He had to find a way out!

He couldn't allow himself to be caged like a wild bird. He loved the outdoors too much. He'd dry up and die like a potted plant if he couldn't get out in the sunshine and fresh air.

He walked to the small window in the center of the wall and put his head against the bars, nudging at them with his forehead. To his surprise, they moved outward a couple of inches. He stepped back and surveyed the window.

Maybe that's what they want! Maybe they want me to get out. Then they can shoot me in the back for trying to escape. Nobody will ever ask questions!

Still, escape was impossible. The window was too high, and with his hands secured behind his back, even an open window could not offer him freedom.

"So whatcha gonna do with him?" he heard Rooster asking down the hall. In all the excitement, they'd left the office door open.

Waiting for an answer, Regret stared out the window. He had a decent view of Main Street and the few shoppers who wandered onto the sidewalk.

"I don't know," Jordy answered. "I thought about takin' him to the county line and dumpin' him off there and tellin' him not to ever show his face in my county again, but that doesn't solve our other problem. Can't keep him from flyin' over Trudy's place."

Rooster laughed. "I already took care of that like you told me to. That plane won't be going nowhere for a while."

So the damage to his bird—the worst of it, anyway—had been intentional! Pure vandalism! Now he was sure not only of the nature of the crime but also of the identity of at least two of the vandals.

Across the street, a blonde in a short red dress stepped out of a men's clothing store. She was wearing dark, cat's-eye glasses and carrying a large plastic bag in one hand and a purse that matched her dress and shoes in the other.

"Well," Rooster drawled from down the narrow hall, "it'd sure solve a lot of our problems if Trudy would sell a piece of her farm to us."

"We've been through that before. Weezer says Trudy wants to keep the property in her family. She still thinks she can save it from Johnny Reb's debts. Weezer's already talked about it with Buck Witherspoon. The bank's gonna take it any day now. You'd think Trudy'd be a little less particular about sellin' it. Now, if you could make some headway with her, old man..."

"It ain't for lack of trying."

"Then try harder. You two were good together once. If you could git it going again, who knows? That land might be yours for a little of nothin', and we'd have a clear path to a tidy fortune! There's a fortune buried on the Dugan place, and I intend for it to be mine. Whether we split it fifty-fifty is up to you."

"I thought we was splittin' it fifty-fifty anyhow."

"That, Rooster, depends on how much effort you put into this little venture. Propose to her. Ain't nobody else gonna marry her."

"She won't marry me, Clayton."

"Then make a deal with her. Marry her and pay off Johnny's debts. But she signs the land over to you."

"No dice, Clayton. She don't feel that way toward me. Not no more. I cain't bring back something that's been over for ten years."

"You need to git in her pants. That'd change her mind."

"She jes' ain't interested in me, Clayton. Too much time's passed."

"Then do sumpin' to git her interested. Maybe I should give you flyin' lessons so you can crash on her place."

Laughter. *Sickening* laughter.

The blonde across the street fidgeted with her purse and finally dug out her keys. *Louisa,* Regret thought, noticing the cut of her hair. He doubted she would help him, but if he could get her attention, maybe she could at least get a message to Hughie. On the other hand, if she was Jordy's wife, then he was probably doubly damned.

"How much longer do you think it'll take before it's finished?" Rooster asked.

"What do you mean, how much longer? I told you, it'd better be as soon as possible. I don't know when the bank is gonna seize the land, and if you're not done by then, we're gonna lose thousands of dollars."

Rooster's voice cracked when he answered. "We'll have it done by then. The rain's jes' put us a little bit behind, that's all. Me and the boys have been workin' day and night to git this thang finished."

To get what finished?

The blonde across the street swung around, her hair bouncing against her cheekbones. A well-dressed man opened the door behind her and beckoned. She smiled enthusiastically and teetered forward to meet him. He said something friendly to her, and she looked down shyly, like a schoolgirl. He laughed, loud enough to be heard from

Regret's jail cell. The man extended one hand and brushed the hair from Louisa's eyes in a gesture that was too intimate to be prudent between a salesman and his customer.

"So how you gonna git rid of this guy, Clayton?"

"Oh, I've got a couple of ideas how. But first I wanna make sure he don't ever wanna come back here. Either we take him across the river and dump him in the middle of nowhere, or we let him go."

"We don't need to be wastin' time goin' across the river, Clayton. If you want us finishin' in the next few weeks, then I need to concentrate on that."

"In that case, I'll leave his cell unlocked tonight. But first—" Regret heard the jangle of keys "—I wanna make sure he knows to take advantage of the situation. Here—go have some fun."

The keys jangled again.

"What'd you want me to do with these, Clayton?"

"Teach him a lesson. One he won't soon forget."

"Aw, man! Why do I always have to be the one to git my hands dirty?"

"Don't be stupid, Rooster. You know how important it is for me to stay uninvolved. My daddy's been sheriff of this county all my life, and when Jim Clayton retires next year, I guaran-damn-tee you, he ain't gonna be the last Clayton to hold that office."

Jordy's crumpled aluminum can arched in a free throw into a metal trash can on the other side of the room just as Trudy walked into the sheriff's chilly office. Then Jordy's mouth dropped open when he saw the rifle in her grasp.

"Tr-Trudy! Trudy, how nice to see you! Could I git you some coffee or maybe—"

"Shut up, Jordy."

"Truuuudeeeee! That's not a nice way to greet your brother-in-law."

"Save it for your fan club, Jordy. I'm in no mood for it."

"Where's little Droolcie? You didn't bring her by to see her favorite uncle?"

"Dulcie's with her Granny Sandlin. I thought it'd be best if she didn't hear what I've got to say today."

"So what brings you into town?" Jordy continued in a falsetto. "Come to do a little shopping? You and Weezer should git together. You know how she loves to spend my money."

Trudy swallowed the bile in her throat. There were few things she despised as much as being patronized by someone considerably less intelligent than she was. Thank goodness Miss Myrtle had called to let her know Jordy had caught the man who had allegedly stolen her truck. And thank goodness Papa had gone fishing and left his car for her to borrow, or she would've had no other way to town.

"Where's R.J.?"

"Who? R.J.? I don't believe we have anybody here by that name. Maybe you should check down at the barbershop."

Did he not know R.J.'s name? Or was he just playing with her?

"The guy who was driving my truck. Don't play dumb with me. Where is he?"

"Oh, him. I'm afraid it's a little too early for visiting hours, Trudy. Why don't you come back after dinner?"

"Did you lock him up?" As she brushed past Jordy, he grabbed her elbow to stop her. Instead of yelping in pain, she stared at him with eyes she knew were deadlier than her rifle. He dropped her elbow and stepped away.

"R.J.? R.J., are you back there?"

"Trudy?" His voice sounded like a wounded bird's.

"R.J.?" She was running now. Her sandaled feet slapping against the concrete floor, she flew past the two cells and the sleeping men inside, past the empty rooms, all the way to the last cell.

Trudy gasped. Regret lay slumped against the block wall, his hands cuffed behind his back and his torn shirt open to expose his bandaged ribs. Rooster, his thumbs hooked through his belt loops, was standing over his prisoner. The blood on Rooster's right fist matched the scarlet on Regret's bottom lip.

"Trudy," whispered the man on the floor.

He was trying to be brave, trying to salvage his dignity. His eyes, grateful but sad, reminded her of Grendel as a puppy, abandoned on the roadside and desperately searching the face of each passerby for the kind eyes of an owner.

Without fear, she'd picked up Grendel in her arms and carried him home to be fed and petted. She wanted to lift Regret in her arms now.

"Trudy." Rooster looked down guiltily. The barred gate between them gaped open.

Her gaze riveted on Regret, she demanded, "What's going on here? He's hurt. He shouldn't even be out of bed!"

"Trudy, Trudy, Trudy," Jordy's voice rang out. "You should know better than to interfere with the law."

She whirled around, her rifle barrel inches from Jordy's face. "What law? He's done nothing wrong! And what's Rooster doing in there? You two sadistic—"

"Your friend resisted arrest," Jordy answered calmly. "He got a little bit out of hand."

"Out of hand? He has a concussion and broken ribs. He can barely move and you've got him handcuffed, Jordy! How could he get 'out of hand'?"

Rooster edged away from the prisoner. "Hey, look, Trudy, I didn't mean—"

"Shut up!" Jordy and Trudy shouted at Rooster at the same instant.

Trudy pointed at the key ring on the floor by Rooster's feet. "Get those handcuffs off him!"

Rooster started to pick up the mass of keys but froze when he looked up and saw Jordy's glare. He wouldn't defy him.

"Put the gun down, Trudy," Jordy said quietly. "You don't want to cause a ruckus, now do you? You put that gun down and leave and as a favor to Weezer, I'll just forget you were ever here."

Trudy shook her head emphatically, dark hair tumbling across her brow and into her eyes. She jerked her head backward, flipping the hair out of her eyes. She dared not lower the rifle.

"Aw, come one, Trudy. You're not actually gonna break this punk out of jail, are you? Hangin' around with him like you are, some people might think you've lost any sense you ever had. Didn't you learn your lesson with the first pilot?"

Trudy's finger trembled on the trigger.

"Boys? Is there a problem here?"

Looking beyond Jordy, Trudy was relieved to see Jim Clayton. Jim was a smaller, leaner, older version of Jordy, but his features suggested he'd once been as handsome as his son. Jim was known for his even temperament and reasonableness. And for his white cowboy hat.

"Sheriff Clayton," she said breathlessly, closing the distance between them to appeal to Jim Clayton's sound judgment. "You've got to let R.J. go, Mr. Jim. I let him borrow my truck. He hasn't done anything wrong. Can't you see he's hurt?"

Jim Clayton eyed Trudy thoughtfully, his solemn expression falling casually over her face and the rifle in her arms. Silently he regarded the handcuffed prisoner on the floor, the man with the bleeding mouth and the white bandages shining through the rip in his shirt. Then he looked at Rooster, red faced and guilty, and finally at his son. Without Jim Clayton's saying a word, his gentle manner challenged Jordy's temporary authority.

"But, Daddy, I caught him red-handed with Trudy's truck!"

"Did she report her truck stolen?"

"Well, no, Daddy, but—"

"Did he break any laws while he was drivin' it?"

"Well, no, but I saw him drivin' it, and I knew it weren't his. I knew it was Trudy's truck."

"Well, hell, boy. How many times have you taken my car without asking? Have I ever had you arrested for borrowin' sumpin'? Least this boy had permission to take her truck."

"Yeah, but, Daddy—"

"Son, I told you and your friends before, this jail is not a playhouse. You can't just lock somebody up 'cause you don't like the looks of 'im. Now, let the boy go, and don't bother him no more."

"But, Daddy—"

"And I don't wanna hear no more 'bout you turnin' on your siren to git through red lights."

Jordy hung his head. "Yes, Daddy."

Chapter 6

She came back for me, Regret was thinking as he followed Trudy and Dulcie on horseback toward the woods. Damn her! He watched her slender form rocking up and down, up and down in the saddle, and found himself growing hard at the sight of her. *Who does she think she is? Who does she think I am?*

She radiated a soft sensuality he'd never seen in another woman. Maybe it was the looseness of her hair or maybe the hint of sadness in her eyes. Maybe it was the appearance of vulnerability balanced against self-assurance. Maybe it was nothing more than the fact she had come back for him—not once, but twice—and no one had ever come back to him in kindness.

His thoughts flickered over Caroline's face with its warm brown eyes and auburn hair. He smiled to himself. The body of an angel, six feet tall. They'd spent almost a year together—longer than he'd spent with any other woman—before her corporation had transferred her to another state. She'd come back for him, all right. Two years later, unemployed, she'd come back in desperation to ask for child support for a little boy six months too young to be his child. A simple operation had made sure her allegations would be the last, but he often wondered if he was no better than his own father. Would it have killed him to make a loveless union with Caroline and acknowledge her son as his own? Probably not. But he was sure he would have been a lousy father.

He rarely thought of Caroline anymore. And even less of her child. At least the kid didn't have to grow up in a loveless home.

If anyone knew what it was like to grow up in a loveless home, Regret did. He didn't remember much about those early years. Most of it he'd blocked out. But he remembered the straps across his arms and chest to hold his screaming little five-year-old body to his hospital bed. And he remembered the two nurses outside his room.

"We need his mother's permission to treat him. Hasn't anyone seen her?" one of them had asked.

"Not since yesterday. Looks like she dumped the kid."

"Poor little boy. What about his father?"

"We contacted the man listed on the child's records. Says he doesn't have a son. I hear the state will be appointing guardians for the boy...."

Guardians had come and gone, none of them able to handle a troubled little boy. He'd come close twice. The Campbells, a military family, had wanted to adopt him, but left for Germany without him when the air force decided to send the family overseas shortly before his ninth birthday. He'd spent his twelfth and thirteenth years with the Sawyers. Just when he'd relaxed his guard and let himself try to love them back, the woman had died in a freak traffic accident, and he'd been shipped off to new keepers before the funeral. After that, he'd blurred the pain by skipping classes and drinking too much—until one day he was eighteen and free.

"How are you doing back there?" Trudy turned in her saddle and flashed a smile of encouragement.

"I'm fine," he lied. What was wrong with her? She just kept *being there* for him! "Who knows? If I keep riding Guildy, I may become a regular cowboy."

Trudy laughed and waited for him to catch up. Grendel trotted behind him with his pink canine tongue sliding out the side of his black-gummed mouth as he panted in the heat. The dog ambled down to the edge of Johnson's Creek and lapped up the water. The current was just as fast as it had been the day before, but the water had receded enough that the two horses crossed without wetting their bellies. The two plastic buckets tied over Guildy's back shifted against Regret's thighs as the horse climbed the opposite bank.

"Are you sure you're feeling up to this?" Trudy asked him.

"If I wasn't sure, I wouldn't be here."

Trudy glanced doubtfully at him. "I was worried about you when Miss Myrtle told me Jordy had arrested you."

"I can take care of myself," he responded instinctively.

"Hmm. Under normal circumstances, I'm sure you could. How many crash landings have you walked away from?"

He laughed. "All of them."

"I'm serious." Trudy frowned back at him. "It could've been a lot worse."

"Tell me about Rooster," he said, changing the subject.

"Not much to tell."

"You were involved with him once, weren't you?"

She shrugged. "That was a long time ago."

Inwardly Regret shuddered at the thought of Trudy in Rooster's arms—arms that knew nothing of tenderness. "Was he your first love?"

"I suppose."

"He hurt you, didn't he?" Regret wanted to ask if it was Rooster Reed who had put the pain in her blue eyes.

"Did he hurt you, R.J.? Today? In that cell?" She turned and waited for his horse to catch up again. She was as good at changing subjects as he was.

"I'll be okay. Not exactly in mint condition, but I've been worse."

"He threatened you, didn't he?"

She surprised him by extending a slender hand toward his face and touching his injured lip with her forefinger. Her head tilted to one side as she regarded him tenderly.

"Was it because of me?"

"Maybe. To tell you the truth, I was more concerned about Jordy. He's the one who's dangerous."

"Jordy? Oh, Jordy wouldn't hurt a fly! Without that uniform, he's just a petulant little boy."

"Why do they want your land so bad, Trudy?"

"They're only trying to help. Jordy and Louisa have offered to buy the farm. I . . . have some debts. I'm . . . facing bankruptcy."

"Then sell."

"No!"

"Why not? Cornerstone doesn't have as much to offer you as you have to offer it. Why don't you sell everything and leave?"

"I can't."

"Sure you can. You could start over in the big city. Atlanta, maybe."

She shot a questioning glance in his direction. "Where you're from?"

He shrugged off the implication. It wouldn't be right to mislead her into thinking there could be something lasting between them. He knew better.

Trudy shook her head. "I could never leave this place. It's part of me and I'm part of it."

"Because of your grandfather? You don't owe him the prime of your life, Trudy. If he can't take care of himself, then have him put in a retirement home or—"

"No!" She glared back at him, warning him not to make such a suggestion again. "He doesn't have anybody else. He needs me. He thought I was going to leave after Johnny died, so he deeded everything to me. And now I'm losing it all. I have to stay. There's no one else he can depend on."

"How about his lady friend in town? He spends more time with her than with you. Maybe she'd be willing to—"

"Whoa!" She grabbed the reins and hauled Regret and the horse back toward her. "Stay close to me."

Regret grinned. "Gladly."

"See that hole over there in the ground?"

He followed her pointing finger. "Yeah."

"It's an open well. One of Papa's mules fell in it back in the 1930s."

"Yeah? How deep is it?"

"Not very deep as wells go, but with all the rain, it'd be full of water. If you and Guildy got too close and fell in, I'd never get the horse out. And you'd drown if you went down with him."

"Point made. I'll stay close to you." Again he grinned devilishly. She'd never know just how close he'd like to stay.

"I never thought that much about the land when I was growing up," Trudy said, urging their horses down a swampy path. "I always took it for granted."

"It's just real estate, Trudy. And it's too swampy back here to be worth much. Why can't you sell just enough to pay your debts?"

"It's not just real estate. It's my heritage. That open well back there was where the turpentine workers from the turn of the century used to drink and wash up after a hard day's work. The pond where Rooster and his goons like to come to hunt is where my great-grandfather used to gamble with the men from town." She turned momentarily to wave toward a grassy knoll beyond the well. "You see that huge oak over there? It's over a hundred years old."

"The one that looks like three acorns grew into one tree?"

Trudy nodded. "One of Great-Granddaddy's gambling buddies was the town banker. Back in 1907 when there was a bank panic, the banker disappeared with about five thousand dollars in deposits. A lot of it in gold. The people in town found him here, hiding in the Dugan woods. They lynched him from that oak. Papa says he can still remember part of the rope hanging from that big limb. If you look close, you can see where the limb bulged out over the rope and grew around it."

"What about the gold?"

"They never found it."

"Did you ever consider dredging that little pond for it?"

"No. I've seen that particular pond dry up several times. I remember Papa kicking around in the dirt a couple of times. He never found anything but a few Indian arrowheads."

"Trudy, you could have a gold mine here on your land."

She turned to him with the smile of a patient mother. "It's not the gold that's important. It's the story of the gold."

"Oh, come on, Trudy. Don't you want to find it?"

Urging her horse onward, she shrugged. "It doesn't matter. It's part of the history. Can't you feel it, R.J.?"

"No. Sorry. I've never had a place to call my own."

"Think of it! My ancestors walked these same woods a hundred years ago! They're long gone, but the land is still here. And if it could talk!"

"I never knew my ancestors. I barely know anything of my own parents or where they were from or if they had other family. I never heard stories about great-grandparents or the good old days. There weren't any good old days."

"Oh R.J., I am so sorry. I keep forgetting how lucky I am to have roots. And to have them right here under my feet."

"You're really sentimental about this piece of property, aren't you?" He wondered what she'd think if she knew how close she'd come to the gas line north of her farm exploding because of the erosion around the pipes.

"Yeah, I'm sentimental about the land. But I never realized it until after Johnny died. Papa was afraid I'd leave with Dulcie. He gave me this long pep talk on how the land was really Dulcie's and I needed to take up the torch from him and take care of the land the way Mama had. If it hadn't been for me wanting to leave, he never would've deeded the whole farm to me." She let out a ragged sigh. "Now I'm responsible for losing it."

Regret remembered the conversation with Louisa. "Your husband's debts?"

"Yeah. After Johnny died, his creditors tried to come after me, but I was living with Papa and didn't have any real assets, so they left me alone. Then Papa deeded the land to me, and I finally had something the bank could take. The loan officer is a family friend. He's done everything he can to delay foreclosing."

"But they haven't taken your land yet."

"It's just a matter of time."

He couldn't think of anything comforting to say, so he said nothing as their horses ambled farther into the shadowy woods.

"We're here," Trudy announced a few minutes later. She dismounted and hoisted Dulcie down next to her onto a dry mound of leaves and dirt. Regret frowned at the thick hedge of bushlike trees laden with clusters of pinkish red berries amid light-green leaves. The hawthorns stood in pools of clear water, where dozens of berries floated in twos and threes. Grendel swished through the water into the shadows.

"These are mayhaws. This little corner of Georgia, plus a few neighboring counties in Florida and Alabama, is the only place on Earth where they grow," Trudy explained.

Regret swung his right leg over his horse and eased himself to the soggy ground. He set the two buckets on the ground and reached for the nearest fistful of berries. Something pierced his skin powerfully, and he instinctively withdrew his hand. Regret frowned at the swelling pinprick of blood dotting his finger.

"Careful," Trudy warned, too late. "They have huge thorns."

He looked back at the berries, perfect and unflawed like thumb-size apples. Amid the green leaves were fanglike thorns, and he understood why his barefoot hostess had finally chosen wearing shoes over feeling the earth—and its needles—beneath her feet. He picked the biggest berry and bit into it, making a face at its tangy sharpness.

Trudy giggled behind him. "They're really not best that way. We'll fill these buckets and take them home to make jelly."

"Oh."

Dulcie took one of the buckets and contented herself picking from a low bush not standing in water, which left Trudy and Regret to share the remaining bucket. Mayhaw berries thudded against the plastic bucket bottom as they snatched handfuls from the lower branches. Several times they reached for the same clusters, touched hands and drew back with uneasy smiles. After filling their bucket with what they could reach, they exchanged with Dulcie, whose bucket contained less than an inch of leaves and a couple of berries.

Trudy raised her head once, like a fawn listening for hunters. "Did you hear that?"

"Hear what?"

"It sounded like a gunshot."

Regret shrugged. "I didn't hear anything."

"Hmm. Must've been that last handful of berries you threw into the bucket." Troubled, she shook her head.

"I guess so."

"That's all we can get this time," Trudy said, frowning at the dozens of tiny apples in the treetops.

Wisps of her dark hair clung to her damp forehead. Her cheeks had become flushed with the heat, and were as pink as the berries in her hands. Regret itched to caress her face.

"Let me try." Regret ducked under the low-hanging, thorny limbs and thrust his hands as far around the small tree trunk as they would go. He wrenched his body backward, not hard enough to elicit the pain in his ribs but hard enough to shake the tree.

Plop! Plop! Plop! Berries rained into the shallow water at Trudy's feet. Giggling, she reached down and scooped up a double handful of fruit and pitched the mayhaws into her bucket. He shook the tree several more times, then moved to the next tree. Their second bucket was full in minutes.

"See? I am good for something." He grinned at her, for the first time seeing laughter sparkling back in her eyes. Laughter he'd put there. When was the last time he'd made a woman laugh?

"Yes. I'm sure you're good for a lot of things, R.J." Her tone seemed less prim than before.

He stood close to her, close enough to bend and kiss her. Involuntarily his mouth pulled him to her as she tilted back her rosy face to gaze up at him. Then she backed away uncomfortably, biting her lip and glancing nervously toward Dulcie, who wasn't watching but was too close for her mother to relax. Then Trudy glanced frantically at the horses and around the bushes.

"Where's Grendel?"

Regret shrugged. "I don't know. I haven't seen him since we got here."

"Grendel? Grendel!" Panic wavered in her voice as she called in all directions. Dulcie joined in, too, crying out her guardian's name in a shrill voice.

Trudy put her fingers in her mouth and whistled, waited, whistled again. The woods were silent except for late-afternoon bird songs and a distant hammering.

"This isn't like him. Grendel would never go off and leave us."

"Maybe he thinks you're safe with me."

Trudy's brow furrowed. "He especially wouldn't traipse off and leave us with a relative stranger."

A relative stranger. Her words stung unexpectedly. For a moment, he'd forgotten he wasn't part of her life.

"Mommy! Mommy!" Dulcie pointed down the path they had come along earlier, and the hairy giant of a dog emerged from the brush. His light-tan coat was wet and freshly stained with red. "Mommy, Grendel's got an owie!"

The dog limped faithfully toward his mistress, his eyes glazed with pain. Trudy knelt beside him, examining his wounded leg. The dog whined as she touched him.

"What's wrong?" Regret dared not approach the injured animal. He'd heard how quickly they could turn on their masters, and it made sense that Grendel would turn on him even faster. Instead he picked up Dulcie in his arms and held her tightly. "Has he been in a fight?"

Trudy patted the dog's head, murmuring something comforting. The animal seemed grateful and nuzzled her chest. Trudy finally looked up at Regret and her daughter. She did nothing to hide the tears streaming down her cheeks.

"He's been shot."

Chapter 7

Miss Clarice stood in the middle of Trudy's kitchen with her hands on her pink-aproned hips and a hint of irritation in her eyes. It was the same look Miss Clarice got every Sunday that she volunteered to come over and cook dinner for Papa.

"Can I help you find something, Miss Clarice?" Trudy asked from the doorway. She didn't really like the idea of another woman in her kitchen—in the kitchen where her mother had cooked and her mother's mother before her, before they both died of cancer—but Miss Clarice's attention pleased Papa when few other things could.

"Where do you keep your sugar, Trudy, dear?"

Trudy smiled indulgently. Miss Clarice had asked the same question on her last visit, two weeks ago. "In the canister marked Sugar, Miss Clarice."

The woman clucked at herself. "So it is." She poured the dark brew of strained tea from the kettle into a tall glass pitcher and then scooped a heaping cup of sugar into the pitcher. Then she stirred ice cubes into the steaming tea, each cube cracking as it hit the amber liquid. "When your grandpa and I get married, I'm going to have to rearrange this kitchen. If I don't, I'll walk myself to death in here the way you've got it arranged, dear.''

Trudy braced herself against the woman's words. She knew that in time Papa probably would remarry. She didn't hold that against him. In his younger days, he'd been quite a handsome man, and even now in his seventies, the widows in town still fancied him. Trudy understood his need for a companion his own age as much as she understood her need for a companion her own age. She just didn't know if Miss Clarice was the right one.

Miss Clarice was a youthful sixty-five, her face and hands unmarred by her decades as a Cornerstone socialite. Her hair, dyed a not-so-subtle shade of red, was the product of a weekly trip to the beauty salon. Trudy could understand what Papa admired physically in Miss Clarice. The diminutive woman doted on her suitor, always offering to cook for him or attend church suppers with him. There was something about her that made him feel alive. Maybe she was what Papa needed. . . .

"Trudy dear, you're almost out of shortening. Don't forget to pick some up next time you go to the—'' Miss Clarice wailed in surprise as she looked up at Trudy and dropped the long, two-pronged fork she held in her hand.

Trudy responded instinctively, startling, looking behind her. She was relieved to find only Regret standing there. He merely smiled and glanced from Trudy to Miss Clarice. Dulcie clung to his chest with her arms wrapped tightly around his neck.

"Hello, pretty," Trudy greeted her daughter with a quick kiss on the cheek. "Did you enjoy your walk in the garden with R.J.?''

"I did! And he showed me how to make a paper airplane!'' Her eyes brightened with adoration. She snuggled against the man in her father's clothes.

"Sorry," Regret said quickly to Trudy. "I didn't realize you had company." He nodded at Miss Clarice, who was staring back at him. "I'm R.J. James. And you're obviously Miss Clarice." He stepped into the kitchen light but didn't extend his hand in welcome. Both arms were full of Dulcie.

"I, uh—"

"Mr. Dugan speaks of you so often. I certainly couldn't mistake his endearing descriptions of you."

Blushing, Miss Clarice wiped her hands on her apron. "Well, Lester is such a dear."

Trudy didn't know whether to giggle or roll her eyes at such blatant flattery. "You charmer," she muttered, just loud enough that Regret could hear her. What was to stop him from using the same flattery on her?

"I didn't realize we had another guest for dinner, Trudy," Miss Clarice admonished gently as she poked at the contents of a frying pan. "Now I'll need to fry up some more chicken."

"R.J. is staying with us for a while," Trudy told the woman.

"You mean he's staying here in this house?"

"Yes. In the guest room, of course."

Miss Clarice frowned disapprovingly. "Oh, I'm sure he is, dear. But you must know how this looks. Especially with a child in the house. Young man, if you really want to make an honest woman of Trudy—"

Regret cleared his throat and put Dulcie down on the kitchen floor. His eyes had turned that deadly shade of green again.

"Ma'am, Trudy is the most honest woman I know."

"Oh, I'm sure she is! I mean, I didn't mean . . . well, you know." Her head popped back up at the hum of a car engine outside. "That sounds like Lester coming home from church now. I'd better hurry and get dinner on the table."

Trudy offered Regret her kindest smile. She wanted him to know how much she appreciated his defending her.

"How's Grendel today?" he asked her. The words sounded strained, angry. He hadn't been angry moments ago when he'd appeared behind her.

"The vet says he'll have to stay there a few more days. The bullet went right through. No permanent damage. He's trying to keep the wound from getting infected worse than it already is. It didn't help matters that Grendel had been tramping through the swamp. The wound had already saturated the bandage by the time we got him to the vet's."

"I'm glad it looks like he'll be okay. I know how much that dog means to you."

"R.J.?" She touched his arm tentatively. Miss Clarice was too busy with the chicken to hear. "Is something wrong?"

"Yes," he hissed.

Papa took off his hat as he stepped into the kitchen in his three-piece Sunday suit. The first person he saw in the room was Regret, and by the look in his eyes, Trudy dreaded hearing his greeting. Then Papa's gaze drifted to Miss Clarice as she busily ushered a platter of fried chicken to the linen-draped table. The expression on his face softened.

After Miss Clarice had set the rest of the meal on the table, the five of them sat down and Papa blessed the food and the hands that had prepared it. Heartily the old man dug into the platter of fried chicken.

"This is delicious, ma'am." Regret smiled solicitously after a few bites of dinner.

"Why, thank you, R.J.! Now, tell me about yourself. What is it you do for a living?"

"I'm a pilot," he answered willingly.

"Oh!" Trudy bumped her glass. Tea and ice cubes spilled across the table.

A pilot. Another daredevil pilot. Sometimes she was able to forget what he did for a living. Why couldn't he have been a farmer or a doctor or a timber cutter at the mill? Anything but a pilot!

Reaching for a dish cloth, she jumped to her feet and began mopping up the mess. Miss Clarice hurriedly poured another glass of tea for Trudy and took her seat again beside Papa.

"A pilot! How wonderfully appropriate!" Miss Clarice cooed. "We could sure use another crop duster 'round here."

Trudy's hands had started to shake again. Every time she thought of Johnny, they shook. Only she wasn't thinking of Johnny. She was thinking of Regret, bleeding, dying in a cockpit.

"Do you think ya'll will ever get married, Trudy, dear?"

"Use your fork, baby," Trudy said automatically to Dulcie. She could feel her cheeks reddening behind the veil of dark hair that hid her face when she looked down. She could feel, too, that Regret's eyes were on her. Angry eyes. "I have no intention of marrying Mr. James."

The older woman leaned across the table like a lifelong confidante and lowered her voice, even though the three other people at the table could hear every word she said. "Why not, dear?"

Regret shoved back from the table and stood up, flinging his napkin onto his plate. "I've had all of this I can stand!"

Miss Clarice gaped at him. "You don't like my fried chicken?"

"I don't like you." His face had turned a purplish red with rage. Ragged breaths rocked his body.

The color drained from Miss Clarice's face. Papa was already half out of his seat.

"Boy, you ain't got no right talking to Clarice like that."

"And you've got no right letting her talk to Trudy like that! How dare you jump to your girlfriend's defense and not to Trudy's!"

Papa stared at him. Was he seeing Trudy through Regret's eyes? A woman and not a child meant to wait on him?

Miss Clarice regained her voice. "Oh, Trudy, sweetie, I didn't mean to pry. I'm so sorry if you took it that way. It's just that Dulcie's such a precious little thing, and a child needs two parents. There's no telling how that sweet little thing will turn out if she doesn't have a daddy's influence in her life."

Regret bent one hand into a fist and the other into a pointing index finger aimed at Miss Clarice. Furious words lay behind his clenched jaw. He shook himself, swallowing the venom, instead. Then he glanced at Trudy, seized her by the wrist and dragged her to her feet.

"Please excuse my rudeness," he snarled at Papa and Miss Clarice, "but this conversation is over. I owe my life to this woman, and I'm not about to sit here—or let her sit here—while you treat her like a child."

"R.J.!" Trudy stumbled down the doorsteps after him, her wrist still tight in his grip. "R.J., let go!"

He didn't. He didn't even look back at her. She nearly ran to keep up with his long strides.

"R.J., stop it! I can't leave Dulcie by herself."

"She's not by herself. Your grandfather can watch her for a few minutes."

Trudy stumbled through the arch of the rose-covered trellis. "But she's too much of a handful for an old man." She nearly tripped as he hauled her into the privacy of the rose garden, well out of earshot of the kitchen. "R.J., stop it. What will Papa and Miss Clarice think...?"

He spun around. His eyes! All green fire and raw anger.

"Do you think I care what they think?"

"I—I care," she stammered.

"Well, you shouldn't. Why do you let them treat you like that?"

"L-like what?"

"Like a doormat. You let them walk all over you. You should've told that old busybody to take her country cooking and choke on it."

"I couldn't do that, R.J." He tightened his grip on her wrist even more. She tried to jerk free, but he pulled her to him.

"Why not? You marched into a jail cell and demanded that your redneck friends leave me alone. Why can't you demand people leave you alone? Why didn't you tell Miss Clarice to mind her own business?"

Trudy looked away. She couldn't bear the brunt of his gaze. "She's Papa's girlfriend. If I said anything to her, it would just hurt Papa's feelings."

"So hurt his feelings! He doesn't care if he hurts yours, does he?"

She forced herself to look into his eyes, which was almost like forcing herself to look into the sun. She could barely stand it. "He doesn't mean to. He's just a product of his time. He grew up in a world where women were subservient and—"

"Fine. That's his world. You don't have to make it yours."

"He's an old man, R.J. He wouldn't understand."

"Then why don't you put him out to pasture?"

She stared at him. "How could you!"

He didn't blink. "Well, he's worthless, isn't he? I mean, he can't even get up and pour his own iced tea! What good is he? You'd be better off without the burden of a feeble, old—"

She yanked away from his grip. "How dare you say he's worthless! That man may be nearly eighty years old, but he's more vital and alive than most men half his age."

The coldness in his eyes wasn't real. He'd known exactly what it would take to break through the walls she put up around Papa. *Damn you, R.J.*

"Let him stand on his own two feet, Trudy. Stop being a crutch. No wonder he treats you like a child. That's exactly how you treat him."

"But... but he doesn't have anybody else but me. I have to be there for him. No matter how hard it is." Tears burned behind her eyes. She blinked them back. "Don't you understand? He gave me his most precious gift—his land. My daughter's heritage. And I'm losing it." Her voice cracked, and Regret's face softened. "I can't let him see how bad it hurts me that I've failed him. I have to be strong." She looked away. "Because he can't."

"Trudy." Regret gathered her in his arms, pressing her cheek to his chest. "Oh, Trudy. You don't have to be a doormat to be a pillar of strength. Walk away. If you're not here, he'll learn to fend for himself. They all will. Come back to Atlanta with me. Start over."

She let go of a shuddering sob, then quickly composed herself. She pressed her head harder against his chest, listening to his steady heartbeat.

He raised her face to his. "Let me take you out of this place."

Slowly she lifted her lids. Did she dare let him see what she felt? Surely he'd read it in her eyes. Her fear of falling. The knowledge that she was on the edge and swaying!

"Don't you think I've thought about it? What it would be like to hop in that little two-seater with Dulcie on my lap and the three of us fly out of here? But I can't. I can't! Not as long as there's a chance of saving this place. I have to fight for it—for Dulcie."

"Then I'll stay and help you fight for it."

"No, I—" She pulled away. "You can't." *Not you. I can't go through this again!*

Brushing the hair from her face, he turned her chin, her mouth, toward his face. "You need me," he whispered.

He was going to kiss her. She knew by the look in his eyes, the warmth of his descending lips.

"No!" She broke free. "A pilot's the last kind of man I need!"

Regret jerked himself out of a nightmare and sat up in bed. His forehead was clammy with sweat, even though the windows of his bedroom were open and the night breeze was cool. He'd been dreaming about his mother again and about the hospital where he had lain strapped to a white, sterile bed, screaming.

I need air! he thought, his lungs heaving in oxygen as he pulled on a pair of Johnny Sandlin's jeans and stood up. The room was dark, as was the rest of the house. He guessed it was well after midnight.

He walked slowly across the room. The floor seemed colder than usual to his shoeless feet. His bare-chested shadow crossed the mirror over the bureau, and he drew a startled breath before recognizing his own reflection.

The living room was quiet as he tiptoed through the house. Light snores came from Mr. Lester's bedroom. The doors had been left open to let the breeze flow through the house. Regret had to be careful of squeaky floorboards if he didn't want the old man rushing out with his rifle.

He paused as he passed Trudy's bedroom. Dulcie's shallow breaths were discernible over the faint swish of curtains on the breeze, but he heard nothing of Trudy. Somewhere beyond the bedroom, somewhere outside the house, faint hammer falls echoed through the night.

What is she doing? he wondered. *Building bluebird houses at this hour?*

Moving to the back door, he found it unlatched. Quietly he stepped out onto the back doorsteps—and almost tripped over a feminine form sitting on the bottom step.

"Trudy, is that you?" he gasped, straining for his balance.

"R.J.?" She was still breathing hard when he sat down beside her. "What are you doing out of bed?"

"Couldn't sleep. How about you? Do you always sit outside in the middle of the night?"

"Shh! Don't you hear it?"

He listened to the darkness, hearing only the distant hammering he'd heard before and a lonely whippoorwill. "What are we listening to?"

"I don't know. It woke me up. I came out to get a better listen."

"I thought it was you, Trudy. Hammering your bluebird houses together."

"Hammering, all right. But not birdhouses. It's been going on a long time."

"Is somebody building a house around here?"

"This time of night?"

He shrugged. "Guess not. Sounds like it's coming from your woods."

"I know. That's what worries me."

Her voice sounded tense, and he didn't want to say anything that might frighten her. "Hard to say, really. Sound can travel a long way at night. It's probably coming from miles and miles away." He decided not to tell her he was sure the hammer falls couldn't be any farther away than his broken airplane.

"You really think so? You're probably right, R.J. I worry too much."

"Yeah. Probably some poor guy who's staying up all night to finish the sun deck his wife's been nagging him about."

As his eyes grew accustomed to the starlit darkness, he saw she was smiling at him. "You're probably right. Thanks for today."

"Today? What'd I do?"

"You made me see how I've been treating Papa. I've been handling him with kid gloves. I'm not going to anymore." She grinned. "And if he doesn't like it, he'll have to get over it."

"Good. I don't like to see people mistreat you. You deserve better than that."

Her expression sobered. "Can I ask you something?"

"You can ask me anything. But I can't promise I'll give you the answer you're looking for."

"Why did you get so upset when Miss Clarice was talking about a child needing both parents? That wasn't just concern for me. You took it personally."

"I suppose that's a fair question. Not an easy one, but a fair one." He hesitated until he had rehearsed the words in his head. "You see, I never knew my father. I met him once and didn't like him very much. And I knew my mother too well. She walked out on me when I was five years old. I was raised by dozens of foster parents until I turned eighteen. And Miss Clarice really hit home with me. And without even meaning to. Some people might blame the way I turned out on a broken home."

"I don't think you turned out so badly. Sometimes going through a lot of pain makes you stronger in the long run."

He took her hands in his. He could see the outline of her face against the night sky. "Can I do anything to make your pain go away?"

"No. You've got your own pain to deal with."

"I know. And I haven't dealt with it. Until now. But if there's anything I can do for you, Trudy..."

"You can't."

"Try me. Tell me who hurt you. Open up to me. Please?"

"You don't want to hear this. It's nothing very exciting."

He kissed the back of her hands. Her scent was stronger than the faint odor of fresh laundry. "I find you very exciting, Trudy Sandlin. I told you something I've never told anyone—that my parents didn't want me. Hell, how can you want a child and name him 'Regret'?"

"Regret?"

"Yeah. Regret James. My mother took one look at me in the hospital and told the nurse my name was Regret."

"That's—that's horrible, R.J. Why would she do that?" Her hands folded over his.

"My father was married to someone else. He didn't want anything to do with my mother or me. She always said I was her one regret."

"How awful for you! R.J., if—"

"Stop it, Trudy. I told you what really hurts in [ ]
your turn. Who hurt you? Who put the pain in th[ ]
tiful blue eyes?"

"When I was in high school..." She stopped. "I [ ]n't
know if I can tell this, R.J."

"Hey, who am I to pass judgment? God knows, I'm the
last person in the world who can cast stones at anything
you've done."

After a long silence, she started over. "When I was in the
tenth grade, a boy noticed me for the first time ever. That
boy's name was Royce Reed, but everybody called him
Rooster."

"The same Rooster who shot at me and beat me up? If I
hadn't been handcuffed and bandaged, he'd need a few
bandages of his own."

"Yeah. That's the one. His father was a poultry farmer.
Still owns a lot of land here. Liked to joke about Royce being his 'little rooster.'" She grinned. "Stupid, huh? Anyway, we dated for about two years—"

"I can't see you dating Rooster Reed. I just, well, frankly,
he didn't seem to be your type."

"Oh, he isn't now. But back then, he was...different. He
was a nice boy back then. A nice-looking boy, too. Well
mannered. Didn't drink. Didn't smoke." She paused, her
words sharp when she spoke again. "Respected other people's property. Respected my morals. The day after he gave
me his class ring, everybody in town knew we were going
steady." Trudy smiled at the memory. "Small towns are like
that, you know. People like to keep up with what's going on.
Or what they think's going on."

Regret nodded, trying to show his attentiveness. He was
distracted by the natural smell of her skin. He wanted to run
his hands up her arms, to her bare shoulders, draw her to
him.

"Rooster was a year older than me, which meant he
would be going to college before me, and I really didn't see
any way that I would be going off to college unless it was on
a scholarship or something. My parents couldn't afford to
send me, and even working a couple of part-time jobs after

:hool and in the summers, I couldn't save enough to pay my first year's tuition, let alone room and board. But when Rooster got accepted at Georgia Tech, I was so proud of him. He really hadn't thought he would make it, but I believed in him. He'd already asked me to marry him, and I promised him I'd wait until he graduated from Tech and came back for me. See, he wanted to be an engineer, and he had all these wonderful dreams. He was going to save the world. Or conquer it—I don't know which.''

"And then you met Johnny and broke it off with Rooster?"

Trudy laughed uneasily. "No, that's not exactly how it happened. I'd always known Johnny. He was Rooster's best friend, you see. Johnny didn't go off to college like Rooster did. Johnny had a good job here in town. He was a crop duster. Used to talk about flying just like—'' She hesitated and took a deep breath. "Just like you do.''

She propped her cheek against her fist. "I missed Rooster so much when he left for college. I wrote him every day, and at first he wrote back about once a week. Eventually the letters stopped coming altogether. By Thanksgiving, we found out my mama had cancer. The doctors gave her about six months to live, and even then she had to go through all kinds of painful radiation and chemotherapy. I didn't tell Rooster about it in any of my letters. It was hard to talk about, and I wanted to wait until he came home. I needed someone to talk to so badly. I needed so badly to be held.''

Regret waited patiently while she composed herself in the darkness. He knew what it was like to need so badly to be held. He wanted so badly to hold her now.

"Since I knew what day Rooster was coming back, I was expecting him to come by and see me. But he never did. He called me a couple of nights later. Said he was coming by to pick me up. Said we needed to talk. I should've known then that something was wrong.''

"You mean, he wanted to break up?"

She ignored Regret's question. "When he came to my house to get me, he didn't come in the way he always had. He'd always been such a gentleman. This time he just sat in the car and honked the horn until I came out. He told me to

get in the car, that we were going for a ride. His ca[...]
like sweet cigarette smoke, and he smelled like whisk[...]
wasn't the same Rooster who'd left, R.J. The Rooster w[...]
left had been so caring. This man was so callous. I didn't
even get a chance to tell him about my mother. Rooster
drove to the lake to park, just like we always had before.
Except when he kissed me, I felt like I was being smoth-
ered."

"The whiskey?"

"He was just so... so greedy. The more insistent he was,
the more I pushed him away, and the more I pushed him
away, the more determined he was to hurt me. He told me
he'd waited long enough for me to consummate our relationship. He said it was high time I gave in to his needs."
Trudy's voice cracked. "He told me about the other girls
he'd been seeing at college—the ones he wasn't supposed to
be seeing because we were supposed to be faithful to each
other. I don't know if he was bragging or lying, but he told
me what he'd done with those girls and that if I expected
him to come back and marry me, then I better learn to give
a little bit, too."

"Because he was a big man on campus and you were a
poor little hometown girl?"

"Something like that. I think once he left home he forgot his upbringing. Anyway, that night he gave me an ultimatum. Something of a variation on the old theme of 'put
out or get out.'"

"And what did you do?"

"I got out, of course."

Regret stared at her, incredulous. "He actually put you
out of the car?"

"Not physically. He gave me a choice, and I chose to get
out. I don't think he expected me to. It was dark outside.
Miles from anywhere. But I don't like to be backed into a
corner. I got out of my own free will. And he drove off and
left me there in the pitch-black December night."

Regret shook his head in disbelief. "That takes a lot of
guts. Especially when you're a teenager."

"It was almost more than I could take, R.J. I mean, you
know how fragile a teenager's ego can be. You know how

horrible it is when your first love rejects you. And on top of all that, Mama was dying. I couldn't burden her with my problems. I didn't dare call home and tell Daddy what had happened."

"How'd you get home?" Regret asked tightly. *Bastard,* he was thinking.

"There's a concession stand at the lake, and even though it's closed during the winter months, there's a telephone booth next to it. I walked through the dark and the mud and the grass toward the streetlight next to the concession stand on the other side of the lake. I had some change in my pocket, but I didn't have anybody to call."

"So you called Johnny?"

"He picked me up ten minutes later and took me back to his parents' house. His mom helped me get cleaned up while they all listened to my story. I told them about my mama's cancer, and Johnny and his folks were so sweet to me. He held me while I cried, and his mom fed me hot chocolate with the little marshmallows, and his dad called my house to let them know where I was and that I'd be home soon."

"Then you started seeing Johnny."

"Yeah. But at first as friends. Rooster had been the love of my life until then, and I wasn't ready for another relationship like that. But I needed somebody to talk to, and Johnny was a great listener. Plus he was so mad at the way Rooster had treated me that he wouldn't have anything to do with him. Rooster went back to college in January, and Johnny and I kept seeing each other. At first just on weekends and later nearly every night. By March he'd asked me to marry him. Mama was in remission then, and we decided on a September wedding. But toward the end of May, Mama took a turn for the worse, and her doctor said she wouldn't make it another month, so we decided to move the wedding up. On the first day of June, she called me into her hospital room and she . . ."

"Shh." Regret squeezed her hand as her voice faltered. "It's okay."

"She took my hand and cried and told me she loved me and that her one dream was to live long enough to see me married. The doctor said she wouldn't make it to the wedding. So that night we called our preacher, and the next day Johnny and I got married in my mama's hospital room. It's awful what cancer can do to the human body, the way it turns a person into a shell of what that person once was. Mama was too weak to hold her head up." Trudy lapsed into silence for a moment. Then her voice dropped to a whisper. "She died a few days later."

Regret slipped his arm around her shoulders and pulled her to him, offering her as much comfort as he knew how. He could only imagine feeling that way about his mother. "Whatever happened to Rooster?"

"Oh, he showed up at Mama's funeral." Her voice sounded strained. "Except for the people in the room with us, nobody knew yet that Johnny and I had gotten married, so it wasn't all over town yet, and Rooster didn't know. He was just coming back from his first year of college."

Her eyes grew glassy in the starlight as she stepped into the past. "He walks up to us at the memorial service and shakes Johnny's hand and dismisses him. Rooster says, 'I'm back now. Thanks for keeping her warm for me, Johnny Reb.' Only Johnny doesn't move. Rooster offers me as much of an apology as he can. Says something about things at college not working out. That he's decided to come back and thought maybe I would be willing to take up where we left off last summer."

Trudy shook herself back into the present and smiled to herself. "I'll never forget the look on Rooster's face when Johnny told him he was too late, that we'd gotten married. Complete disbelief. Betrayal. Not just by me, but by his best friend, too. Rooster actually suggested we get our marriage annulled."

"And that's why Rooster is the way he is today?"

"Part of it, I guess. I used to think it was the whiskey and drugs, but now I think it's just bitterness. You see, Rooster somehow got the idea in his head that leaving this little hole in the road and going off to college somehow made him better than the rest of us. Kinda like Louisa did. As long as Rooster and I dated, he didn't drink. I had my standards, you see. I wouldn't date a boy who drank or took drugs or fooled around. But once he got off to college, all his friends were having keg parties, and he didn't want to be left out, so he started drinking. He'd always been a good student in high school, but in college the only thing he was good at was partying. And by that June he'd flunked out. So you see, only part of Rooster's dream came true. He became a 'rambling wreck from Georgia Tech,' but then he flunked out, so he never became a 'hell of an engineer.'" She made a gesture imitating the college's fight song.

"I guess he never got over you."

"Not for lack of trying. He's been married a couple of times. Didn't work out very well."

Regret kissed the back of her hand. "Dulcie—is she your only child with Johnny?"

"Yeah. My miracle baby. I can't have any more."

"You can't?"

Trudy shook her head. "Johnny and I'd been married for seven years, and we still hadn't had any children. We didn't worry much about it, though. We just figured that was the way things were meant to be. Before I knew it, I was twenty-five and I'd never been to a gynecologist because I'd always been too, um, shy. It's kind of hard to get undressed as a woman in front of the family doctor who delivered you and nursed you through chicken pox and the flu. Then all of a sudden I was pregnant with Dulcie, and I had to go see a doctor. My doctor called me and told me that one of my tests had come back abnormal and that I might want to consider not having this baby. I had some cancerous cells on my cervix and it would be better to abort and try again later. But to me, after waiting seven years, Dulcie was like a miracle baby, and I just couldn't give her up. Of course, since Mama had died of cancer, I was scared to death. I really thought I was going to die, R.J. I'd had a good life with Johnny, and I figured I'd have Dulcie and that would be it. I'd die having her or something, and somehow I would live on in her. After that, I always thought it would be me, not Johnny, who would go first. It wasn't easy carrying Dulcie, and I did have a lot of problems. On top of that, she came a bit early."

Regret squeezed her hand harder.

"After she was born, my doctor sent me to a specialist in Alabama. He used this new type of laser surgery. The cancer is all gone now, but I'm still a little paranoid it'll come back. The doctor said to get a checkup twice a year, but I go four times." She smiled sadly at him. "Life is even more precious now that I have Dulcie. But you see, the cancer did some damage, so I can't have another baby. My doctor says it's very doubtful I could ever carry another baby past the first trimester."

"Does Miss Clarice know about all this?"

She nodded. "She plays bridge with my doctor's nurse. Apparently, I was the topic of discussion one night."

"Oh, Trudy." Regret brushed the hair out of her eyes. "Didn't you report the nurse?"

"I could have. But what good would that have done? She was gossiping out of pity, and if the doctor had fired her, she would have gossiped out of vindictiveness. Plus, R.J., it's a small town. I'd get a reputation for being a spiteful you-know-what."

"You should've done it anyway."

"No, R.J. I have to live here. I have to get along with people. But at the same time, I don't dare let them see how weak I am."

"Trudy…" His hands moved up to her face, cupping her cheekbones in his palms as he mined for secrets in her starlit eyes. "You're not weak. Not at all. You have such incredible strength! You've faced so much tragedy, so much more than I have, yet you keep going as though it doesn't bother you at all. I don't think I could have found the courage to face cancer, let alone bring a child into the world in spite of the risk."

"It was worth the risk."

"Take another risk, Trudy. Take a chance on me."

She looked away. "I . . . want to."

"Don't you think I'd be worth the risk, too?"

"If I could freeze time. If I could forget what might happen tomorrow. Maybe then."

He brushed his lips over her forehead. "Then forget about tomorrow. Seize this moment as though there were no tomorrow." He kissed each eyelid and pulled back to look at her. "Don't you want me, Trudy?"

"You'll just fly out of here in a few days. You'll forget all about me."

"No, I won't. I won't go. Don't you want me?"

"You're a pilot. A daredevil."

"But don't you want me?"

"You're liable to get yourself killed."

He wouldn't let her go. She didn't want to be let go. "Be honest with yourself. With me. Don't you want me?"

"Yes! I want you." Her voice was husky in the dimness. "But—"

"But what?"

"I think I'm falling in love with you."

He smiled at her. She seemed so frightened. "That's not so bad, is it?"

"It's terrible, R.J. I don't think I'm strong enough to let myself love you."

"You're strong enough for both of us." Running his thumb along the pout of her lower lip, he searched her eyes for signs of surrender. "You'll never know how much I admire your strength."

She pressed her face to his. "Show me," she whispered, closing her eyes.

He pulled her tousled head down, bringing her lips to his. He searched her mouth for a passion to equal his own.

"Mommy? Where are you?" called a thin voice from inside the walls. "Mommy? Monster's in my room!"

Trudy pushed away reluctantly. "She's had another bad dream."

"She'll be okay," he murmured as he pulled Trudy back to him. "Stay with me."

She raised her hands like a shield against his desire. "Sorry," she mumbled as she ran inside the house.

Sometimes she was stronger than he wanted her to be.

Chapter 8

I can't do it. I can't fall in love with another pilot. I won't let myself.

Trudy turned off the cold water that splashed into the kitchen sink and swished her hand around in the coolness. Beside the sink were the two plastic buckets filled with the mayhaws she and Regret had picked the afternoon Grendel had been shot. She dumped half of the first bucket of berries into the water, and they thudded in, plopping back to the surface and rolling in the water under her touch as she stirred them.

The water was as cold as Regret's kiss was warm. She couldn't stop thinking of the kiss, wondering what might have happened without the excuse of Dulcie's nightmare.

I won't, she told herself again. Just thinking about his touch brought back the heat deep inside. Dangerous heat. Heat that would make her think he was worth the risk after all.

I have to think of Dulcie. She was too young to remember Johnny. But if Regret tried the same fool stunts Johnny had, Dulcie would remember him.

"Mommy?"

"Yes, pretty?"

"Whatcha doin', Mommy?"

Trudy skimmed a handful of leaves off the water. "Washing mayhaws so we can make jelly. You want to see?"

Hugging a home-sewn doll to her chest, Dulcie considered her mother's offer and then shook her ponytailed head. Trudy wore her hair in a braided ponytail, too, but mainly because she planned to spend the day in a hot kitchen.

"Would you like to help Mommy bake bread later?"

Dulcie shook her head again. "Where's R.J.?"

So that was it. Dulcie's first crush. Trudy couldn't blame the tyke, now, could she?

Trudy swirled both hands through the water, picking out debris and examining the plump little apples. Dulcie used to ask about Papa, who on this day had gone to the fields to work, or about Grendel, who was still at the vet's. Dulcie used to be interested in everything Trudy did, reveling in being "Mommy's little helper." Now she had a new playmate in Regret, who took her for long walks to look for birds and flowers or played chase with her in the backyard. The two of them had spent most of the previous day photographing a nest of fledging bluebirds on the garden fence.

"Mommy?" Dulcie tugged at Trudy's skirt. "I said where's R.J.?"

"In his room, baby. Now, you stay out of there. He's busy right now. Besides, it'll soon be your nap time."

"Okay, Mommy." Dulcie wandered away, lingering distractedly at the window to watch several mourning doves that had scattered across the yard.

R.J. had taken the truck into town that morning to pick up some photographic supplies, and although Trudy had worried that he might run into Rooster and Jordy again, he'd come home safely. He'd even chatted with several people in town and found them to be likable and earthy. He'd brought back half a dozen intimidating boxes of supplies, most of which Trudy knew nothing about. She did understand that he intended to turn the guest room temporarily into a darkroom and that he planned to develop some important pictures. She couldn't imagine what was so important about these pictures but hoped they'd explain what he

wouldn't. He'd held something back from her. He'd said he
was an aerial photographer and a pilot. But he'd never explained exactly what it was he was taking pictures of the day
Rooster Reed had fired into the air and the two-seater
Cessna had glided to the ground.

Then she heard a cry of desperation from the guest room.

"R.J.? What happened?" But she knew in an instant
when she saw him in the doorway of the guest room. He was
holding a recalcitrant toddler in his arms, a mixture of affection and glumness on his face.

"I should've locked the door," he explained.

"Oh, Dulcie." Trudy took the little girl from his arms.
"I'm so sorry, R.J. She's ruined your pictures, hasn't she?"

"Well, not all of them. To tell the truth, I was almost
done."

"That's no excuse. I should've kept a closer eye on her. I
turned my back for one minute...."

Regret touched her shoulder, and a shiver ran through
her.

"It's okay. Really."

"I sorry, Mommy," Dulcie said with a pout as she cud-
dled against Trudy. "I just wanted to help."

Regret assured her that everything was all right, but still
Trudy felt guilty that she'd let her daughter interrupt his
work. She couldn't bring herself to return his smile. "It's
past Dulcie's nap time," she said sternly.

"I don't wanna go night-night," wailed Dulcie, starting
to kick and fret in Trudy's arms.

"Cut that out, Dulcie," she warned. Her two-year-old
was terrific most of the time, but Trudy always felt so in-
adequate when her child was less than perfect. Couldn't she
be all sweetness and light in front of Regret?

"Mommy, I don't wanna go night-night." Dulcie broke
into a full-fledged whine, kicking harder against her.

"Cut that out, Dulcie. I'm not kidding."

Immediately Dulcie stopped kicking and looked up at her
mother with wide, innocent eyes and said, "I'm not a kit-
ten, either, Mommy."

Regret's eyes locked with Trudy's, and she and he both
burst into laughter. So much for being a stern mother!

Trudy hugged the child again as she put Dulcie into her crib. They executed their twice-a-day ritual of night-night hugs and kisses that were blown, caught and rubbed in. But this time was different—this time Regret joined their family ritual.

"Are you keeping busy today?" Regret asked after they had closed the door to the bedroom and Dulcie had quieted down.

"I always keep busy."

"Are you doing something for yourself today? Or for everybody else?" He brushed a stray lock of hair from her face. She caught it nervously and tucked it back into her ponytail.

"Both. I'm making jelly out of the mayhaws we picked."

"Can I help?"

Taking a deep breath, she broke free of his light-jade eyes and stepped back. "Uh, sure. Why don't you join me in the kitchen when you're done?"

Why did I do that? she wondered as she walked back toward the kitchen. Once she turned on the pressure cookers, the kitchen would be even hotter than it already was. And once Regret walked into the room and stood close to her, the room would only get steamier.

She finished washing the two buckets of berries, taking care to pick out the stems and stray leaves, and set four large boilers on the stove. Trudy transferred the berries to the boilers, filling them with enough water to cover the berries and turning on each unit to a low boil. Gradually steam rose from the pots, dampening her face with a light mist as she bent over them. Already her loose dress clung to the cleft in her back and the valley between her breasts.

"Are those the fruits of our labor?" asked a low voice behind her.

She felt a pair of cool hands rest on her shoulders, but she didn't look up. Instead she stared intently at the contents of the four boilers. The bubbling water turned a light, clear pink with the juice of the berries. A faint breeze played at the back of her neck, and she realized that he was trying to cool her off—but what he was really doing was heating her up!

"Y-yes," she stammered.

"What can I do to help?"

Awkwardly she handed him a potato masher and showed him how to mash the softened berries to extract more juice. He leaned obediently over the boilers, performing just the way she'd shown him. The heat lingered in his wavy blond hair, soaking the curls and pressing them to his brow. She noticed that a spark of playfulness had replaced the danger in his green eyes. He grinned up at her from his chore.

"Am I doing it right?"

"Oh, yes," she said, without looking at the berries.

Then she shook herself out of a coming daydream and showed him how to strain the juice through a cotton bag into four waiting pans. As instructed, he carried the large boilers and the remaining pulp from the berries to the sink to make room for the rest of the process. Then he watched with what Trudy interpreted as fascination as she carefully measured out the juice and sugar into saucepans and, stirring, brought them to a low boil before sprinkling pectin into the rosy concoction. She looked up at him and smiled as she brought the pans to a rolling boil.

Dulcie's asleep, she thought. *And Papa's in the field. There's no one here but the two of us.*

"Do you do this often?"

Trudy caught her breath. "Do what?" *Think of getting you alone?*

"Make jelly."

"Oh. Several times every April. The berries don't last long."

She turned off the stove and removed the saucepans from the units. After they'd cooled for a few seconds, she picked up a serving spoon and skimmed the foam from the liquid. Her hands trembled as she wielded the spoon with less grace than usual. Conscious that he was watching every movement, she spooned the liquid into the waiting trays of sterilized jelly jars. He sealed the lids for her.

"All done," Trudy announced when they had stacked dozens of gleaming jars on the countertop.

Regret ran his fingertips over the warm jars. He seemed as proud of their yield as she was. "What now?"

"Now we bake bread."

He turned her around to him and took her hands. "There's something I'd like to share with you first."

Expectantly she bit her bottom lip and gazed up at him. If he wanted to kiss her, she wasn't prepared for it. Johnny had never been one for deep kisses and she'd forgotten the art, if she'd ever mastered it at all.

"Trudy, there are two great loves in my life. You know them already. Flying is the first."

Flying is always a pilot's first love. They get in the sky and forget all about wives and babies at home. They get so tangled up in breaking free of gravity that they do something stupid and get themselves killed! They think they're immortal. They only die faster.

"Are you okay, Trudy?"

"Yeah." She fanned herself with her hand. "Just a little warm."

He led her to the table where he had left several stacks of four-by-five photographs. "Photography is my second love."

She picked up an aerial view that she recognized as her own farmhouse. The cascades of purple wisteria and the stark white of the dogwoods in the driveway stood out against the bright green of the lawn. She noticed the shiny silver of new tin that patched the barn roof. The fuchsia of azaleas in her garden. And there, plainly in view, were two dressed-alike girls waving back at the camera.

"R.J., it's—it's beautiful!"

"You can keep that."

"Thank you. It may be all of my farm that I get to keep." Her voice cracked. "But at least I'll have a picture of what was once mine."

"Shh." He laid his hand over hers. "We'll figure out something."

She shuffled through the photographs in the first stack and saw several more of her farm, the cows, Papa on his tractor with Grendel close behind. Most of the pictures were of views she didn't recognize.

"What are these?" she asked.

"Other farms between Atlanta and here. I told you. I'm an aerial photographer."

She laughed. "When you first crashed, I thought maybe you were running drugs."

He frowned. "Hardly. Actually, I have several jobs, but I've managed to combine them into one. See, I take these great shots of farms while I'm flying and then later drive back through Georgia and sell the photographs to the land owners. I also sell pics of the little towns I fly over to their chambers of commerce, and they use the pictures to promote the town to new industry."

"I know where this is," she said, picking up a photograph. "This is north of here. Up where Johnson's Creek starts."

He nodded and took the picture from her. "This one— and the ones like it—go off in tomorrow's mail. This picture is the reason for my being so far south."

She studied it more closely. "Looks like...the gas line?"

"Yeah. I'm also contracted to fly troubleshooting missions for a gas company. And this creek is trouble waiting to happen." He pointed to a washout around the pipes. "See that erosion? I report problems like that so the gas company can come in and build the land back up. Otherwise the exposed pipes could leak or break or maybe even explode."

Trudy shuddered. "Explode?"

"Oh, nothing to worry about now. I got through to my business partner, and he relayed the message to the company. Everything's been taken care of."

She thought back on the stormy night when she'd found him passed out, the phone in his hand, and she nodded. Regret James was a businessman. A perfectly legitimate businessman. She sifted through another stack of photographs and drew back in surprise.

"I don't think that one's for a gas company or for a farmer, R.J."

He laughed and proudly held up the photograph of two sapphire-hued bluebirds sitting on a rusty fence. "No, Trudy, this one is for me. I also sell my work to magazines. I'm what's known as a stock photographer. I sell most of my work to aerial and agricultural magazines—anything with a rural emphasis. This one—" he pointed to the pair of bluebirds "—should be worth a pretty penny in a wildlife contest I know of."

"It's beautiful!" She raked through the stack of pictures, mostly of nature scenes, several of Dulcie and her blue eyes as she danced in the rose garden. "You can really sell these?"

Regret nodded. "I'll sell most of the pictures over and over. Fifty dollars here, seventy-five there. A picture may be worth a thousand words, but it's even better if it's worth a thousand dollars."

"What about this one?" She held up a picture of herself, lost in thought in the strawberry patch. "I don't think you'll make much off of this one."

"On the contrary, Trudy." He lifted the print from her fingers and took her hands in his. "That's by far the most intriguing photograph I've ever taken. See your eyes? Full of dreams and hope and... and a little sadness. I won't be selling this one. I'll keep it for myself."

His next words tore at her heart.

"To remember you by."

She pulled her hands away from his, certain that he could read the fire in her cheeks. "I—I wanted to get the bread baked before Dulcie's nap was over."

He looked disappointed. "I'll help."

Regret followed her back to the countertop, where he watched with a bored expression while she cleared away the pots and pans she'd dirtied to make jelly and shifted them to the sink to be washed later. She took a large, glass bowl from the cupboard and combined meticulously measured flour, sugar, yeast and butter in the bowl. Leaning casually against the warm oven door, Regret watched her add hot water to the mix.

"I thought you were going to let me help," he teased.

She reached for a farm-fresh egg.

"Or do you insist on doing everything yourself?" He studied her movements, her shoulders, her hips, the way she brushed the damp hair from her cheekbones.

"Can you crack an egg?" she asked, more because she needed something to say than because she needed the help.

"Can I crack an egg? Of course I can crack an egg!" He tried to sound miffed, but the laughter in his voice betrayed his playful intent. Then he winked at her. "If you give me instructions."

"Sorry," she said, cracking the egg herself, "but instructing you on anything you'd need instructions on would take up far too much of your time."

His expression softened, his green eyes half-mast with yearning. "Time's one thing I have plenty of." He touched her arms, and she shuddered, turning away quickly to her bowl and busying herself with stirring the ingredients.

"Have you ever tasted anything like that jelly?" Her voice broke. It was all she could think of to say.

"Never," he purred. She reached into a wooden bowl and dusted her hands with sifted flour. "It's like the first fruit of Eden."

His eyes were on her. She didn't look up, but she could feel the burn of his gaze. "We'll have jelly biscuits when I'm done." Trudy dumped the bread dough onto a floured board and sank her hands into the doughy softness, molding it into a ball and then kneading it. Two masculine hands, powerful in their grip, rested on her shoulders, kneading her flesh, molding her desire into a ball of want.

"I'll bet you've made this recipe a hundred times before," he whispered. "I'll bet you can make bread without even thinking about it."

Trudy laughed nervously and pulled away, kneading the dough frantically. As it stuck to her fingers, she reached for more flour from the smooth wooden bowl and sprinkled the powder onto the flattened dough.

"Sometimes making bread requires *a lot* of concentration." She felt the warmth in her blushing cheeks. Realizing the context of what she'd said, she quickly added, "When I was a little girl, I used to stand here in a chair beside the stove while my grandmother made cat-head biscuits."

"Made *what?*"

Trudy dared to glance up and found an expression of disbelief on his face. "Cat-head biscuits," she repeated. "Because of their *size*, R.J. What did you think I meant?"

He shrugged. "Oh, I don't know. I thought it might be another one of your South Georgia delicacies. Like mayhaw jelly."

Covering the kneaded dough with a dishcloth, she pushed the gooey mix to one corner of the cabinet. Her hands were still masked in flour.

"Now what?" he asked brightly.

"Now we let the dough rise in a warm place."

Regret's voice dropped again, low and guttural, as he turned her around to face him. "Then it should rise fast— because it's very warm in here."

She pressed her floured hands against his chest, leaving imprints on the shirt that Johnny had once worn. "It'll take about thirty minutes." She was surprised to find her voice breathless. She dared not look at Regret.

"So we've got thirty minutes to waste?" He raked his lips across her brow as he bent close.

Trudy pulled away. "I...I really need to wash those dishes."

"I'll do them for you. Later."

His gaze would not release her.

"Dulcie," she whimpered.

"Dulcie's asleep. And your grandfather won't be home all afternoon. And even ol' Grendel's at the vet's. It's just you and me."

He kissed her damp forehead. She closed her eyes as her head tilted backward.

"R.J., I—"

"Shh. Hush, Trudy. I know you want me. I can feel it."

Laughter caught in her throat. "I bet you've said that to a hundred other women," she joked. He didn't answer. She knew that he probably had said it, and it probably had been true in a hundred other cases. But with his bandaged ribs, even now in the sticky humidity of her kitchen, Regret

James embodied every plea for affection her so-long-untouched body craved. Yes, she wanted him!

"I can handle it," she whispered back, both admitting and denying her attraction to him.

"I don't want you to handle it. I want you to handle *me.*" He seized her hand as he pushed close against her, holding her hand against the bulge in his jeans, crushing her palm against his desire. As his mouth nuzzled hers, he slowly parted her lips and pressed his tongue inside, tentative at first and then more boldly.

Her pulse thrashing in her ears, she broke the seal of his kiss as she bumped into the cabinet behind her. She was trapped between the stove and his hot embrace.

"I can't," she said, her voice husky.

"Of course you can." His encircling arms tightened around her.

"I couldn't take it if...if I let you into my heart... and...something happened to you."

He crushed her against him. "Nothing's going to happen to me."

"I...can't."

"What are you so afraid of?"

The edge of the cabinet jammed into her back and hurt, but she hardly noticed any sensation other than the one his green eyes stirred inside her. "Of you," she blurted out. "Of falling in love with you."

"Is falling in love with me so bad? Don't you want me?"

"I do...."

He assaulted her neck with soft kisses. She tossed her head back in surrender. "More than anything?"

"More than I should." She offered him an affectionate kiss on the lips, light and platonic—the way she had always kissed Johnny.

"You can do better than that," he whispered. "Kiss me, Trudy. *Really* kiss me."

Her mouth met his, responding eagerly to the urgency of his tongue. Her white-powdered hands moved across his chest and around the taut muscles of his shoulders.

His fingertips brushed across her cheeks and into the soft, wet tendrils of hair that lined her temples. Gentle fingertips wove through her dark hair, unraveling the braid until her hair fell loosely at her shoulders.

"I don't want to lose you," she murmured between kisses.

Regret pulled away to look at her, his eyes delving into her soul. She couldn't read the emotion in his face. Was it pity? Or admiration?

"You won't lose me," he promised gently. "I have no intention of leaving you."

Oh, R.J., she wanted to say. *It's not that you might walk out on me. It's that you might fly away—and into the ground.*

She slid her arms around his neck and pulled him down to her, returning his deep kisses. Her eyes closed to everything but the feel of his skin against hers. "My baking will go to waste if I don't get back to it."

"I'm not stopping you, Trudy."

He cupped one hand over her breast. A little moan escaped from her throat.

"Then again, I can always bake bread."

Instantly his hand moved from her breast to the hem of her loose-fitting dress, up along her bare thigh, lingering over her white cotton panties before it trailed across her hip, across her trembling ribs and back to her breast. Caressing her breast warmly, he teased her nipple with his thumb.

A screen door slammed, and Trudy startled away from Regret. "Wh-what was that?"

Regret froze, listening. "Sounded like the back door. Maybe it's your friend Louisa."

Dread coursed through her, down to her knees. All Trudy needed was for Louisa to spy on her "cooking" with the good-looking pilot. Louisa would never understand. Or worse yet, Louisa would understand.

"Trudy? Where are you, girl?" called a feeble, exasperated voice.

"Papa." She pushed free of Regret just as her grandfather stepped out of the shadows and into the kitchen. She felt guilty and knew she looked it, too.

"Girl, didn't you hear me calling you?"

Trudy stepped back to the stove and tidied the counter with a dishcloth. Maybe Papa wouldn't notice floured handprints on Regret's chest and shoulders. "No, Papa. I didn't. I was right in the middle of...baking bread."

"Where's my great-grandbaby?" asked Papa. He walked to the refrigerator and brought out a gallon jug of lemonade. He gulped the icy liquid from the spout of the jug. His face was caked with field dust, and only the sweaty creases on his brow and around his squinted eyes seemed clean. Papa had removed his straw hat before he'd come into the room. The upper hemisphere of his head gleamed pale and tender.

"Dulcie's still down for her nap." Turning her back to both the men, Trudy washed the flour from her hands. Moments before, she'd stood alone with Regret, ready to give herself to him willingly. Had Papa seen them through the kitchen window? Could he read the unfulfilled want in the stiffness of her movements? Could he decipher the oh-so-dirty thoughts that still pounded through her head?

"Well, you need to wake her up," Papa instructed as he returned the jug to the refrigerator. "Dad-burned tractor broke down again. I think I got it rigged good 'nough to get me to town, but I need you to follow me on the truck and bring me back while Donny Ray and his boys fix it."

"Right now? Papa, I'm baking bread. I'll be glad to drive you in another thirty minutes or so—"

The old man shot her a despairing look. It was the same one he had practiced on her mother and on her mother's mother. It was the brand of disapproval from a generation that had never understood the importance of women's work, particularly when there was any delay in a task Papa deemed more important. Trudy wasn't as much worried about bread baking as she was about being quizzed on the way home with Papa. She was sure he'd see through her and certain that he would send Regret packing—probably with the aid of the .12-gauge shotgun he kept in his closet.

No. She wasn't her mother and she wasn't her grandma. She wasn't Papa's servant, either. He could just blooming wait until the bread was done. Maybe by then she could manage to compose herself.

"I'm sorry, Papa. You'll have to wait."

"I'll go with you, Mr. Lester."

Regret seemed to sense the sudden flustering in her movements. Surely he knew what his touch did to her.

"Trudy's got plenty to do this afternoon, and I'd like to be of some help to you, Mr. Lester. It's the least I can do for all your generosity."

Papa eyed him suspiciously and pursed his thin lips. "Awright, boy. Come on. I ain't got all day."

Chapter 9

"Stay with me, R.J. Please? Pretty please?"

Dancing blue eyes gazed up at him, begging. Regret bent over the crib rail and kissed Dulcie on the forehead.

"If only your mommy would ask me to stay with her..."

The child blinked up at him. "My mommy won't ask you to stay with her?"

Regret bit his lip in response. He cringed at the thought of a two-year-old repeating his heartfelt wishes to Trudy. Or in front of Trudy's Papa, heaven forbid. He was in enough trouble with Papa as it was. Yesterday afternoon, he'd followed Trudy's grandfather on a puttering old tractor into town to a tin-roofed mechanic's shop. Donny Ray and his boys were to repair the tractor after Regret gave Mr. Lester a ride home on the truck. As it turned out, Donny Ray was a man in his seventies and his two sons, both in their early fifties, knew the old man as "Uncle Lester."

Donny Ray had nodded solemnly while giving the tractor the once-over. "Lester, why don't you and the boy hang around a while? I think we can squeeze you in next if you don't tell nobody."

Regret had been prepared for a fifteen-minute ride back to the farm and whatever questions Lester Dugan might ask him on the way home. He hadn't expected to sit in a dusty, greasy shop for almost three hours, listening to anecdotes of rural life during the Great Depression and vivid descriptions of who hadn't come home from World War II. Mr. Lester had helped himself to a grape soda at the bottom of a refrigerated drink box. Then he had parked himself on a wooden chair with a torn cane seat. Seeing no place else to sit, Regret had hoisted himself onto the drink box and sat swinging his legs.

"What are your intentions toward my grandbaby?" Mr. Lester had asked after chewing on a piece of hay for several minutes.

"Intentions?" Was the old man talking about marriage? Regret didn't have any intentions about marrying Trudy. In fact, he'd never had any intentions about marrying anyone. The first step, Regret had reasoned, was to find someone who wanted to stay with him as much as he wanted to stay with her. And that had never happened. Until now. "Oh, we're just friends," Regret had added quickly.

Lester Dugan had coughed dryly. "I seen the way you two look at each other. Ain't nothin' jes' friendly 'bout it. Trudy's been through enough already. I don't want to see her hurt again."

"I'd never hurt her, Mr. Dugan."

"You won't mean to, but you will. She's taken a likin' to you, and you ain't gonna be here for long. If you'd been a truck driver or a farmer, it wouldn't have mattered none. But you fly in here in that airplane, and she cain't help herself."

"What's my plane got to do with it?"

Mr. Lester had looked away uncomfortably then. "Hasn't she told you about her husband?"

"Some."

"She had to save you, boy. Had to. She couldn't save Johnny." Mr. Lester had lifted the grape cola to his lips again, this time draining the bottle.

"She tries to save everybody, doesn't she, sir? Me. You. Her mother. Her bluebirds." Regret had dared to catch the man's gaze. "Your land."

"It ain't my land no more. I gave it to her when Johnny died."

"But she's about to lose it. The bank will take it if she can't pay off her husband's debts."

"They cain't take it away from her. It'll always be her land and her children's land—no matter who owns it."

"But, sir, if someone else owns it, she won't be able to take Dulcie for long walks in the woods or pick mayhaws in April or watch her bluebirds fledge." Regret had narrowed his eyes at the old man. "And you won't have land to farm."

Mr. Lester had risen then from his chair and retrieved a second grape cola from the drink box. "This is my last year farmin' anyway."

"Trudy says you say that every year."

"And I mean it every year, too. I got a little bit of money to live on. And some for Trudy if she needs it. We've both got our social security. And Trudy could git a job in town at the dime store if she had to."

"You know it would kill her to lose that land."

"I know it, boy. But I cain't do much about it. If I was thirty years younger, things'd be different then. Wouldn't be none of them rascals from town out here botherin' Trudy. But I don't git around like I used to. And I cain't work off a farm debt now like I could when I was your age."

"I've heard there's gold buried on your land. If Trudy could find that—"

Mr. Lester had snorted, raising his hand in protest. "That's just a story, boy. They been tellin' it since 'fore I was born. Every ten years or so, the story gets started up again, and I have to run off all the local fortune hunters. Cain't tell you how many times they've dug up my woods. Gertie used to run 'em off with my shotgun."

"Gertie?"

"Trudy's grandma."

"Your wife?"

"For almost forty-five years. Finest woman ever to set foot in the state of Georgia. And Trudy looks just like her."

"R.J.?" Dulcie's soft voice brought him back to the present. "Will you stay with me?"

He smiled down at her and traced her delicate eyebrows with one forefinger. "You need your nap. When you wake up, we'll make paper airplanes, okay?"

Dulcie seemed satisfied with his explanation and rolled over, hugging her teddy bear, but Regret was still troubled. There had to be a way to help Trudy save the woods where her ancestors had walked. It meant so much to her. And nothing to him. He was almost jealous. He'd never been blessed with a sense of roots. He doubted he ever would be.

There had to be a way to stop the foreclosure. He had his own debts to pay, and getting his bird back in the air wouldn't be cheap. But he had the money. For nearly thirteen years, it had sat in the stocks and bonds Hughie's father had set up for him, dividends reinvesting and the accounts growing far beyond the original one hundred fifty thousand dollars. But he'd sworn he'd never touch it.

A scream from the kitchen jarred his senses. *Trudy!* He ran through the house, the wooden boards shaking under his bare feet. There was no time to get the rifle out of Papa's bedroom, not that his aim was half as accurate or as practiced as Trudy's when she lined up pinecones on the fence posts.

Standing in the door of the kitchen, Trudy was gripping a butcher knife in her right hand and a broom handle in her left. Her back was arched like an angry cat's, and although her dark hair hung loosely to her eyelet-covered shoulders, Regret found nothing sweet or demure about her survival instinct. Trudy Sandlin was pure tigress when it came to protecting her territory.

"Who are you?" she demanded in a growl.

Regret couldn't see the trespasser from where he stood.

"Are you one of Rooster's hunting buddies? I told you boys before to stay off my land, and you'd better stay out of my house!"

"T-take it easy, baby," a familiar male voice pleaded.

Relieved, Regret felt his entire body relax. "It's okay, Trudy," he assured her softly, laying a hand on Trudy's shoulder.

Startled, she jerked around. Regret jumped back as the knife slashed in front of his ribs. Her wild blue eyes tempered with sudden recognition. Her hands flying to her face, she dropped the knife and broomstick.

"R.J.!" she shrieked. "I could've hurt you!"

He stared down at the slit in his shirt and the gleaming white of his bandages.

"I could've *killed* you!" she added.

"It's okay." He embraced her awkwardly and quickly released her. "I should've known better than to frighten you like that." With Grendel still recuperating at the vet's, Trudy had been jumpier than usual about protecting her property.

"R.J." The intruder stepped out of the shadows where Trudy had cornered him. "Damned glad to see you, buddy." Trudy still stood between them. The man dared not come any closer.

"Hughie." Regret grinned at him. "I see you've met Trudy."

Hughie nodded. His hands were still shaking and his knuckles were white from clutching the corner of the counter behind him. He was tall and thin, almost thirty years old. He had a hint of a mustache that never thickened and scraggly brown hair that would have fallen to his shoulders without the black mesh cap to tuck it under. His T-shirt and jeans smelled of oil; his scuffed cowboy boots were the same hue as his brown eyes. Hughie Waddell was probably Lester Dugan's idea of a hippie, minus the peace symbols. As thin as Hughie was, the old man would've described him as having the kind of body you could hold up to the sun and see the seeds inside him like peas in a pod.

"This is your... your..." Trudy swallowed hard. "Your business partner?"

Regret laughed suddenly. "I can guess what this is all about. Hughie has a habit of forgetting to knock." Regret bent and picked up the butcher knife and laid it on the table. Best to get it out of Trudy's reach in case Hughie said something to offend her. "Yep. Hughie's been my business partner for ten years."

"It's—it's nice to meet you, Hughie." She extended one hand meekly, but he didn't venture forward to shake it.

"I'm sorry if I scared you. I've had a few unexpected visitors lately, and I thought you were one of them."

"Forget about it," Hughie said after a nervous glance toward Regret.

"Did you have a good trip?" Trudy asked him.

Hughie shrugged at her question. "One speeding ticket just south of Atlanta. Other than that, pretty good."

Trudy shifted on her feet. She seemed to want to make a good impression but knew it was too late. "You've been driving for hours. You must be starved. We just ate a little while ago, but I could warm up something for you." She gestured toward the stove.

Regret laughed again. "Hughie's always hungry. Hey, Hughie, you should try one of Trudy's jelly biscuits." He winked at his friend. "I helped make 'em myself."

Hughie stepped awkwardly to the table and leaned against a chair. "You? Damn, buddy! You in love or something?"

Feeling the color rise in his cheeks, Regret slumped against the wall. Hughie had seen women come and go from his life, but he'd never seen one stay. Regret had beheld each of them with appreciation and contempt, never staying close to any one of them long enough to know if he was really in love. So many of them, in his younger days, had recklessly fallen in bed with him, laid claim to him, begged him to stay, and none of them knew anything more about him or who he was than how he was in bed. He'd sampled from some of the finest women he'd ever seen, but not one of them had he let near his heart. Was that why Trudy Sandlin kept pushing him away? Because she was afraid of becoming a relic of his present as so many others had of his past? Or did he want her so badly because she was the only woman who'd never asked him to stay? Why did he always crave the one thing he couldn't have?

Trudy was watching him, her eyes sympathetic, as she waited for him to say something. Finally he muttered, "Hughie's the best airplane mechanic in Georgia. There's not a bird he can't fix."

"Oh?" Trudy brightened for a moment. "Why don't you have a seat, Hughie? I'll fix you something to eat."

"Jelly biscuits?" Hughie smiled warily at her.

"If you'd like." When she was finished preparing them, she spread a generous dollop of mayhaw jelly on each of the four warm biscuits and arranged them on a flowered china plate in front of him. Graciously she served him a tall glass of iced tea, sweetened with real sugar. Hughie's first bite was tentative, the second enthusiastic. "Will you need a place to stay tonight?" Something in Trudy's tone suggested a hidden motive.

"Nope. I just wanna take a look at our bird, and then I'll be driving on back tonight. Can't afford to be away from the business for too long at a time. Not like ol' R.J. He's been shirking his business duties back home. Least now I know why."

Regret glared at him.

"So this airplane of R.J.'s . . . it's yours, too?" Trudy sat down next to Hughie, her eyes anxiously following his movements.

"Yep. We're fifty-fifty partners."

"You must be . . . very close."

"Me and R.J.?" he asked between mouthfuls. "I reckon so. Practically brothers."

"Practically?"

She shot a questioning glance at Regret, and he cringed. Trudy really didn't need to know all that. He turned a kitchen chair around and sat backward in it, his chest pressed against the chair back.

"You two have known each other a long time." Trudy was fishing. "Did you grow up together?"

"Yeah. Kinda," Hughie conceded. "But not in the way you think. We weren't little kids together or nothing like that. We didn't even meet until we were grown. Well, *almost* grown."

"Hughie," Regret growled, warning him not to continue.

Trudy ignored him. "How did you and R.J. meet?"

"In jail."

Regret groaned inwardly. "You're enjoying this too much, Hughie. There's no sense in scaring Trudy just because she got you on the wrong end of a knife."

Without warning, Trudy shivered. She tried to hide her hands in her lap. "Wh-what were you in jail for, Hughie?"

"Oh, I wasn't in jail. R.J. was."

"Hughie!" Regret bounded to his feet.

"What was R.J. in jail for, Hughie?"

She wouldn't let it pass, would she? *This is what I get for keeping my business to myself.*

Hughie grinned, then said quietly, "What do you think he was in jail for?"

"I—I don't know."

"Come on, Trudy! Don't you have any idea? The guy's been living here in your house, probably creeping around in the dark at night. Haven't you figured it out yet?"

Regret was curious to hear her answer—and afraid of what she might say. What kind of man did she think he was? A rapist? A murderer? "Leave her alone, Hughie. She doesn't deserve to be teased."

"Aw, come on, R.J.! It's not every day I get held at knife point." He winked playfully at the woman. "Or broom point!"

"Car theft," Regret confessed. "I stole a car."

"Oh, and not just any car," Hughie chimed in. "He stole my father's Mercedes. I mean, I wasn't even allowed to touch that car except to wax it, and this foul-mouthed kid a little older than me steals his car and then wrecks the damned thing!"

Trudy frowned, no doubt reevaluating whatever trust she'd credited to Regret.

"But why would you steal a car?"

"I wanted to get as far away from my foster home as possible as soon as I turned eighteen. I hitchhiked to Atlanta and then decided to pick up some transportation that was a little more reliable than my thumb. So I stole a car a few miles west of there. I was a stupid kid, Trudy."

"Yeah, I'll say he was stupid." Hughie finished his third biscuit. "If he'd been smart, he would've picked something a little less flashy. They caught R.J. in less than an hour after Daddy reported the car stolen. The next morning, my daddy hauled my butt down to the jail to show me what could happen to me if I didn't finish high school and straighten up. R.J. was just standing there. Just staring out the window of his cell. Looked like a lost puppy. Daddy took one look at him and dropped the charges.''

"Hughie's father took me home to live with them until I could decide what to do with my life. Told me I had to work off my debt to him." Regret stared down at his feet. "My debt to that man only got deeper. The next year, Hughie graduated from high school. He liked to tinker at his daddy's airport, and I liked to fly, so his daddy set us up in business together. His daddy's the closest thing I've ever had to a father. And Hughie's the closest thing I'll ever have to a brother."

Trudy braced her hands under her chin and stared wistfully—too wistfully—at Hughie. "R.J. says you're the best airplane mechanic in Georgia. Is that true?"

Smiling sheepishly at her, Hughie ran his forefinger over the dewy condensation on the tea glass. "I don't like to brag none," he lied, "but there's not an airplane—or a car—that I can't fix."

"Don't speak too soon," Regret warned. "You haven't seen ours yet. It's pretty badly smashed up. Like I told you, some of Trudy's, uh, friends decided to ground me for a while. That bird's gonna take a lot of tender loving care to get her back in the air."

"Don't you worry none, R.J. I'll mend her—body and soul."

"So you're really, really good," Trudy asserted again, her voice brimming with hero worship.

Her adoration was beginning to annoy Regret, maybe even make him a little bit jealous of the attention Trudy showered on the scraggly faced man whose five-o'clock shadow lingered from the day before.

"Yes, Trudy. He is really, really good." Then Regret added wickedly, "With airplanes."

She laid an unsteady hand on Hughie's wrist, and jealousy scorched Regret's cheeks.

"I want to show you something," she whispered to Hughie with the quiet, awe-filled intimacy of a lover's voice.

Minutes later, Regret followed the two of them across the backyard toward a rusty-roofed barn. Refusing to join in their animated chatter, he walked a discreet six feet or more behind them. His throat clenched at the sight of Trudy's bare legs and feet as she danced over the pale-green grass. Enough of a breeze stirred the spring air to lift the dark tangles on the back of her neck and play in the eyelet folds of her loose-fitting dress. She was more suited, he realized with a sudden sinking dread, to a down-to-earth, feet-on-the-ground guy like Hughie than a head-in-the-clouds dreamer like him. A country boy at heart, Hughie could appreciate the slower pace of life Cornerstone, Georgia, offered and find in it a peace he would not in the suburbs of the big city. If it wasn't for the business he shared with Regret, Hughie would likely spend the rest of his days tinkering with engines and molding car bodies in a small town similar to Cornerstone.

Trudy jangled the rusty latch on the double barn doors and tugged them open, heaving against the tall grass that had grown thick at the footings. The musty smell of old hay greeted Regret's nostrils as he stepped up to the dark, open space beyond the doorway.

"Well, I'll be damned," he heard Hughie say as his own eyes adjusted to the darkness. "What are you doing with that thing in your barn? You should've sold it for parts. Or scrap."

"We paid a lot of money for it. It's not any good to anybody but me. And I never could bring myself to get rid of it."

"It's yours?"

"It was my husband's," Trudy whispered reverently.

Regret saw her hands start to shake. He blinked at the twisted metal in front of him, at last focusing on a broken propeller.

"Do you think you can fix it?" Trudy asked Hughie eagerly. Her voice was giddy, her eyes hopeful, watery.

"The damage isn't too bad," Hughie said slowly from the shadows. He circled the plane once, rubbing his hand over the dents, the scratched Confederate battle flag painted on the side and the words "Johnny Reb." He pulled hard on the door to the cockpit. Reluctantly it opened, and he crawled inside. "Holy—" His words were lost as he half stepped, half fell backward out of the cockpit. Hughie stumbled out of the shadows. His face was pale. He scrubbed his sweaty palms against his jeans. "I'd love to meet the poor devil who walked away from that one."

Trudy's lips twisted involuntarily, almost smiling and then puckering. "My husband . . . Johnny. He didn't walk away. He . . . he died in my arms."

"Jeez. I'm sorry. Was he a good pilot?"

Her eyes misted. "The best."

Regret swallowed the lump in his throat. How many times had he joked with Hughie that Regret James wasn't just a good pilot but the best?

Hughie dug into his shirt pocket for a cigarette. "What'd he hit? A utility pole? Radio tower?"

"Just a tree."

Lighting his cigarette, Hughie inhaled thoughtfully. "That explains the smashed-in canopy."

Trying not to be too conspicuous in his actions, Regret moved slowly toward the cockpit. Part of him wanted to argue that it was bad luck to look at another pilot's handiwork, but his curiosity won out. He had to see what had given Hughie the shakes.

"Johnny could be a daredevil sometimes," Trudy was saying as Regret smoothed his palm over the cold metal of the fuselage. "He didn't think there was anything he couldn't do. Once he was in the air, he was invincible."

Kinda like me, Regret mused silently.

"I stopped watching him fly a long time ago. It used to scare me to death to watch him fly under guy wires.

"'Didja see that, Trudy?' he used to say. 'I oughta charge people to watch. Ain't nobody seen a pilot as good as me.'

"And I'd say, 'Johnny, you've got to be more careful. You've got to think of me and the baby. What would we do if you got yourself killed?'"

She stared at the plane, love and hatred mixing with the tears. She didn't seem to see Regret at the cockpit door.

"Two years ago, he was spraying the Meltons' cotton field. He pulled up too late, got tripped up in a utility wire and lost control. Clipped the top off an oak."

Regret stared into the dim cockpit. A bloody handprint, perfectly preserved, waved from the inside of the door.

"Johnny didn't come home for dinner that day," Trudy continued, her voice trembling. "Johnny was never late for dinner. I knew where he was supposed to be working, and that's where...that's where I found him. He was calling my name."

She stopped talking for a moment, her words choking in her throat as Hughie averted his eyes, distantly interested in a blackbird on a faraway fence. Regret watched a teardrop run down her cheek.

"But I was too late."

Regret shut his eyes tightly, seeing in the darkness what he thought Trudy must've seen that day. For a moment, he saw himself mangled in Johnny's duster. He thought of all the fool stunts he'd tried and how easily it could have been him, bleeding to death, rib cage crushed, instead of Johnny Sandlin. Without Trudy's determined rescue, he might have died in the Dugan woods where Trudy's ancestors had played poker and searched for embezzled gold.

"Trudy." Regret opened his eyes, releasing his pent-up breath in a heavy sigh. She sniffed and brushed away the tears. She wouldn't look at him. He jumped down from the cockpit door and in three strides folded her into his arms.

"Don't." She stiffened. "Don't...touch me."

A horn beeped four times in the distance.

"Th-that must be the mail." She wriggled free of him. "I'll be right back."

Watching her plod through the grass toward the house, Regret was almost relieved to see her go. Witnessing Trudy's pain only made him feel sad and helpless, and the loss of her husband was a hurt he couldn't take away. She was the kind of woman who felt things far too deeply to forget those she loved when they were gone. He'd have to remember that. How could he let her feel too deeply for him when he didn't—couldn't—plan to stay? Or could he?

"Damn, buddy. You got it bad."

"What?" He blinked at Hughie.

"For her. Trudy, I mean. What's she got the rest of 'em ain't had?"

Smiling to himself, Regret nodded. Yeah, he had it bad. He'd never been able to hide his feelings from Hughie. From everyone else, but not from Hughie. "She's got spunk. And heart." He grinned. "And the damnedest blue eyes I've ever seen."

"So?"

"So what?"

"So when are you gonna consummate this little affair?"

His grin faded, and his mouth twisted cynically. "Maybe I'm not."

Hughie laughed, and for a split second, Regret hated his friend.

"If you haven't taken her to bed yet, it's because she won't let you!"

"Maybe it's because I don't deserve her."

He ambled back to the duster.

"Of course you don't." Hughie sobered. "You really do have it bad for her, don't you?"

"Yeah. But don't worry. I'll get over it."

"But you don't want to." Hughie drew hard on his cigarette. "I can tell." He motioned to the smashed crop duster with his free hand. "I could probably fix that. Probably as easy as I can fix whatever you did to ours. Ain't quite so good at mending broken hearts."

"I want you to fix them both. The planes, that is."

"Aw, come on, R.J. You know how long that'd take? How much that'd cost? Just so you can impress the girl!"

"I want you to do it," Regret persisted. "And that's not all."

Hughie finished one last drag on his cigarette and stamped it out on the dirt floor of the barn. "Why do I get the sinking feeling you're about to ask the impossible?" he asked, shrugging at the sky and making a face.

"I want to buy this place."

"Buy it! For what? You're no farmer! And I didn't think you wanted to set up a business in the middle of nowhere. What would you do? Crop dusting?"

"Actually," Regret said slowly, slamming the cockpit door and leaning against the bent double wing, "I wasn't thinking of buying it for myself. The bank's about to fore-close on it. I want to buy it for Trudy."

"Have you lost your cotton-picking mind? Why would—"

"I owe it to her, Hughie. If it weren't for her, I wouldn't be standing here talking to you right now. She saved my life. I want to do something for her."

"Send her roses like you do all the other women—" Hughie broke off the joke when he saw Regret's glare of warning. "You're finally going to spend it, aren't you?"

"I don't know."

"I don't suppose it would cost *that* much to buy this place."

"Say about seventy thousand dollars. Give or take a few thousand."

Hughie removed his cap and fanned himself, his scraggly hair tumbling down to his shoulders. "That's hardly a drop in the bucket. I say give it to her. Money's not doing any-body any good just sitting there. Somebody might as well enjoy it if you're not."

"You know I can't touch that money."

"I know you won't."

"If I spend a penny of it, I'm no better than he is."

Hughie clamped the cap down backward over his head. "You let that woman lose her home, and you're certainly no better than—"

"Shh!"

Trudy was coming back toward them, ambling through the thick grass, which caught at her bare feet. In one hand she clasped a white envelope.

Regret stepped up to meet her. "What's wrong?"

Her blue eyes wavered with the tears of a woman walk-ing a fine balance between strength and despair.

"Trudy?" He reached out to touch her shoulder, and she threw her arms around him. "What's wrong, beautiful? Is it bad news?"

He encircled her loosely in his arms and held on. She didn't push him away. She sobbed into his chest.

"Very bad news."

Chapter 10

Her world was crumbling around her. Three days had passed since she'd received the letter from her insurance company, and every day she felt her land slipping farther and farther away from her. In a world where nothing was constant but the earth under her feet, she'd been as steadfast to the Dugan land as it had been to her. Miles of South Georgia had once been tended by the hands of Dugans and the hands of their descendants. Now all that remained of the Dugan heritage was the farmhouse, a few peanut fields and the woods where her great-grandfather had played poker with the town banker. She found it ironic that the land on which the errant banker had been lynched for his misdeeds would soon belong to the Cornerstone State Bank.

She crossed the dirt road from the Meltons' place, where she'd left Dulcie and walked somberly toward the barn. Regret was waiting patiently, leaning against a rear tire of the four-wheeler and twirling a hammer in his hands. Behind him, in the small trailer, was a stack of birdhouses that they intended to erect in the woods before the bank took her land.

At least my bluebirds will have a home.

One look at the four-wheeler laced her heart with dread. She'd never sought insurance on it and had never intended to. Louisa's well-meaning offer to have it added to Trudy's farm insurance policy had garnered an unexpected response. Not only had the insurance company denied Louisa's request for all-terrain vehicle coverage, it had also unilaterally canceled Trudy's policy on the entire farm. For an industry that dealt with risk management, the risks of driving what it considered an accident-prone toy far outweighed the benefits of the hefty premiums Trudy and her family had paid over the years.

Regret smiled at her, and she felt the familiar chill course down her spine. She enjoyed being with him more than she cared to admit but knew they had no future together. She couldn't allow another pilot into her heart, and she couldn't clip his wings. Better if he just flew off and left her behind. That's what he'd do anyway when his plane was fixed. Fly off and leave her with a broken heart. Fly back to—to wherever he'd come from. She knew so little of his past. But most of it she could guess. There was probably a long string of women he'd flown away from.

"Did Dulcie mind being left behind?" he asked.

"Behind? Oh, you mean at the Meltons'?" *Not "behind" as in you leaving us behind and disappearing into the sunset.* "Not at all. Miss Naomi's got a big bottle of bubbles."

Trudy stifled a smile. She wasn't in the mood for smiling, but she could hardly believe that Regret James, a man who claimed to have no fatherly concerns, had taken such an interest in Dulcie.

All the more reason not to let her guard down.

"That trailer's a little bumpy," he noted.

She could feel his green eyes toying with her. "Mind sharing the driver's seat, Trudy?"

"Suit yourself." The troublesome snake of yearning twisted deep inside her chest, luring her toward the apple of his mouth. Resisting his temptations, she climbed onto the four-wheeler. He swung his leg over the seat and scooted up close behind her. She caught her breath. Keeping her guard up was going to be harder than she'd imagined.

Following the path, she took him deep into the woods, deeper than she'd ever taken him. That last time on the path it had been muddy. The mayhaw bushes and swampy underbrush had still been bright red with berries. The apple-like fruits were gone now, and without a recent rain, Johnson's Creek and the land near it were dry.

He slid his hands around her waist. The vee of his legs rested against the lowest point of her backbone, warming her from behind. A hardness slowly rose between them as his hands moved up to her breasts. Soft kisses flitted across her shoulder. She concentrated on driving.

The four-wheeler hummed steadily into the darker woods. By the time the trees overhead were too thick for the sun to trickle down through the leaves, she thought she heard something else in the woods. Surrounded by a thicket of scrub oak, she braked and killed the engine.

"I knew you couldn't ignore me much longer," Regret said from behind her, nibbling her ear. "Kiss me, Trudy."

"Shh! You hear that?" Listening, Trudy held her breath. And he was right: she couldn't ignore him much longer.

"Hear what? I don't hear anything." He went back to nibbling her ear.

Shrugging him away, she dismounted. In the breezeless pathway, the sound grew more distinct. A gentle, but determined thudding. Not unlike her plans for hammering the birdhouses to the perimeter fence posts.

"That hammering," Regret whispered, verbalizing her thoughts. "I've heard it several nights this week."

"So have I."

"It's not that far from here. Does anyone else live back here?"

"Not for miles. A tributary of Johnson's Creek leads into a lake not far from here. Alligator Pond it's called."

"On your property?"

"Yeah. I don't go back there much myself. It's too wet, even for a four-wheeler. And the wildlife's not very hospitable. Papa tried to fill in the pond one time with junk from around the farm, but that just made it snakier."

Regret bounced off the four-wheeler and joined her. Twirling the hammer in his hands, he stared out toward the sound. "You think that's where the hammering's coming from?"

"I don't know. Must be coming from the other side of Alligator Pond. The creek borders my property line. No way anybody could get on my land from that side. They'd have to swim the creek and half of Alligator Pond."

Regret dug his hands into his jeans pockets. He turned to look back in the direction they'd come from, then frowned at the trail ahead. "Will this path take us to it?"

"Near there. Close enough you can smell the swamp without having to worry about the 'gators."

"Then let's take a ride that way."

Trudy shook her head. "They'd hear our motor. They'd be gone before we could get close enough to see what the hammering's all about."

Trudy and Regret exchanged glances. Too many nights she had lain awake in her bed, listening to the distant hammers and the occasional chain saw. She'd even thought of slipping off into the woods by herself to find the source of the sound, with nothing but the glow of a lantern in her hand and moonlight overhead.

"I'll go," Regret said simply. "It could be dangerous. We don't know who or what's down there, and I don't want you hurt."

Nodding, Trudy gazed down the path at the darkened shade looming in front of her. "There are worse things in these woods than alligators."

Trudy wrung her hands while she waited. She should've brought her rifle with her, she thought. At least that way she could have offered it to Regret. He wouldn't know how to take care of himself in the woods. She should have accompanied him. He probably didn't know anything about moccasins and rattlesnakes. The last time they'd gone into the woods, Grendel had come limping back to her, his fur bloodied with gunshot. Grendel had been her protector, a role Regret now assigned himself. She hoped Regret had better luck in the woods than Grendel.

She checked her watch. Only fifteen minutes had passed. Hammers still pounded deep in the woods. A good sign, Trudy decided.

When twenty minutes had passed, she found herself pacing the clearing, kicking acorns out from underfoot. Twenty minutes was enough time to follow the trail as far as it would go, then come back. Unless he'd left the path and made his way through the underbrush to the dubious Alligator Pond.

Thirty minutes after he'd left he returned, red faced and puffing. Wherever he'd been, he'd run all the way back. She met him at the edge of the clearing.

"R.J.! What'd you find?"

He didn't answer at first. He bent over, bracing himself against his knees and breathing hard. His boots and jeans were muddied almost to the knees.

"You went down to the lake, didn't you, R.J.?"

"Had to," he gasped. "I couldn't...get close enough...to see otherwise."

"See what?" She wanted to touch him, to brush the damp hair from his brow, to tug away the shirt wet with perspiration from his chest.

"Your...friend. Rooster. And two other men. They've cut a...road through the woods. They're building some kind of...bridge over that creek you told me about. They're almost done."

"A bridge? To what? There's nothing back there but swamp. It's too wet to do much of anything."

"There's a dredge on the other side of the fence. That's your property line, I guess." He sucked in another deep breath. "Looks like they mean to bring it across the bridge."

Hammers still thudded faraway.

"Did they see you, R.J.?"

"I don't think so. I'm sure they would've come after me if they had."

Raking her fingers through her hair, Trudy shook her head. She couldn't understand. "I've never run them off my land for anything but hunting."

"Well, they were hunting for something, all right, but it sure wasn't anything small and furry. They had guns and metal detectors."

Metal detectors! Trudy remembered the one Rooster and the Tabors had carried with them the day Regret's plane had crashed.

"The gold," she whispered. "They think they've found the gold!"

"Now, let me git this straight...." Pushing his white cowboy hat high onto his brow, Sheriff Jim Clayton leaned across his desk and studied Trudy. Something in his eyes told her that he wanted to believe what she had just recounted, but he was uncertain. Not uncertain of her sincerity, but of her eyesight. "You say your friends are coming on your land without your permission."

"No, that's not what I'm saying." Shaking her head adamantly, she shifted in the uncomfortable straight chair. Regret, with Dulcie asleep in his arms, stood behind her. "What I'm saying is Rooster and the Tabor brothers are coming on my land without my permission. I never said they were my friends."

"Of course they're your friends, Trudy," interjected Jordy from his desk. Although it wasn't part of his official uniform, he was wearing a black baseball cap backward. Leaning back smugly in his chair, he propped two muddy black boots on his desk and smiled at her. "We grew up with those boys. Went to school with them. Hell, you almost married one of 'em fresh outta high school."

"They are not my friends," insisted Trudy to the sheriff. "And I didn't invite them onto my land."

Jordy shrugged and popped open a soft-drink can. "Maybe not this time. But they've been huntin' on your property before." He shot a wicked glance at Regret. "Your husband has been known to invite his friends to hunt. Back when he was alive, that is."

"Is that true, Trudy?" The sheriff aimed his no-nonsense gaze at her. "There's this thing called the law of estoppel. If you've set a precedent by letting them hunt on your land whenever they want, they can't arbitrarily be stopped from doing it again."

"Are you telling me I have no choice, simply because I haven't been able to stop them before or because Johnny used to invite them over?"

"It sounds like a misunderstandin' to me. I'll agree that the boys are bein' rude about it, but they probably thought that you gave them permission once, and now they can come and go as they please."

"That's not how it is, Sheriff Clayton! I've never given them permission. They just come on my property any time they feel like it. They shoot my birds, they trample my fences, they—"

Jim Clayton held up one palm to stop her. "Then why don't you speak to them about it, Trudy? I'm sure if they realized how much damage they're doin', they'd be happy to fix the messes they've made and make everything right with you."

"Sure, they would," piped up Jordy. "You know, Rooster would do almost anything for you to git you to take him back as a boyfriend." Jordy looked up at Regret. "Or bedmate," he added calculatingly.

Trudy felt the sudden radiance of anger from behind her, but Regret didn't move. She'd asked him to stay quiet. She had a better chance of getting help from Jim Clayton if she, a hometown girl, did the talking.

"Sheriff Clayton." She turned back to the thin man on the other side of the desk. "Never mind about them hunting on my land before. This time they shot my dog. They could've killed him."

"I'm sure it was an accident, Trudy. Those boys wouldn't do sumpin' like that on purpose."

"You know, Trudy," Jordy interrupted, "I've known Rooster Reed a lot of years, and he was probably tryin' to impress you. Johnny Reb and me used to go huntin' in the Dugan woods while you and Weezer did your girl-talk thing over iced tea in the kitchen. Remember how we used to bring back a mess of doves for you gals to cook? Maybe Rooster's doin' the same thing to impress you. I bet it's been a while since you've had a man—" he smirked at Regret "—bring you the spoils of huntin'."

She whipped around to face him. "Jordy, why don't you mind your own cotton-picking business? Don't you have anything better to do than sit there and annoy me?"

Jordy shrugged, feigning hurt feelings. "You wound me, Trudy. You really do."

Trudy ignored him. "Sheriff Clayton, they weren't hunting birds out of season this time. They've been cutting down trees and building some kind of . . . of bridge over Alligator Creek."

Jordy howled from behind her, laughing until soda spurted out of his mouth and down his tan deputy's uniform. "Oh, Trudy! You're such a comedian! Everybody in town knows the bank's gonna take your farm any day now. Why would Rooster make improvements to your land when you're gonna lose it anyway? Even Rooster's not that stupid!"

This time Jim Clayton ignored his son's comments. "Trudy, did you actually see this . . . bridge? With your own eyes?"

"Well, no."

"Or the trees you said they cut down?"

"No. But I've heard the chain saws and the hammering."

Jordy, still dabbing with a white handkerchief at the spilled soda on his shirt, stood up and leaned against his desk. "Chain saws and hammerin'? Gee, Daddy, that sounds like Bruce and Alice's house to me. Alice has got another one in the oven. Bruce is plannin' on closin' in the carport to make another bedroom. That's probably what Trudy's been hearin'."

"No." Regret had been silent until then. "I saw it with my own eyes."

"Well, see? There's the problem." Jordy laughed again, his eyes meeting Trudy's for a split second before he looked away. The mirrored sunglasses, his trademark, were missing.

Regret glared at him. Trudy knew he hadn't forgotten that Jordy had snapped handcuffs on him and thrown him in jail for no reason.

"They're going to bring a dredge across the bridge," Regret continued, undaunted. "They're looking for something in Alligator Pond. They've got metal detectors, too."

"Aw, Daddy," Jordy began again. This time Regret's glare silenced him.

"Look, Sheriff. Trudy came to you for help. I expect you to give it to her."

"Well, boy," the sheriff drawled, "things are done a little bit differently in this neck of the woods. We try to talk things out before jumping to conclusions. Best for everybody if we just take this thing real slow. Once tempers settle down, things'll work themselves out."

"I don't think so, Sheriff. This is more than a minor disagreement. Did you know they shot at my plane? I believe even in your neck of the woods, Sheriff, there's a law against that kind of thing."

"Aw, Daddy," whined Jordy. "He's lying. Ain't nobody shot at his plane."

"Shut up, son. Mr. James, you want to be a little more specific?"

"I crash-landed because of a bunch of good ol' boys trying to impress Trudy with their guns. Then they smashed up my plane to keep me from flying over the farm and seeing what they were up to."

Grumbling, Jordy threw up his hands with his most practiced martyr imitation.

"You got any proof of that, Mr. James?"

"I heard them admit it myself."

"Aw, man!" Jordy kicked at the chair leg. "He's lying! Why would me and Rooster wreck a plane? Fly-boy, you're nuts if you think anybody will believe you."

Jaw set, Regret squinted across the room at Jordy. "We'll see what the FAA says when they come in to investigate the cause of my crash."

"Now, hold on, boys." Sheriff Clayton held up one nervous hand. "No need to bring in the big guns. Nothing we can't settle right here." He raised his eyebrows. "Now, Mr. James, what would Rooster and his friends be dredgin' for in Alligator Pond that's important enough to smash up your plane? Nothing back there but swamp."

"Sheriff Clayton?" Trudy suddenly felt foolish. "You remember the story about the poker-playing banker? The one who disappeared with all the gold the bank was using as collateral for bank notes?"

"Never met him myself, Trudy, but I've heard my daddy talk about it. Got himself lynched right there in your woods, didn't he?"

"That's the one, Sheriff. He was hanged before he could say what he'd done with the gold. Rooster and his friends think they've found it."

Jim Clayton stiffened. "But that's just a story. He was half a mile from Alligator Pond when they found him, according to what my daddy told me. Wasn't enough time for him to throw nothin' in the pond and come back to meet his poker buddies."

"You know that and I know that." Trudy was nodding. "But Rooster and his friends don't know that."

The sheriff leaned forward and patted Trudy's hand. "Why don't you let them dig to their hearts' desire? They'll realize nothing's there and go away for good."

"You know what I think?" Jordy waltzed across the room from his desk and leaned forward on two palms. His face was only inches from Trudy's, and she drew back at the strong smell of bacon on his breath. "I think it's all a lie."

"Leave me alone," she growled back. "Stop defending Rooster. You know what he's capable of."

Jordy and his bacon breath leaned even closer. "He ain't the one who's lying, girl."

"Now, Jordy." Jim Clayton frowned up at his son. "You know Lester Dugan's granddaughter ain't no liar."

"Well, of course not, Daddy. I know Trudy would never ever lie about a thing like this. Not intentionally. But this here friend of hers is another matter."

She could tell by the look in Regret's eyes that he was ready to lay Jordy flat on the floor with his fists. But with Dulcie sleeping in his arms, starting to stir, he turned his back on Jordy and shushed Dulcie back to sleep.

"Trudy," he said, "it's time to take Dulcie home."

Jordy snatched at his soft words. "He's already tellin' you what to do, I see."

"You leave R.J. out of this!"

Jordy rose to his full height. His dark eyes twinkled. He enjoyed looking down at her. "Trudy, you're the one who brought him into this. Are you so desperate for a man that you'd take up with the first thing in pants to—"

"Shut up!"

"You know what I think, Daddy? I think this here fly-boy made up that story about the bridge to keep Trudy out of his way while he looks for the gold. Everybody around here knows that there ain't no gold. Everybody but him. Are you blind, Trudy? Cain't you see he's trying to swindle you—even if there ain't nothing for him to swindle? I'll bet you've already let him in your pants—"

"Shut up, Jordy! You don't know what you're talking about!"

"You cain't bring back Johnny Reb."

Without the rage that flared in her vision, she would have burst into tears. "I'm not trying to bring back Johnny."

"Trudy." Regret touched her sleeve. "Don't let this moron push your buttons. Let's go home."

"'Course you're trying to bring back Johnny Reb. You won't even give Rooster Reed the time of day. But you let this here fly-boy into your house. Probably into your bed, too."

"Shut up!" She knew Regret was right. She was being baited. But she couldn't restrain her resentment. She'd put up with it for so long. For too long!

"That's enough, boy," Jim Clayton warned quietly.

But Jordy either didn't hear his father or chose to ignore him.

"What about him reminds you so much of Johnny Reb, huh, Trudy? His blond hair? Is that it? You'd desecrate the memory of your dead husband because this here guy's got blond hair?"

"Shut up! Just shut up!" She struck at him with both fists, and Jordy caught her wrists in a cruel grip. If she'd had her rifle, she would have raised it to his chest without hesitation.

"Or is it because he's a fly-boy like Johnny Reb was?"

"It doesn't have anything to do with Johnny! Now, let me go!"

Jordy's voice fell to a tremor. "It has everything to do with Johnny Reb. Look at him, Trudy. Look at him. He can never replace Johnny Reb, no matter how hard you try." He turned her around, forcing her to face the man who held her sleeping daughter protectively in his arms.

"It has nothing to do with Johnny," she repeated.

Jordy released her bruised wrists. "Go ahead, Trudy. Fool yourself all you want. But you know as well as I do that Johnny Reb would roll over in his grave if he could see that swindler holdin' his little girl."

Jordy stalked out of the room, leaving Trudy to collapse, sobbing, into the straight chair. Jordy had won. She'd let him win. Losing Johnny was a wound most of Cornerstone knew about, including Jordy. But most people knew better than to ask to see her wounds. Jordy had been determined to make her lose control. And she'd fallen for it. She'd let her emotions get the best of her.

Jim Clayton awkwardly took her hands and patted them. "Maybe he's right, Trudy."

"R.J. would never lie to me." She didn't dare look up at him. She wouldn't let him pity the tearstains on her cheeks.

"I meant about Johnny. About your feelings. Maybe they're clouding your sense of reality. Nobody could blame you if they were. Finding Johnny like that . . ."

She shook her head emphatically. "It doesn't matter what I feel. I didn't come to you for counseling, Sheriff. I came to you because people won't stay off my land, and they won't leave me alone. It's your responsibility to help me."

"Okay," Jim Clayton said somberly. "I'll keep a closer watch on those boys. But I want you to promise me you'll give it another chance. If you'll tell them to stay off your property—and that you mean it—I'm sure they'll listen and respect what you say."

"But, Sheriff—" *But, Sheriff, you don't respect what I say!*

"No buts." He brushed the underside of her chin affectionately. "They just don't realize that when a pretty girl says no, she means it."

"Sheriff—"

"Trudy, this isn't a police matter. Not yet. You need to work this out with your friends."

"She will," Regret assured him, laying a warm hand on her shoulder. "If you won't take care of Trudy, then I'll have to."

If it was the last thing Regret James did, he was going to help Trudy "work out" her problems with her "friends," as Sheriff Clayton had so delicately worded it while ignoring Trudy's plea for help. The friend he planned to start with was Louisa Clayton, Jordy's wife.

Trudy had been unusually quiet since the sheriff's brush-off a few days before. He knew she must be feeling like a child reprimanded for being the target of bullies. She'd been silent for another reason, and Regret suspected she was sorting through the resurrected emotions around Johnny's death and the helplessness she'd felt when she'd held her dying husband. Was she afraid to feel the same thing for him? Was she afraid of pulling him out of another airplane some other time and place and rocking him in her arms while he bled to death? When was she going to stop thinking of him as a pilot and start thinking of him as a man?

But that was exactly how he viewed himself. As a pilot.

Hell, he thought. *Maybe her only interest in me is because I'm a pilot.*

Trudy had a healing touch for everyone but herself, and as Regret felt the wounds of his own childhood closing over, he wanted to do the same for the woman who'd not only saved his life but had given him an ability to trust—maybe even an ability to love—that he'd never known before.

He parked in front of a burgundy brick storefront with a gray canopy over the darker gray door. The antique brass rectangle centered on the door read Louisa Sandlin Clayton, Insurance Agent. Regret paused between the truck and Louisa's professionally landscaped office. He mused for a moment on the bodily harm Jordy could commit on him if the deputy saw Regret entering or leaving Louisa's office. Then Regret dismissed the thought—for the sake of Trudy—and barged ahead to the door.

"Come in," Louisa said from behind a dark, masculine desk. She was bent over the fine print of one of her insurance policies, her white-blond hair falling across her face, not quite hiding the harshness of her makeup. She didn't look up.

He waited patiently at the foyer door. They were alone, and he stood between Louisa and the solace of escape. Whomever she was expecting, it wasn't him. Smirking to himself, he slammed the interior door behind him.

"R.J.!"

He saw the shudder run through her.

"What are you doing here?" She reached for the black decorator telephone on her desk, knocking the receiver off its cradle with her trembling hand.

"Who are you calling, Slick?" Regret asked. Before she could think of an answer, he snatched the phone cord out of the wall and held it up to her.

"N-no one."

"You look like you've seen a ghost. Do I resemble your brother that much? Do I look like Johnny to you, too?"

She narrowed her eyes at him. "How dare you take my brother's name in vain!"

"Sorry." He dropped the silver cord to the floor and sat down casually in the leather-upholstered chair closest to her desk. "I'm only repeating what I've been told."

"What—what have you been told?"

"That Trudy is interested in me only because I look like her dead husband."

Louisa chewed on her crimson lower lip.

"Well? Do I? Do I look like Johnny?"

"No. Not really. Maybe from a distance."

Regret straightened, encouraged. "Trudy doesn't see me from a distance. She usually sees me up close. Closer than anyone has ever seen me."

The blonde squirmed in her seat. "You never should have come here."

"You're right, Slick. And I never intended to. But when Rooster shot me down—"

"Rooster *what?*" Her mouth open, she stared at Regret.

"He fired toward my plane. Birds hit the propeller of my plane and the oil lines were torn out, and I came down like a rock."

"Too bad it wasn't a burning rock."

"Trudy says it was an accident." He noticed that Louisa was frowning. She didn't believe him. "Do you think it was an accident, Louisa?"

"I—" She looked away, then shrugged. "I don't know. I—I'm sure it was. Are you sure it was Rooster?"

"Trudy says it was him. She was there."

Louisa glared suspiciously at him. Then she fidgeted with her red painted fingernails. "And what were you doing there?"

"My job."

"Your...job?"

"I'm a troubleshooter for the gas line. I was flying too low when I crossed the path of the infamous Rooster Reed."

"My brother used to fly too low." Her words were barely louder than a whisper.

"I'm sure you loved your brother very much. Is that why you're so dead set against Trudy's interest in me?"

"Trudy could do better than you, mister."

Regret smiled at the woman. "I won't deny that. But do you think Rooster Reed is a better choice for her mate?"

"He loved her once."

"And threw her away."

"Whatever. Trudy needs someone to take care of her," insisted Louisa.

An image of Trudy aiming her rifle at Jordy in that ice-cold jail flashed in his brain, and he laughed aloud. "Trudy can take care of herself."

"Since when? She's going to lose the family farm in a few months. Maybe weeks. It's almost like vultures are sitting on the fence posts, waiting. Everything's closing in on her. God knows, I've tried to help."

"How? By buying the land out from under her, when she doesn't want to sell? Was that the best you could come up with?"

"Trudy told you that?"

"She didn't have to." He wouldn't tell Louisa that he'd been eavesdropping. "Why does everybody want to buy her land? Farmland's not worth that much. Swamp's worth even less."

"Not if it has gold on it." Louisa gasped. She'd spoken without thinking.

Regret glared back at her. "I'm glad you're so concerned about your sister-in-law's welfare," he retorted. "Maybe she does need someone to take care of her. Protect her. Maybe I'm that someone."

"And who's going to protect her from you?"

The violet eyes appraised him in his borrowed clothes. Her face passed judgment on him, declaring him little more than a vagrant.

"What could you possibly do for her?"

His lips twisted into a secretive smirk. "Maybe I have the means to help." He watched the confidence fade from her eyes.

"R.J., if you really want to do what's best for Trudy, then you'll leave Cornerstone and go back to whatever rock you crawled out from under."

"Best for Trudy? Or best for her so-called friends?"

"You'll only break her heart and leave her with nothing."

"I have no intention of breaking her heart. And I don't intend to leave her with nothing."

"You're not the man for Trudy." Louisa licked her red lips and stood up, leaning across the desk and tilting her head seductively to one side. "You're not her type."

Regret swallowed the surprise in his throat. What kind of ploy was this? And why? "And what is her type?"

"Oh," Louisa said slowly, thoughtfully, as she slithered around the corner of her desk, "someone less... tantalizing."

"Y-you think I'm tantalizing?" If there was one thing Regret knew when he saw it, it was a come-on, and especially a bad one.

"I sure do." She moved in front of him, leaning backward against her desk. She smiled just a little, but the smile was a bit too smug. He noticed she'd undone the top button of her silk blouse and her third finger rubbed against the hollow at the base of her throat. Something in him stirred involuntarily.

"Trudy's got something you don't, and you can't stand it, can you? She's got *me*."

"She could never satisfy a man like you." Louisa licked her upper lip, slowly running her tongue from corner to wet corner.

Why would Louisa do this? he wondered. Was it jealousy? Or desperation? Did she want him out of Trudy's life—and out of Cornerstone—so badly that she'd prostitute herself to get rid of him? Didn't she know she was making a fool of herself?

"Don't do this, Louisa."

She glanced over her shoulder at the stack of papers on her desk and lowered her head, her eyes raised in invitation. In one swift move, she raked the papers onto the floor. They tumbled across the room, leaving a wide desktop, shiny and bare. Regret clenched his fists, his breath suddenly unsteady.

Louisa waited, but he didn't move. Tossing her blond hair out of her face, she said, "Don't you think I'm your type?"

Fervently he nodded. Louisa Clayton was his "type," all right. He thought of the women in his past, all beautiful but every one an empty shell. Holograms. Like Louisa. Flash and no substance.

"So what's stopping you, R.J.?"

She circled him, one foot in front of the other, her hips rocking from side to side as she moved. Standing behind his chair, she laid ten burning fingertips on his shoulders and kissed the bare skin of his neck as he bent his head forward. Her wet tongue slid up his neck to his hairline and then to the lobe of his ear. He moaned before he could help himself. Her fingers lingered at his nape.

"You like that, don't you, R.J.?" she asked with self-assurance.

"Mmm. You have wonderful hands, Louisa." He paused. "Now, get them off me."

"What? Don't you like it when I touch you?"

"Oh, I like it very much." It was true. He did enjoy her touch. And had he not met Trudy, he would probably by now be wrinkling Louisa's dry-clean-only suit on the Oriental rug. "I'm sorry, Slick. I'm just not interested."

"Of course you're interested," she purred. "I can tell by the goose bumps on the back of your neck."

"Then let me put it this way. It's not worth my time and certainly not worth your energy for you to have your hands all over me while I try like hell to convince myself that it's Trudy and not you. In fact, I think it would take far too much effort for me to keep that illusion going long enough for me to... keep it up."

Her meandering fingertips stopped dead, barely touched his shoulders. "You're turning me down?" she asked incredulously. "You're turning me down for little Trudy Sandlin?"

"In a word, yes."

The light touch disappeared from his shoulders completely. "Well, I'm afraid you got the wrong idea about me. I certainly wouldn't have gone through with it."

"Why, Louisa," he said flatly, glancing up at her with an accusing smile, "you're nothing but a tease."

"There's only one man in my life," she retorted, "and that's my husband. Jordy Clayton. He's a sheriff's deputy. He's going to be the next sheriff of this county when his daddy retires."

"Yes, I know. I've met your husband. Believe me, I understand perfectly why you'd get your kicks teasing other men."

"Other men? You don't know what you're talking—"

"Other men, Slick. I watched you one day for fifteen minutes while you flirted on the street corner with the fellow from the menswear shop."

Louisa's face went ashen. "You saw— Well, it doesn't matter what you saw. You didn't see anything."

"No. I'm sure I didn't see... anything."

"Ted's just a good friend. He makes me feel pretty."

"Pretty is as pretty does."

"Are you saying—"

"I'm not saying anything, Louisa. Except that you're vain and selfish. But I'm sure if I looked hard enough under all that makeup, I might find a real woman with a real heart."

"How dare you! You know, I could tell my husband you came on to me and—"

"You could say that, all right, and he'd probably believe you. I'd just have to mention your friend Ted."

"You wouldn't do that."

"Try me."

She flipped her hair out of her eyes. Louisa was trying too hard to be casual. She didn't realize her jaw was quivering.

"You can't do that. Jordy means everything to me. I'd do anything for my husband. Anything."

"Yes." Regret nodded, understanding. "I'm sure you would. Even cinch the sale of Trudy's heritage if that's what he wanted."

"Well, let's just call us even, and you can be on your way."

"Even? Not quite, Louisa. We're far from even. But I intend for us to be when I leave here."

Chapter 11

Trudy flung her arms around him as soon as Regret sauntered through the kitchen door. She gave him a friendly, but platonic, kiss on each cheek and stepped back, grinning.

"Wow! What did I do to deserve that?" His arms twitched as though they wanted to wrap around her and never let go.

"You were handy, and I felt like it."

"That's all? You mean if the mailman had beat me here, he'd be getting all these great hugs now?"

"Uh-huh. So where have you been all morning?"

Regret shrugged and eased into a comfortably loose embrace. "I had to run a few errands." He glanced around the kitchen. "Where's my little Trudy look-alike?"

"Dulcie's spending the day with her Granny Sandlin." She smiled at him, hoping he'd take the hint. "And Papa won't be home until late."

Absently studying the ceiling, he puckered his lips thoughtfully. "Late. I've heard that one before." No doubt he was thinking of the day they'd made jelly—and almost love—in the kitchen and Papa had interrupted them.

"He's gone to Dothan to pick up spare parts for the tractor. Miss Clarice went with him so he could take her shopping. Can't you just imagine Miss Clarice dragging Papa all over a mall?"

Snickering, he agreed. "Is that what's put you in such a good mood?"

Trudy frowned. She really hadn't thought of it before, but she had been in a pretty lousy mood after Jordy's daddy had treated her like an unsociable little brat. When Regret had left the house hours ago, she'd been quiet and brooding. Now she couldn't stop herself from bubbling over with enthusiasm. "Louisa called here a few minutes ago."

"She did?" The spark disappeared from Regret's eyes. He didn't like Louisa for some reason, but then, he probably didn't know her as well as Trudy did.

"I'm insured again!" she announced.

"Really? That's good news."

"Are you kidding? That's great news, R.J.! She called her headquarters and told them it was a mistake, and she fixed everything!"

Nodding, he smiled. "I'm glad she could repair whatever damage she's done."

"You had something to do with it, didn't you?"

He shrugged. "Maybe. Why?"

"I've never known Louisa to admit a mistake. I know she didn't mean to get my insurance canceled. She was just trying to help. But I don't think she would ever have fixed things if you hadn't done whatever you did."

"You're not still thinking of selling out to Louisa, are you?"

Trudy fidgeted with her collar. "No. I think I'd rather see the farm go to the bank. Louisa wouldn't appreciate the land. And Jordy, well, he'd either cut down the woods and sell the timber or he and men like Rooster Reed would spend their spare time killing everything with four legs or feathers. Even if I have to sell out, I'd like to keep the land in the family. It's just too bad that the only family I've got to sell it to doesn't understand its value. But I'm grateful that Louisa at least tried."

"You wouldn't be so grateful if you really knew your sister-in-law. You admire her, don't you? I'll never understand why."

"Louisa's always been so perfect. Men notice women like her. She's so beautiful and worldly."

Moving closer, Regret lifted Trudy's chin with one finger. "She's nothing compared with you."

Trudy felt her cheeks burn and pulled away. "I could never be like Louisa—"

"Thank God," Regret interrupted.

"She's so polished and strong. I'm so...simple."

"Your sister-in-law is tarnished. Weak. You, Trudy Sandlin, have far more to offer."

Trudy turned away, embarrassed, but Regret eased his palms onto her shoulders and turned her back to him. "It's your warmth, Trudy, and your simplicity. Those are two wonderful traits that can't be learned. They're completely natural." He sucked in his ragged breath. "And sometimes very erotic."

Staring down at her bare feet, Trudy wasn't sure what to do or what to say. She wasn't adept in the games of seduction. She twisted away, pretending to look out the window.

"I have a hard time understanding your devotion to Louisa. She's so unlike you."

"She's Johnny's sister. She's family. And around here, family watches out for family."

"Trudy." He slipped between her and her view out the window. "We need to talk about Louisa and Jordy."

Dread burned in her cheeks. She fixed her stare on a button on his shirt. Whenever anyone told her "We need to talk," it was always bad news. For good news, people yelped it out the moment they entered the room.

"You were right, Trudy. I went to see Louisa about getting your insurance reinstated. She wasn't an easy person to convince."

Still she stared at the button. She'd trusted Louisa for ten years. Considered her the sister she'd never had. Did she really want to hear this? It was bad, and she knew it was bad. "What happened?" she asked in a whisper.

Regret paused, long enough that she thought he'd changed his mind. She glanced up at him in time to see the struggle in his eyes.

"She tried to seduce me."

"No," Trudy croaked out. Nausea knotted in her stomach. She'd always come in a distant second to Louisa. Even now. Even with the man she—

Trudy forced her gaze upward to his face. "And were you seduced?"

"What do you think?"

"You said she wasn't easy to convince." Bitterness tinged her voice.

Somber-faced, he studied her. Finally he shook his head. "She made an offer, but there weren't any takers."

Trudy exhaled, then relief filled up her lungs. Pressing her forehead against his chest, she slipped her arms around his waist. His hands stroked her back.

"Then you believe me?"

She nodded. "If you said you turned her down, then I believe you."

Warm hands stroked the back of her head, fanning out her hair over her shoulders.

"I meant about her coming on to me."

"Oh." Trudy hadn't questioned Louisa's behavior. She'd taken it for granted. Maybe she'd known all along that Louisa wasn't the person she'd wanted to believe she was. Maybe she just hadn't wanted to face the truth.

"Trudy?" He raised her chin, then kissed the bridge of her nose. "Your sister-in-law is a very troubled woman."

"A very troubled woman," Trudy repeated, still stunned. "But she's got everything."

"Well, something's missing. I'm not sure what it is, but I'd guess she and Jordy are having problems. Maybe he's lost interest. I think she desperately needs attention, and she's not getting it at home."

"Oh, R.J. That would just kill her if Jordy left her. She's always bragged about what a great catch he was. She'd do anything to hang on to him."

"Even sell out her brother's widow." His eyes had turned cold again. "She's been giving you the hard sell about getting rid of the farm, hasn't she?"

Trudy nodded. "She's willing to buy the place and let me keep the house."

"Why?"

"She's fami—" Trudy stopped. Louisa hated the farm. She was determined to have concrete under her heels, not grass. "I thought it was because she was trying to help me out."

"When has Louisa ever done anything for you that wasn't out of self-motivation?"

She tried to think of a time when Louisa had been there for her. Not since high school.

"Why doesn't she just loan you the money? She's got plenty of it. At least, that's what she says."

Trudy's mouth went dry. "She hasn't offered."

"Of course not. She wants your land."

"Louisa doesn't care about the land. She wants to buy it for Jordy. She says it would make him really happy."

"Yeah, and I'll bet he'd be a little easier to live with. And it would tip the marital scales in Louisa's favor if Jordy owed her. You know why it would make him so happy?"

Jordy's words echoed back at her: *"Why would me and Rooster wreck a plane?"* Him and Rooster. She and Regret had gone to Sheriff Clayton's office to complain about Rooster and the Tabor boys. They hadn't once mentioned Jordy.

"You think he's the one behind the search for the gold?" she asked as the realization swept over her. The fourth man with Rooster and the Tabors. The one with jeans and long legs. The one hiding in Rooster's truck while she confronted the other three rednecks. Jordy. He'd stayed out of sight so he wouldn't jeopardize Louisa's thrice-a-week negotiations for the land. "It's not the land they care about—or Dulcie and me. It's the stupid gold." Her hands knotted into fists.

"And Jordy's willing to do anything to get it. Scrap my plane. Beat me up and dump me over the state line. Even convince Rooster Reed to marry you so they can split their findings fifty-fifty."

Trudy felt the color drain from her face. No wonder Rooster had been so insistent. She clutched Regret's shirt. "What am I going to do, R.J.? I can't let them have my land! I won't sell it to them, but they can buy it for peanuts at the foreclosure auction. And there's nothing I can do to stop them."

"Yes, there is." He lightly kissed her forehead, then her lips. "You can let me help."

"It's not your fight."

"It is now. You've got something, Trudy, that I've never had. Roots. I have no idea where my ancestors walked a hundred years ago. I've lived in a dozen different cities, but I've never missed a one when it was time to move on. I don't get nostalgic, Trudy. There's nothing in my past or in my present that I'm sentimental about. Not even my bird." He wiped the hair out of his eyes and looked up at a distant point on the ceiling. "Yeah, I hate the mess it's in, but if I couldn't fix it, I'd scrap it. I sure as hell wouldn't lock it away in a barn because I couldn't bear to part with it."

Trudy inhaled deeply. She was sentimental about everything. Sometimes she wished she could be more like Regret, more detached.

"Nothing means anything to me, Trudy. And I didn't realize it until I met you. You and your farm and your bluebirds and your mayhaws and your roses! I can't let you lose all that. I won't let those bastards take all that away from you and Dulcie."

Slipping her fingers up through the blond waves that spilled over his eyes, she smiled up at him. "What are you going to do? Hang around and be my bodyguard?"

"Maybe."

She expected him to grin, but he didn't.

"For a while, anyway."

"You've got a business to be getting back to. Hughie called today. Said he'd be down next weekend with parts to start fixing your plane." She let her hands glide down his chest. "And then you'll be gone. You'll fly out of here and never come back."

"I'm not going anywhere." He caught her hands, held them against his chest. Through the thin fabric, she could tell that the bandages underneath were gone. "I'm staying right here with you until you're safe."

"Safe?" From what? Her own feelings for him?

"From Jordy and his thugs."

"I've tried everything already. I'd hoped Sheriff Clayton would help. But he still thinks of me as the little girl who used to sit on Daddy's shoulders and watch the parades in town. Even if he took me seriously, I'm not sure he'd do anything about it. People here consider him to be a peace-keeper, not an enforcer. Some people take the path of least resistance. Well, Sheriff Clayton *is* the path of least resistance."

"Maybe it's time we went to a higher authority."

"'We'?" She couldn't stop the smile that stretched into a cheek-to-cheek grin.

"With pictures. Indisputable proof of what they're doing. We'll give Sheriff Clayton one last chance before bringing in the 'big guns,' as he calls them."

Then her smile faded. "But what good will it do to stop them now? The bank could foreclose any day. The land won't be mine anymore."

Pulling her close, he kissed her forehead. "The land will always be yours. I'm going to see to it."

She rubbed her cheek against his soft shirt. "Aren't you forgetting something? I'm broke."

He stiffened. "I'm not. I have a—a little money tucked away."

"R.J., I couldn't ask you to do that." She broke free and backed away. He didn't know what he was offering. He couldn't know. A way out. A reprieve from Jordy and Rooster. A chance to keep her roots alive for Dulcie.

"You don't have to ask me."

"You have no idea how much money we're talking about here."

"I think I do."

"I'm not talking about several hundred dollars. I'm talking about over seventy thousand dollars."

He smiled. "I know."

"You don't have that kind of money to throw around!"

"I have more than you think. See, Trudy, this—" he waved his hand at the open window and the distant woods "—this is your inheritance. Mine isn't so grand. Mine's just cold hard cash."

"You're...rich?" He didn't have the arrogance of a rich man. At times he seemed more like a street waif.

"My *father* called it a gift." Regret's jaw tightened. "But I know what it really was. Guilt money. A self-imposed penalty for all the years I spent wishing for a father and he spent avoiding me. I swore I'd never touch that money. If I did, I'd be no better than him. I've changed my mind."

"R.J., I couldn't. That's *your* money. From your father." Any gift from a father would be precious, wouldn't it? Even money. "It must mean a lot to you."

"Yeah. It represents the roots I never had." He pulled her back to him, brushing his thumbs across her cheeks. "The only way it'll ever mean anything to me is if I can buy back your roots for you."

She swallowed hard. This man with the wounded heart was offering her the chance to reclaim her heritage. This lost child who'd never known a real home understood what her home meant to her.

"I might never be able to pay you back."

"You've already paid me back."

"No, I can't take charity. Not even from you. Especially not from you. I will pay you back."

He rolled his eyes. "You don't have to. I wouldn't touch the money at all if it weren't for you. At least now I can put it to good use."

Trudy didn't flinch. She'd always worked for everything she had.

"Oh, all right. I'm sure we can work something out. Maybe as part of the deal, I'd get the crop duster."

"It's not worth much. Especially in the shape it's in now. Besides, I don't think I could get rid of it. This is where it belongs."

"This would always be its home port, Trudy. I could put a runway in the pasture."

"But why? So you could fly down here and visit me?" The words tumbled out of her mouth before she could stop them. They weren't words she wanted to admit to. Not yet, anyway. How could she dare presume that Regret James would go to the trouble and expense of dropping in on a small farm in South Georgia merely to see her? What was she to this rambling man that he would ever return once he'd left her home? That moment would come so soon, and time was short and opportunity brief. She knew she'd never take advantage of the moment, particularly if he didn't take advantage of...

"Maybe I could expand my business. My work is—I guess you could say—portable. Being an aerial photographer means I can live anywhere I like." He grinned. "I'll just fly to my job."

She frowned up at him, not believing a word. "You're really thinking of moving to Cornerstone?"

"I'll admit, the thought has crossed my mind. Airspace around Atlanta can get rather crowded." He nodded toward the window and the green fields beyond. "I don't know, Trudy. I can't help but think that this might be a really nice change of pace. And I think Hughie would like it here, too."

"But if I sell you the land..."

"I'd get Johnny's plane, maybe a nice chunk of pasture and a couple of barns I could use as hangars. You'd keep the house, of course. And the peanut fields. And I don't need the woods or the swamp."

"That's all you'd want?"

"You get to keep your ancestral land. I pay my debt to you, and you pay off Johnny's debts." He shrugged as if there were nothing else to debate. "Strictly business."

She turned away, surprised at the sting of his words. Hurt suddenly blurred her vision, turning into hot teardrops spilling down her cheeks. He saw the wet trails on her face before she could hide them.

"Trudy..." Lifting her dark hair from her shoulders, he touched her tenderly on the back of her neck. "Please don't cry." She hung her head. His lips grazed her neck. She wouldn't look at him! "I know you're happy about this, but—"

"Do you?" she asked bitterly.

He hesitated. He seemed startled by her reaction. His hands moved to brush away a tear, but she swatted back at him.

"Trudy, what's wrong? I thought you'd be happy. This is what you wanted."

"What I wanted!"

She had turned to flee. He grabbed her wrist and pulled her back. "Trudy, what did I say? What's wrong?"

"Everything!" Again she wrested herself from his grip, fighting the draw of confusion in his eyes. He closed in on her. She tore away.

"Trudy!"

Fighting the blindness of her tears, she rushed toward the blur of sunshine from the open door that led to her bedroom. She stumbled, falling into the room and whirling to slam the door behind her. It struck something hard, immovable, refusing to close, refusing to lock. She pressed all her weight against it.

"Trudy!"

Regret's hands pried themselves through the opening, followed by elbows and shoulders as he stepped into the room with her. She shoved hard against him, deliberately against his injured ribs. He flinched but held his stubborn posture.

Grabbing her flailing hands, Regret kicked the door closed behind him. Now she couldn't push him out of the room! She couldn't even push him away. He pulled her to him, his gaze delving hers. "Strictly business, Trudy. I swear it!"

His scrutiny was unbearable.

"Damn you," she choked out.

"What did I do wrong, Trudy? I just told you I found a way for you to keep your farm. Aren't you happy?"

She couldn't speak. Her throat had closed too tightly.

"It'll be a legitimate business deal. I promise. I wouldn't dare think that it'd be anything more than business."

Tears spilled down her cheeks again—only this time, with her wrists secured by Regret's grasp, she couldn't wipe them away.

"Okay," he said, releasing her. She'd stopped fighting him. "If you don't want me to help you, I won't. But tell me what I've said to hurt you."

Violently she shook her head. "I'm sorry, R.J." She wiped at the corners of her eyes with the back of her hand. "It was stupid. I don't know how I could've let myself lose control like that."

"I kinda like it when you lose control." He dabbed at a stray tear with his thumb. "Come here, you." He encircled her gently in his arms as he pressed her head against his chest. "Tell me what happened just now. Don't you want me around?"

She nodded against his chest. It heaved steadily under her cheek. She listened to the rhythmic thumping of his heartbeat.

"Good. I was afraid you didn't want to see me again."

"N-never," she sobbed.

"Then why were you crying? Those certainly weren't tears of happiness."

"I just thought—" She stopped to sniff back the tears. "I just thought that maybe you wanted to buy my land so you could be near me. It's stupid, I know, but I guess I all of a sudden wanted our friendship to be more than 'strictly business.' I wanted you to want to come back here because of me—not because you needed a second airstrip or a 'change of pace.'"

"Oh, Trudy." He cupped his hand over her hair and stroked her head again and again. "I do want to come back here because of you. If it were strictly business, I could find someplace a lot cheaper to settle down or to build another airstrip. So if I do come back here, you'll be the deciding factor."

"I don't want you to come back because you think you owe me for pulling you out of that plane. I don't want you to be obligated to me."

"I do owe you. And I am obligated to you, Trudy. But that's not why I'd want to see you again. I don't know that I can give you everything you deserve. Now or ever. But I'm not ready to leave you."

"Then don't."

She dared to look up at him. His expression was a little sad, a little hopeful and full of yearning. His hands slipped down over each of her temples, weaving fingertips through her hair as she gazed up at him. His playboy grin had turned somber as he pierced her defenses. His gaze raked her face, soothing her at the same time he shook her resistance. Self-conscious, she felt herself tremble in his arms, and the knowledge that he knew she was trembling shook her even more.

His mouth moved gently against hers. Its underlying urgency was masked in tenderness.

"R.J." She sighed, tossing back her head in surrender. Her eyelids fluttered closed, and she lost herself in his embrace.

Arms encircled her, lifted her, carried her to the soft cushion of her white chenille bedspread and laid her there as gently as an autumn leaf drifting to the ground. Her eyes closed more tightly as she struggled to hold this sweet dream. Without thought, her lips parted in invitation.

"You look so beautiful," he breathed over her, his body molding to hers as he lay atop her, supporting his weight with his elbows.

Underneath him, she smiled, almost laughed into his warm kiss. So long alone, she'd forgotten what pleasures a man's hands could offer as they skimmed her face.

She opened her eyes, reassured to find him still there, like a dream but solid with reality. If he could only read her eyes, he'd not doubt how much she wanted him. The frozen rapture of his face told her that yes, he knew, and yes, he was the man to fulfill her fantasies.

Awkwardly she slid her hands past his wounded ribs and over his muscular shoulder blades, between his shirt and skin. She'd forgotten how to touch a man, if she'd ever known how.

Without breaking their gaze, Regret shifted above her, making room for one stealthy hand to unfasten the dozen tiny buttons on the front of her dress. His fingers moved with an agility of their own, popping open each lock with his thumb and forefinger, not needing to see what he was doing. He unfastened the last button at her waist and let his fingers glide up the bare landscape of her open bodice to the white cotton bra that restrained her. He pressed his fingertips underneath the elastic binding, prying away the fabric, exposing her, liberating her. He broke their gaze as his mouth plunged to feathery kisses on her bare neck. Shivering under his touch, she closed her eyes, unable to stop the pleading moan in her throat.

His lips moved down, moist on the valley between her breasts. They ascended one sensitive mound and lingered, lapping at the dewy rosette of nipple. Squeezing her eyes shut, she tensed beneath him.

This can't go on much longer! The thought screamed through her head.

"R.J."

"Shh. Don't talk."

His hand brushed against her waist as it expertly found her white cotton panties. His forefinger smoothed the upper perimeter of the elastic band, then eased down to the banding around her thigh, tracing it from her hip to the waiting wet heat and crossing the boundary into her dark and private land.

Trudy cried out in lusty surprise.

"Shh," he urged gently. He buried his mouth in hers, devouring her gasps as his probing fingers promised her greater pleasures. His bulging jeans rubbed against her thigh, teasing her.

"No." She twisted free of his kisses. "We can't."

"No one else is here," he whispered, the urgency evident in his voice.

"It's not safe," she rasped.

"There's nothing to worry about, Trudy. I promise."

His fingers distracted her. She struggled to focus. "No, it's not safe. I need protection. I—"

"There's nothing to worry about," he assured her again.

"R.J., I—"

"Listen to me." Reluctantly he separated from her, looking into her eyes. "There's nothing to worry about."

"Nothing to worry about," she repeated mechanically.

"Darlin' there ain't nothin' for you to worry about," she heard Johnny say in the back of her mind. *"I'm the best damned pilot ever to fly over Cornerstone."*

Regret kissed her cheek. "Are you okay?"

She pushed him away, hands against his chest. For a moment, she imagined shattered bone inside the muscular chest, soft under her touch. Like crushed eggshell. Like Johnny.

"Trudy?"

She sat up quickly, turning a chilly shoulder to him, clasping her unbuttoned dress to her.

"Trudy?"

No, she wouldn't spend the rest of her life waving goodbye to a man who might not come home. She wouldn't spend the rest of her life cringing every time she heard his plane overhead, wondering if he was hotdogging it through the narrow space between the utility lines and the ground.

Pilots were like that. They thought they could do anything. They thought there were immortal. They weren't.

And Trudy couldn't spend the rest of her life scared to death that one day she might again have to pull a broken pilot from a crumpled plane.

"Trudy? What's wrong? Where are you going?"

She wanted to cry.

Chapter 12

Getting the cold shoulder from a woman was nothing new to Regret. Women had been giving him the silent treatment all his life. His mother. A dozen foster mothers who'd barely known he was there. The rich debutantes who wouldn't give a bad boy the time of day. He'd found long ago that the best way to avoid rejection was to walk away first. If the morning after would be too awkward, then he'd stayed too late already.

Maybe that was what had happened with Trudy. Maybe he'd stayed too long. Maybe he'd been overconfident that he could make her forget Johnny and dream only of him. Somehow he was sure that if only he could have made love to her, then he could have won a place in her heart.

"R.J., I want uppy."

Dulcie was tugging on his pants leg, and he felt guilty for hardly noticing. He'd been too busy watching Trudy as she furiously hammered birdhouses onto the fence posts near the old turpentine well. She didn't need his help. Worse, she didn't want it. She'd assigned him the chore of entertaining Dulcie—which he found to be no chore at all—and keeping her safely away from the muddy pond and the open well.

He scooped up the little girl in his arms. She was as much a puzzle to him as her mother. He wasn't the kind of man who enjoyed children, yet Dulcie brought out the best in him. He'd convinced himself years ago that fatherhood was a mistake he'd never make, and he'd seen to it that he'd never again be mistaken for a father. And yet, holding Dulcie in his arms, he almost wished...

"R.J.?" Dulcie smashed her tiny palms against his cheeks and grinned. She pressed her mouth against his face in a sloppy, sticky kiss. "I love you, R.J.," she blurted out in unabashed adoration.

Oh, God, what have I done?

It wasn't just Trudy he'd let fall in love with him, but a child. An innocent little girl who wanted nothing more than to be loved and played with and tucked into bed with a story and a kiss. That's all he'd wanted at that age, wasn't it? And what had happened? His mother had walked out on him. How soon before he would walk out on Trudy—and Dulcie? How would that little girl ever understand being left behind? He hadn't.

His heart melting, he squeezed Dulcie against him. Maybe he'd been too hasty in his decision never to have children. If he'd known how he'd feel about this child, maybe he would have forgotten what he'd said about his own father.

Dulcie loved him unconditionally. No one else had. And one day he'd repay her by disappearing from her mother's life.

Maybe I should go before it's too late. Before Dulcie's old enough to remember me. Before Trudy hates me enough to want to forget me.

Trudy glanced up, ceasing her hammering to watch her daughter's flirtations. Then, catching Regret's gaze accidentally, she quickly turned back to her task. Regret bit his lip, hating to think how uncomfortable she felt around him.

He couldn't figure out what he'd done to deserve her wrath. He'd hurt her, but wasn't sure how. They'd been moments away from making love, and she'd turned completely cold to him. He sighed aloud. Maybe it was for the best. Maybe that was just a sign of things to come. He'd finally open up to her and she'd lose interest. Just like everyone in his past.

"I wanna ride on your back," begged Dulcie.

He swung her upward onto his shoulders, then caught his breath at the unexpected pain still lingering in his ribs. Dulcie latched onto his forehead to hold herself upright. Her legs dangled on his chest.

"Just don't go potty," he warned playfully.

Trudy glanced up again. Her expression was one of hurt and longing. Turning back to the nail between her forefinger and thumb, she brought the hammer down hard, a thundering blow ringing out in echoes through the woods.

Yeah, she'd probably like to take that hammer to his skull right now.

Yesterday she'd run out of her bedroom. She hadn't cried again, but he could tell she had been fighting back the tears. Trudy hadn't spoken a word to him for the rest of the day.

This morning, she'd been revving the engine of the four-wheeler when he'd stumbled out the back door after her, asking her where she was going. She surely wouldn't have told him if he hadn't asked.

"To finish putting up my birdhouses before they take my land," she'd shouted over the roar of the engine. Dulcie, wearing a helmet that matched Trudy's, had been grinning at him from her mother's lap.

"Mind if I come, too?" he'd asked.

"Suit yourself."

Still, despite her flippant dismissal, he could tell that she wanted him with her. Grendel's leg was infected, causing him to spend more time at the vet's than originally thought necessary. The vet had felt it best that she not take him home yet. There was a good chance, according to the vet, that he wouldn't make it or he'd lose the leg. Regret was a poor substitute for the monstrous canine protector, but he could at least keep Dulcie occupied while her mother decided whether to give in to the feelings she tried so desperately to hide. As for protection in the woods, Trudy carried her rifle, loaded and ready in case she discovered Rooster Reed or his cronies—the ones the sheriff had called her "friends"—waiting in the underbrush. She'd left the rifle leaning against the back tire of the four-wheeler with strict instructions to Dulcie not to touch it and stricter instructions to Regret to see that she didn't.

"Trudy?" He followed her from the fence to the cart behind the four-wheeler, where she selected another birdhouse. "Can't we talk about this?"

She walked determinedly back through the grass to the fence and picked up her hammer again. She was barefoot. As usual.

"Trudy, please."

"There's nothing to talk about."

"We need to talk about what happened yesterday."

She swung the hammer, splintering the wood with the nail. "I don't want to talk about it."

"I do."

"Fine. There's a fence post over there. Talk to it all you want."

"Trudy..."

Dulcie kicked against his chest. "I want down."

Regret set her back on the ground, and the child ran to collect more fallen acorns in the clearing. Silly little chipmunk. He turned back to Trudy.

"We need to talk."

"No, we don't. I told you, there's nothing to talk about."

"Did I say something wrong?"

Another blow rang out. "No."

"Is it something I did?"

"No."

"Something I *didn't* do?"

"No." Another blow sounded. "Just leave it alone, okay?"

"I can't leave it alone. I can't leave you alone."

Her jaws tightened. "You will."

"What's that supposed to mean?"

"I would've let you make love to me. And then it would've been too late to turn back." She straightened her back and drove in another nail.

"Turn back from what?" Her feelings?

Trudy looked up at him, her eyes misting over. "There's no future for us."

"I don't know about the future. All I can count on is the present."

"Well, in the future, either you'll walk out on us or you'll pull some stupid stunt and get yourself killed the way Johnny did. Dulcie's very fond of you, you know. How do you expect me to explain to her that you've...gone? You'll probably leave without even saying goodbye." The hammer pounded down again, drowning out the echo of "goodbye."

"I wouldn't do that." But he would. He had before. It had always been easier that way. Both on him and on the woman. But a child...

"And what would I tell Dulcie when you're gone? She doesn't remember Johnny, but she'll remember you."

Regret shrugged. He'd miss Dulcie almost as much as he'd miss her mother. If he left.

Trudy sighed and stared out across the yellow fields of the neighboring property. "It's too late already. I let her fall in love with you. Now there's nothing to do but let her be hurt."

"Dulcie? Or you, Trudy?" He could tell. She'd fallen in love with him. Dulcie Sandlin was a two-year-old child. She'd be hurt. She'd probably cry. But in time she'd forget him. Her mother never would.

"Why don't we just stop talking about tomorrow and whether I leave or not and enjoy the time we have," he suggested.

It was so like him to remind a woman of their present together, he thought, suddenly angry with himself. Especially since he knew they had no future together. At the wise old age of thirty-one, he didn't even bother to lie to a woman and promise her a life with him. After all, she'd only get tired of him and leave him. Or she'd let her flashy guard down and disenchant him. It was no use—he was destined to be alone.

"There'll be plenty of time to be sad later," he told Trudy. "Let's just enjoy now, okay?"

Part of him desperately wanted a future with Trudy—or at least near her. The rest of him was just as desperately afraid. He'd actually let himself be drawn to her emotionally before physically, and that was a feeling that jolted him to his core.

"R.J., I *have* to think of tomorrow. I don't have the luxury of living only for today. I have Dulcie to think of—" She stopped abruptly, listening, her breath held in.

"What's wrong?"

Bewildered, Trudy glanced around. "Where's Dulcie?"

"Right there by the—"

She was gone! The little girl had been gathering acorns only seconds before, stuffing them into her apron pockets until her dress sagged to her ankles. A small mound of nuts lay in the empty clearing.

Trudy glanced first at her rifle. Still there. Untouched. Then she glared at Regret, her eyes flashing in accusation. "I thought you were watching her."

"She was here a minute ago," Regret mumbled defensively.

Her glare cut too close to the bone. "I trusted you, R.J.! You said you'd watch her."

"Hey, she's not *my* responsibility." He regretted his words immediately. He had volunteered responsibility, hadn't he? And he'd turned his back—only for one minute, but for one minute too long. "I told you, I'm not the fatherly type," he added bitterly.

"Obviously not. I depended on you and—" Then her face softened. "I'm sorry. That was cruel of me. I learned a long time ago not to depend on anyone else. You're right, R.J. Dulcie is my responsibility, not yours."

Regret, you jerk, he thought.

"No, it's my fault. I shouldn't have said that. I told you I'd watch her."

"Oh, my God!" Trudy gasped, her worried gaze falling on the grassy circle around the turpentine well. Dropping her hammer, she bolted to the open pit. "Oh, my God, my God, my God!" She fell on the hard ground next to the opening, peering down into the murkiness.

He fell to his knees beside her. He couldn't tell how deep the well was, only that it was dim and slippery beyond the sunlight at its rim.

"Dulcie!" Trudy cried into the mouth of the well, but the word echoed back at them.

Regret cupped his hands and called down, "Dulcie! Where are you, sweetness?" He shifted on his elbows, knocking a green acorn into the darkness. *Plip!* The surface below rippled in concentric circles, and he realized that he was staring into a pool of water. How deep, he could only guess, but certainly deeper than Dulcie was tall.

"Dulcie!"

The anguish in Trudy's cry tore at his heart. If the child was down there, it was his fault. He'd been right all along—he'd make a lousy daddy. He couldn't be counted on, not even for a minute. What right did he have to want to be Dulcie's father? He couldn't even keep his eye on her for one minute without letting her run off and get into trouble.

Trudy twisted on the grass, squirming as she started feet-first into the pit. Regret grabbed her arm.

"What do you think you're doing?"

Eyes glazed, she whimpered, "I've got to get to my baby!"

"A rope? Do you have a rope in the cart? A chain?"

Trudy shook her head. "Nothing."

"Then you stay here. I'll go down after her. It's my fault."

"She could be hurt. She could be..."

"Mommmmmmmmeeeeeeeee!"

The sound didn't come from the pit. It came from faraway and aboveground.

"Dulcie!" Trudy's features, taut with worry, relaxed. Tears spilled down her cheeks. "She's not down there. Thank God!" Trudy glanced below at the slippery darkness and pulled herself back up onto the grassy rim. Her bare feet were muddy where they had skimmed the walls of the abyss.

"Mommmmmmmmeeeeeeeee!"

Dulcie's voice carried no fear. It was more like the six o'clock in the morning wake-up call she gave Trudy when she wanted to get out of her crib and Trudy wanted to sleep late. Or if she needed help getting to the bathroom. Or if she'd found a bee on a flower and wanted to show it to her mommy.

His heart lighter, Regret helped Trudy to her feet. Dulcie had probably found the world's largest pinecone while he and Trudy had been hunched over the open well, fearing the worst.

"Dulcie, baby, where are you?" Trudy quickened her pace toward the thicket beyond the clearing. Something maternal in her gait suggested she couldn't wait to hug her toddler.

"I over here, Mommy! Lookie what I found!"

Breaking through the thicket, Trudy stopped abruptly, and Regret bumped into her from behind. Over her shoulder, he saw his little dark-haired angel, smiling up bright eyed at Trudy, her hands extended, full of acorns.

"Lookie, Mommy! Puppy dogs!"

In front of the child crouched two snarling dogs, neither of them puppies. The German shepherd was bigger than Dulcie, maybe waist-high on Trudy. Growling, he nervously surveyed the little girl and then the adults behind her. The pit bull a few feet behind the larger dog showed no fear of Regret or Trudy and circled around them, stalking them.

Regret wished desperately for Trudy's hammer. For a big stick. For any weapon. Alone, he could sprint out of danger, maybe up an oak if he had to. Even with his injured ribs. Trudy, with her long legs and bare feet, could probably scurry over the wire fence faster than he could. But Dulcie... The smaller dog was closer to Dulcie than he was, and the German shepherd could reach her in a single leap.

"Dulcie," Trudy began, her voice shaking, "I want you to listen to me, okay? I want you to be very still."

Dulcie cocked her head. "Why, Mommy? The doggie's hungry. Maybe he wants some of my acorns." The child toddled toward the pit bull.

"No!"

Dulcie's face crumpled under her mother's harsh command. Then her blue eyes turned defiant, the way a two-year-old's can be when challenging a parental "No." Tentatively Dulcie held out her hand to the closer dog, not realizing the danger behind the growl.

Regret felt the woman's body next to his chest, felt her stiffen with intent to shield her child, felt the tremble in her knees. He saw the dog dig into the leafy mulch, crouching on its haunches. Its gaze shifted uneasily from Dulcie to her mother and back to Dulcie.

"Here, doggie." Dulcie smiled trustingly at the animal and thrust a handful of acorns at him.

Regret saw the spring in the dog's legs at the same time he shoved Trudy out of his way, almost knocking her to the ground. He stumbled forward. He couldn't feel his legs under him. He scooped up Dulcie, surprised, squirming. The pit bull bit into the air. Dulcie had stood there a moment before.

He spun on one foot, kicking the dog off balance as it lunged. Regret was running backward. Dulcie screamed in his ear. Trudy screamed from someplace far-off.

The pit bull lunged again. Regret kicked again. Dulcie seemed enormously heavy, weighing him down. He fought to keep moving, his ribs protesting.

The German shepherd leaped forward, striking Regret in the knees. He stumbled backward, still kicking at the smaller dog. The pit bull seized his jeans leg. Regret shook him off frantically. He had to get Dulcie to safety!

The rusty fence behind him—a good twenty feet away—was far too distant to reach. Trudy's hammer still lay on the ground beside the fence post where she'd erected one of her bluebird houses.

Fifteen feet away! If he could reach the fence, if he could scurry over the high border and down onto the thick yellow grasses, the pit bull wouldn't be able to follow. Maybe not even the bigger dog.

Ten feet away! In the whirlwind of movement he'd lost sight of Trudy. He prayed she had the sense to climb a tree or run for the fence ahead of him. If he could only get Dulcie to safety and not have to worry about Trudy!

Six feet away! Hot breath burned against his skin as he felt the pit bull's viselike jaws closing on his ankle. He felt the teeth sear into his flesh. He swung forward, pitching Dulcie over the fence and into the grass with his last surge of adrenaline. She tumbled across the tufts of grass and pulled herself up crying but unhurt. The two dogs brought him down like a hunted rabbit.

Dulcie's safe!

With the heel of his free boot, Regret kicked the pit bull, sending him spinning dizzily backward. Snarling and wheezing in its befuddlement, it came back at him. He kicked at it again. This time its teeth caught in the leather of his boot. The dog flailed from side to side as Regret shook his foot—to no avail—to free himself.

The hammer! Still too far away! He'd have to crawl ten feet or more on his belly to reach it. Suddenly the idea of Grendel as a protector appealed to him. Dulcie's guardian angel would never have let two strange dogs near her. And unlike Regret, the dog would never have let her wander off unattended.

Again he kicked at the pit bull, striking it hard in the head and knocking it senseless for a moment. The German shepherd pounced on top of him, seizing Regret's forearm in his black-gummed jaws. Regret twisted in pain, unable to throw off the huge dog. The smaller one dug into his other arm a moment later.

God! They're going to rip me apart!

He'd always wondered how he'd die, but he'd thought it would be in a plane crash or at the hands of a jealous man, not under the unfailing jaws of two wild beasts. Wild? In his agony he saw the murderousness in their brown eyes and heard the soft clanging of the dog tags on their collars. Not so wild that someone hadn't tamed them!

Dulcie's screams filled the air above him. *Better me than her,* he thought, resigning himself. He had so little to show for his life....

A shot echoed through the woods, once then twice. The pit bull collapsed on top of him without hesitation. The German shepherd released Regret's arm and limped toward the thicket. A third shot brought him—twitching—to the ground.

Trudy stood at the back of the four-wheeler. Her white knuckles were tight around her rifle. Dropping it to the ground, she ran toward him. She seemed so far away, yet she was growing closer with each wave of pain.

"R.J., R.J."

She lifted his head in her lap, stroked his face. He opened his eyes and half smiled up at her. Her eyes were limpid with a pain of their own.

"Can you hear me, R.J.?" Panic rang in her voice.

Regret nodded. Glancing down, he saw what had upset her. The blood. Blood like she must have seen the day she'd found her husband bleeding to death in his cockpit.

Disgusted Trudy shoved the carcass of the pit bull away. He couldn't tell if the blood was his or the dog's. Probably both.

"Mommy?" Dulcie sounded frightened. He couldn't see her. He wanted to see her, make sure she was okay.

"I've got to get you to a hospital," Trudy whispered raggedly. She slid her arms underneath him to sit him up.

"No. No hospitals." He held up one shaking hand in protest. "You, Trudy. You do it. You take care of me."

"Not anymore, R.J. I can't do it alone. You're bleeding a lot. You could die."

"No hospitals." He grabbed her bodice with his bloody hand. "I'd rather die here in your arms than go to the hospital."

"That's how Johnny died," she murmured. "In my arms."

"Sorry, Trudy." He sighed. "I didn't mean... Please. No hospitals."

"Look at me," she said firmly, her palm caressing his cheek. He struggled against the pain to keep his eyes open. "You have to trust me."

His strength ebbing with each pounding wave of pain in his arms and ankles, he closed his eyes. Yet, in spite of the pain, he was smiling. The words formed effortlessly, and either he said them or dreamed he said them.

"If I could trust anyone, Trudy Sandlin, it would be you."

Chapter 13

For Regret James, the closest place to hell on Earth was a hospital room. Cold. Lonely. Antiseptic. Even the bed next to his in the semiprivate room was empty. Other patients might have been grateful for the privacy, but to him, it only emphasized the sense of abandonment he'd felt all his life.

Fiercely he flicked off the television set mounted on the wall opposite his bed. He was tired of game shows and talk shows and useless chatter. Even lifting the remote control fatigued him, sending twinges of torture through his bandaged arm.

"I'm sorry," the emergency-room doctor had said. "I'm afraid there'll be scars. Probably for the rest of your life."

Scars for the rest of his life, Regret mused. *Aren't scars always for the rest of your life?*

He wasn't vain about it. And that surprised him. The scars would be more like puncture wounds, the doctor had assured him. Once they healed and turned a silvery white, they would barely be noticeable under the blond hair of his forearms. Only the most observant lover would run a light fingertip over the injured flesh and question its history. But those scars meant that Dulcie was safe, if not a little bruised, and for that he would willingly wear them like tiny medals of bravery.

Where was Trudy? She'd promised to stay by his side—and she had until the emergency-room staff had ordered her to leave. They'd coldly reminded her that she wasn't anything to him. Not his next of kin. Not his wife or sister. Certainly not his mother. And what business did she have bringing a two-year-old child with her and a wounded man? One of the nurses had quickly washed Dulcie's scraped knees, cleaning off the grass stains where she'd hit the ground on the other side of the fence, and covered the marks with funny-face bandages. Then she'd called Dulcie's Granny Sandlin to look after the child while Trudy filled out hospital admission forms for Regret and talked to a local veterinarian about the two dead dogs in the back of her truck. Regret knew that Trudy felt miserable about having to kill an animal, even though she really hadn't had a choice. The animals were trained hunting dogs, not pets, and they'd targeted Regret and little Dulcie as their quarry.

Someone knocked softly at the door. It wasn't a nurse or any of the hospital staff. Of that he was certain. The medical staff tended to barge into the room with a loud knock and a handful of pills. He knew this knock. He knew the soft rhythm, firm and gentle at the same instant. Slowly the door opened, and Trudy's smiling face caught the fading sunlight coming through the window across the room.

"Hi. How's my hero?"

She crossed the room briskly, bending to kiss him quickly on the forehead before setting a milk-glass vase of honeysuckle on the nightstand next to his bed.

Lifting his arms a few inches, he smiled back at her. "Not too bad, all things considered."

She eased herself down on the bed beside him, her eyes soaking up his torn arms in an expression of sadness and gratitude. "I don't know what I would've done if you hadn't been there," she choked out.

Regret knew. She would have been the one in the hospital bed, her pretty face and delicate arms scarred for the rest of her life in her effort to save her little girl. "Don't cry." He stroked the back of her hand with his fingers.

Trudy blinked furiously. "I won't."

"Is Dulcie still with her grandmother?"

She nodded. "I made arrangements for her to spend the night there."

"The night? Why?"

Her smile broadened. "So I can spend the night here with you. I've asked if they'll put a cot in your room so you won't have to be alone."

She understood! He hated hospitals—feared them irra-tionally—but she would stay with him. She *wanted* to stay with him.

"I talked to the doctor and the vet. The doctor wants to keep you until at least tomorrow for observation, but the vet thinks you should be safe."

"Safe?"

"Yeah. Rabies, you know? Both dogs were current on all their vaccinations."

She glanced toward the window, purposely looking away from his face. He caught her hand and squeezed it, gasping at the fire in his muscles. "You're not telling me every-thing."

Trudy sighed and pursed her lips. "I talked to the sheriff again, too. For all the good it did. He still thinks this is something between the hometown boys and me. I got his attention this time, though. He knows it could've been me—or Dulcie—who was attacked instead of you."

"Those were Rooster's dogs, weren't they?"

She shook her head. "Wayne and Claude's. The vet traced their tag numbers for me. I doubt their dogs would be that far from home unless the Tabor boys were close by. It's going to be hell to pay when they find out I killed their hunting dogs."

"Don't tell them."

"Too late. The sheriff's already taken it upon himself to make the call. He promised there wouldn't be any trouble. He's going to remind Wayne and Claude that you could bring charges against them. If you wanted."

"Maybe a little later. I'm too tired right now to go stir-ring up trouble." He gave her a halfhearted wink.

"It won't be you causing the trouble, R.J. I've already had one run-in with Claude over dogs." She grinned at the memory. "Grendel ran him off my land last fall. You should've seen Claude attempting to jump a barbed-wire fence. Got his hand all cut up trying to get away from Grendel." Her face darkened. "I wouldn't be at all surprised if it was Claude's gun that shot my dog."

Regret rubbed his hand soothingly over hers. He could listen to her voice all day—and night.

"Something else is strange, too, R.J. Those were hunting dogs, but Wayne and Claude have never brought them to my woods before."

"No need to. They weren't hunting game. Metal detectors can sniff out gold a lot better than dogs can."

"But why are they still looking in Alligator Pond? We told Jordy it's just not possible for there to be gold in the pond. His dad agreed. The banker who got lynched didn't have time to make it that far into the swamp and back to the edge of the woods."

"Well, they found something in the pond. That's for sure."

Trudy's jaw dropped abruptly. Then laughter suddenly pealed from her throat. "I think I know what they've found. And it's sure not gold!"

Puzzled, Regret studied her. "I take it it's not buried treasure."

She laughed again, this time more softly. "There's a saying that one man's trash is another's treasure." Her deep blue eyes sparkled in the waning light from the window. She was enjoying herself. "Country people don't have the same sanitation services people in town do. For instance, the city of Cornerstone will pick up your trash if you have a town address. But if you live out in the county, the way we always have, you take your trash to the county Dumpster. Then there's the really big stuff you aren't allowed to take to the Dumpster, so you bury it on your own land. Back, oh, ten or fifteen years ago, Papa dumped a bunch of old rusty fence wire and tractor parts into Alligator Pond to help fill in the swamp."

Regret understood her sudden good humor. "Rooster and his pals think they've found gold, but what they've really found is your grandfather's garbage dump. You know, I think the sheriff was right. You should let them dredge to their hearts' content." He grinned at the image forming in his brain. "I'd love to be there when they drag up a roll of fence wire. Kind of like a championship fisherman catching an old boot, huh?"

Trudy giggled.

"You look so happy tonight, Trudy. Lately you've been too sad. But I think you've been sad most of your life."

Ignoring his words, she bent and kissed his forehead again. "It would make me even happier to see you out of this hospital bed."

"Hospital." He sighed. "God, I hate hospitals."

"I know. You keep telling me that. But you've never told me why. Just that you had a bad experience when you were five years old."

"Trudy..."

He rubbed her hand between his palms, reveling in the warmth of her flesh. She was watching him with those patient, motherly eyes. He felt foolish lying so close to her in his green hospital gown.

"Trudy, do you remember what I told you about my mother? She never wanted me. Ever. I was her 'one regret.' She never let me feel wanted or loved when I was a little boy. But I loved her. And I think I was a good kid, too. At least then I was. Probably because I wanted so much for her to love me back."

Trudy looked down at him with broken-hearted sympathy. She was listening to him the way no other woman ever had. And he could tell her things he had told no other woman.

"When I was five years old, I got sick. My mother didn't take me to the doctor right away. She talked about it, but we didn't have any money. I got sicker and sicker. Finally she took me to the hospital, and they told her I was going to have to stay there for a long time and it was going to cost a lot of money. She told them she didn't have any money. Last time I saw her, she was sitting by my bed just before I fell asleep. When I woke up, she was gone. Nobody could tell me where my mother had gone. Or why. But I was all alone. And have been ever since.''

Trudy swept the hair from his brow. Her soft touch brushed against his cheek in tender healing.

"What about your father? Couldn't he help?"

"My father never acknowledged me. Whereas I was my mother's 'one regret,' I was my father's 'one indiscretion.'" His voice sounded so bitter he barely recognized it. "The hospital contacted him as my next of kin. He disagreed. After that, I went from foster home to foster home. And my foster parents probably hated me just as much as I hated them. I was determined to make them all pay for the wrongs done to me. That's what the social workers said, anyway."

"What about your father? Why didn't you go after him when you were older? Make him acknowledge you?"

"I found him. Found out I didn't want to know him."

"Your mother told you who he was?"

"Never. She wouldn't talk about him when I was little. And I never saw her again—alive—after she left me at the Children's Hospital."

Trudy studied the curves of his cheeks with her calming fingers. "Then how did you find him? Did he come to you?"

"Hardly. My mother died when I was seventeen. A long, slow death. Alone in a hospital. Ironic, huh?" He laughed bitterly, more out of habit than hatred. "She died owing a lot of money. Her creditors tracked me down. Trying to collect. They didn't care that I was just a kid myself."

"Did they make you pay?"

"With what? I was living with foster parents at the time. I didn't have a cent to my name. But my foster parents did encourage me to check on my mother's estate. You know, see if I might be heir to something other than her debts. I found out she never married. She lived her whole life in a small rented place. One of her neighbors said he'd kept the only thing that was hers—a cedar box. There wasn't much in it. A picture of her when she was young and pretty. And letters.''

"From your father?"

"*To* my father. From her. Stacks and stacks of them. She'd mailed them, and they'd been returned, marked Refused."

"Poor woman."

"I opened the letters and read them. Read them all. There were photos of me as a baby. Most of the letters were impassioned pleas for money. At first all she wanted was his love. But she couldn't take care of me by herself. She needed his help, and he refused to give it."

"But see? She did love you. She was young. It couldn't have been easy for her."

Regret ignored Trudy's attempt to sway his bitter feelings for the woman who'd given birth to him. "She must've become more and more desperate as the years went by. He still wouldn't see her. It must've eaten away at her."

"Like it's eaten away at you?"

His bandaged arms tensing, Regret howled back, "She left me!"

"She was alone, too. Granted, she should've found a way. But some people aren't that strong. You can't spend your whole life not trusting people because of what she did."

"Can't I?"

"What about your father?"

"I knew who he was by the name on the letters. My daddy wasn't a poor man. The day I turned eighteen, I left to find him."

"Was that before you stole Hughie's father's car?"

Regret winced. "No. Right after. Hughie's dad helped me get a job with the company my father worked for. I stayed there a few months. Long enough to know I didn't like the man."

"You should've approached him, R.J. Told him you were his son."

"I did. He was a senior vice president of the company, making lots of bucks. I figured, why would he believe some tall-tale-bearing kid from the mail room? But I was bold. Bold the way eighteen-year-old boys are bold. I confronted him anyway. What surprised me most was that he didn't even bother to deny it. The expression on his face didn't even change one bit. No 'Hello, son, it's nice to meet you.' Not even a handshake. He just reached into his pocket and brought out his checkbook. Said he figured it cost about a hundred thousand to raise a kid and maybe another fifty thousand to get a college education that would keep me self-sufficient and off his doorstep. Then he said he was about to be promoted to executive V.P. and he didn't want a surprise from his past spoiling his future with the company. So he wrote me a check and then fired me.''

''And that's the money you were going to use to buy my farm?''

He nodded. ''Hughie's dad put the money in stocks and bonds for me, so there's a lot more now. I swore I'd never touch the money. Never have, either. Never had a reason to until now.''

''What about your father? It's been thirteen years. Maybe things have changed. Maybe he'd want to see you again.''

He hadn't squelched the excitement in her eyes. The wheels turned inside. Trudy Sandlin was scheming of yet another way to make him whole.

''My father didn't want anything to do with me when I was born. Or any time after that. He was too afraid his relationship with my mother would ruin his marriage and his career. Well, his wife left him and his company fired him for mismanagement. In the end, he had nothing. Not even a son. He died almost two years after he wrote me off as easily as he wrote that check.''

Trudy frowned at him, then patted his hand. ''It's too bad he didn't live longer. Maybe in time he could've made up for his failures.''

Did she have to see the good in everyone? ''There's no making up for that kind of failure, Trudy. Nobody deserves parents like the ones I had. Not even me. That's why I did what I did.''

Trudy leaned in closer, curious. With the window at her back, she was a sensuous silhouette with bright eyes.

''What did you do, R.J.?''

''I made sure several years ago that I would never pass on this legacy of . . . of unwant to a child of mine.''

"I don't understand, R.J. You told me before, you don't want children. But you're still young. You could change your mind."

Regret laughed without amusement. "A little late to change my mind now. When I was twenty-seven-years old, I went to a doctor in Atlanta and told him I wanted a vasectomy. Only time I've ever willingly gone to a hospital." What he didn't tell Trudy was that he was more afraid of bringing an unwanted child into the world than he was of hospitals. "He told me I was too young. He said I should wait. Think it over. But I'd been thinking it over my whole life, and I knew then that I should never have children."

"Y-you had a vasectomy?"

Even in the dimness, he could see the confusion on her brow. "Yeah," he went on. "The line ends with me. No more unwanted children."

"Don't you think that maybe you were... a bit hasty?"

He'd considered that once or twice. He'd realized too late that if he ever met a woman who really did want a life with him, she'd probably want a family, too. The one thing he couldn't give any woman now. He'd damned all probability of a woman wanting a life with him. Unless she already had children....

"I don't want to be the way my father was to me. I don't want to ever hurt a child by turning my back on him." He thought of Dulcie. "Or her. I'd make a terrible daddy."

Trudy flung herself forward, kissing him on the forehead, on both cheeks, on the chin. "Oh, R.J.! You'd make a terrific father! Just look how well you do with Dulcie!"

"No," he said, but it was true. He loved playing horsey with the child, loved hearing her squeals of delight when he picked her up upside down, loved the night-night hugs and sticky kisses, loved the way her little-Trudy eyes lit up with devilment when they wrestled on the living-room rug. He loved doing all the daddy things with her he had always longed for his own father to do with him.

"She loves you, R.J. And whether or not you're willing to admit it, I think you feel the same way about her."

He nodded reluctantly. "She has us all wrapped around her little finger."

"Why didn't you tell me about your vasectomy?"

Shrugging, he lifted one weary hand to trace her profile. "It didn't seem to matter. Besides, you told me you couldn't get pregnant."

"I didn't say I couldn't get pregnant. I said I couldn't carry a child to term. Big difference."

"Oh." He raised his other hand, tracing the outline of her jaw.

"Yesterday you kept telling me everything was taken care of and I kept telling you that I needed protection. I thought you were being . . . reckless. You should've told me about your vasectomy."

"Would it have made a difference?"

"Very much. I thought you were selfish not to take precautions when I'd told you I couldn't risk getting pregnant."

A smile tugged at the corner of his mouth. "Is that what it was? I thought I'd scared you off by coming on too strong. You probably thought I'd love you and leave you. But, Trudy, I can't just walk away from you."

Lightly she ran her fingertips over his bandaged arms and ribs. "I don't think you can walk away from much of anything right now."

"My ankles are bandaged, too," he acknowledged, grateful for the levity she offered. "Between the plane crash and the fist fight with Rooster and now a dog attack, you're never going to know me as a whole man."

"I'll be the judge of that." Mischief glinted in her eyes.

Trudy slipped off the edge of his bed and, kicking off her sandals, padded softly to the open curtain that separated Regret's bed from the empty one a few feet away. With a wicked grin, she tugged at the white curtain, and it swung around in a semicircle, enveloping Regret's half of the room.

"What are you doing?" Regret hesitantly asked as she crawled back onto the bed beside him.

One corner of her mouth curled upward. Her hands started at his shoulders and raked tenderly down his chest to where the sterile white sheet covered his hips. Through the grayness of early evening, her gaze bore into him, her intent unmistakable as she firmly grasped the sheet covering him and snatched it downward and off his bandaged ankles. With one swift movement, she wriggled out of her white, cotton panties, dropping them to the floor beside the nightstand and the sweet-smelling honeysuckle.

"It's time you got over your fear of hospitals," she whispered hoarsely, straddling his gowned hips.

Only the coarse green hospital gown separated him from the moist heat under her skirt.

"Trudy," he gasped, grabbing at her playful hands. "Not here! Someone could come in."

"Shh. Then you'd better be quiet."

Her hands moved down to the hem of the gown, rumpling it as she shoved it upward to his chest. Still she stared into his eyes. Her mouth had frozen into a hint of smile, lips parted, her lower teeth pressing against her upper bite in anticipation.

"Trudy, I'm serious. This isn't the time or place."

"It's the perfect place. And it's definitely time."

She shifted over him, easing down slowly until the vee of her legs met with the punctuation of his stiffness. She hesitated, her mouth opening in a fast draw for breath, then slid down on him until he was tight within her fever.

Regret moaned without control.

"Shh!" She clamped one hand over his mouth, then replaced the hand with a deep and probing kiss. His arms, stiff with white gauze and tape, folded around her as she shifted downward, parallel with his body, promising delicious friction at the cleft of her pubic bone.

In an unsteady rhythm, her hips rocked against his, each push jolting his desire, chafing his senses with a yearning he could not fight. The want welled inside him, building geometrically until his hips began moving against her with a will of their own, matching each thrust for frantic thrust.

Closing her eyes, she broke free of his returned kisses and lifted her face from him. Her dark hair fell in a loose veil around his face, shutting out the invading white sterility of the hospital room.

"Oh, Trudy," he groaned under her, feeling her body tighten on top of his, listening to her gasping for air, watching her bite into her bottom lip between heaving breaths. "It's just like I knew it would be!"

His bandaged arms strained upward to the fruit of her breasts, finding them bound underneath her buttoned blouse. Desperation in his fingertips, he could barely feel the fire in his wounded arms and ribs for the fanning flame in his groin. He slid his hands between the fabric and skin, caressing the plums of her nipples.

She whimpered at his touch and opened her eyes. He lost himself in their unfathomable depths of blue, no longer caring that he was in a hospital bed or that a nurse might barge in at any minute. If anything, the idea of it excited him even more. To be hopelessly, helplessly, Trudy's when she finally abandoned control to him!

"I'll never walk away from you." Framing her face in his palms, he pulled her mouth down to his.

Her body racked above his with lusty spasms as she fell whimpering into his arms, against his aching chest. Her hips slowed to an almost imperceptible pulse as her mouth found the tender underside of his neck where no beard grew. Fluttery kisses marked a trail across his collarbone and upper chest as she pushed herself upward, back onto her knees. Her slow thrusts quickened again, this time for his pleasure rather than hers, although by the tightening of her body on his, he could tell her movements caused her no pain.

The muscles of his thighs tensed under the fevered embrace of her legs as she drew him into her, refusing to release him even as his own body shuddered and released into hers. Clenching his teeth, he swallowed the moan rising out of his chest. He dug his hands into her back, crushing her against his heart, against his soul.

Chest heaving, she lay quietly on top of him. Regret smiled to himself, thinking through the haze how warm the cold room had become. He smoothed her long hair against his shoulder, realizing that the curls were damp with her effort. Delicately he kissed her misted forehead and wrapped his arms even more tightly around her.

After a long time had passed in the growing darkness, he whispered hoarsely, "Making love to you has got to be the most incredible experience in my life.'' He laughed softly, then joked, ''It's even better than flying.''

''R.J.—'' Deadly serious, she lifted on her elbows.

He could no longer see her face, but her voice resonated against his chest as she bent close to him again and kissed the evening beard on his jaw.

''R.J., I need you to do something for me.''

''Anything, Trudy.''

''I want you to stop flying.''

Silence hung between them. ''What?'' He sat up in bed. Had he heard her right? Was she teasing?

''I want you to stop flying.''

''Stop flying? Are you crazy? I might as well stop breathing!''

''That's what I'm afraid of.''

''Trudy, flying is who I am. And I will never give it up.''

''Please? I couldn't stand it if I lost you.'' She had started to shake. ''You know you'll get yourself killed up there.''

''I won't. I'm a damned good pilot.''

''So was my husband. I won't lose you, too. You have to stop flying. Please? For me?''

He should have known he couldn't trust her. He'd thought she was special, but she wasn't. She wanted to take away the one constant in his life. She was just like everybody else. Just like everybody else in his miserable past. And as soon as his wounds healed and he could get out of this hole-in-the-road town, she'd be part of his past, too.

''Never.''

Chapter 14

The man in the black sedan honked the horn a second time before Trudy could kill the engine of the four-wheeler. Moments before, she had backed the four-wheeler, minus the cart, out from under the tin-roofed shed and started across the backyard toward the woods. Dulcie squirmed in her lap, trying to see if she recognized their unexpected guest, while Trudy muttered unhappily to herself. She'd left Regret asleep in the guest room, and the high-pitched blasts would likely cut through the density of the sleeping pills the doctor had given him to keep him in bed and off his swollen ankles. He seemed to want to sleep. It was an excuse for avoiding her.

"Who is it, Mommy?" Dulcie asked, while the man sat patiently in the car. No doubt he was looking for Grendel, having always before been greeted by the woolly monster with well-honed teeth.

Trudy recognized the Cornerstone Bank logo on the side of the sedan and groaned to herself. "Shh," she said aloud to Dulcie.

The toddler twisted in her lap to assure herself that the rifle was still secured to the bar behind the seat. "Shoot 'im, Mommy," she suggested in earnest.

"No, baby. He's a nice man." Trudy gestured for the man to get out of the car, but she didn't dismount from the four-wheeler. Buck Witherspoon would have to come to her.

The driver's door opened slowly, cautiously, and the man unfolded himself. Buck Witherspoon looked around nervously. He was still an attractive man, fortyish, with a full head of brown hair graying at the temples. On the farm he was out of his element in his long-sleeved, white button-down shirt, dark slacks and conservative tie. Trudy knew it had to be important for him to drag himself away from his vice-president's desk at the bank. She knew why he'd come.

"Er, good afternoon, Trudy. I, uh, you still got that big dog?"

"Go on and get out of the car, Buck. He's not here right now. He's at the vet's until tomorrow. Somebody shot him."

Relief replaced the stiffness in his shoulders. "Oh. Sorry to hear about that. Uh, you going somewhere? Did I come at a bad time?"

There would never be a good time for him to come after her land, she thought to herself. "I was just going to drop Dulcie at Miss Naomi's and then go down to the woods to take some pictures." *Pictures Sheriff Clayton will be very interested in.*

His eyes surveyed her neckline, not out of sexual interest but because Regret's camera hung heavily between her breasts. She felt the inquisitive nature of his eyes on her and abruptly drew her hand to the camera strap.

"Mighty nice camera you got there."

She knew what he was thinking. He was wondering how she could afford such a fancy piece of equipment when she hadn't been able to make a payment on Johnny's debts since the previous season's harvest.

"It's not mine," she said quickly. "It belongs to a friend. He's been teaching me how to take good pictures."

Buck nodded, satisfied with her answer. He didn't come any closer, just remained at the corner of the black sedan, as though it offered him some sanctuary.

"Trudy, you know I think the world of you and your grandfather."

"We've always liked you, too, Buck."

"And Johnny—God rest his soul—wasn't much of a businessman, but he was a good husband to you and would've been a good daddy to that little girl of yours if..."

"If he'd lived. I know, Buck. Johnny really appreciated the way you were always there for us when we needed to borrow money. You always believed in him. And I'm grateful for that."

"And your mama—God rest her soul, too—was a fine woman. Heck, she taught me to read when I was in the first grade. She was a mighty fine grammar-school teacher. Sunday-school teacher, too."

"Don't make this any harder on yourself than you have to, Buck. Just say what you came to say."

He looked crushed at her attempt to ease his discomfort, as though he would have preferred Trudy lift her rifle to her shoulder and pierce his heart or, at the very least, curse him. She didn't plan to do either.

"Okay. I wanted you to hear it from me. I wanted you to know that I tried, but—"

She could read it in his eyes. "The bank is foreclosing."

"First Tuesday of next month, the farm will be sold on the courthouse steps." Buck looked away shamefully. "I've done everything I can to stall it."

"Last time we talked, you said you thought we'd be able to wait until after the fall harvest. Papa's already got this year's crops planted. At least give us the chance to harvest them and make another payment on Johnny's debts."

"God, Trudy, I've tried! If your family weren't so well thought of here in Cornerstone, I wouldn't have let it go on for this long. Anyway, I can't wait another six months for another payment."

Trudy swallowed the lump in her throat and hugged Dulcie to her. She knew what would happen. She'd seen it happen in the early 1980s, when the land value of the local farms had dropped and so many young farmers had declared bankruptcy or lost their homes to foreclosure. Her land—the land where her ancestors had walked a hundred years ago—would be sold on the courthouse steps to the highest bidder for a smidgen of its financial worth. She'd still be responsible for the remainder of Johnny's debts, only this time, she'd have no farm, no home, no roots, no hope. And people like Jordy and Rooster Reed and the Tabors could buy her land if they wanted. They could cut the timber, kill the animals for sport and dredge every inch of Alligator Pond for fabled gold. She shuddered at the chill that curled in the pit of her stomach.

"I'm so sorry, Trudy. I tried. Honest to God I did. But I've got auditors coming in, and it's gonna be hell to pay if I don't take care of this before they find the outstanding debt."

"What if I'm able to pay it off before you foreclose?"

Buck frowned at her. "I don't see how. Selling birdhouses or a little mayhaw jelly in town won't even pay the interest for—"

"I meant, what if I'm able to pay it off in full?"

"With what, Trudy? We've been through this before. You don't have any assets other than this farm. You could move to town and live off your social security checks, I suppose. We can't—and won't—touch that. Other than that, everything, right down to your daughter's piggy bank, will go toward Johnny's debts."

"I've made a new friend. He thinks he can help me."

"Mr. James. The pilot."

"Yes. How'd you know—"

Buck reddened. "Miss Clarice. Well, you know how she talks. But that's an awful lot of money." His eyes narrowed pensively. "Must be an awfully good friend."

"Yes. He is."

"Why haven't you approached me about this before? Here I've been holding off on foreclosure, and you've known that you could get the money—"

"I haven't withheld anything from you, Buck. Mr. James and I have been discussing it since only a few days ago, and to tell you the truth, I don't know if his offer still stands. I haven't had the guts to ask him."

"You haven't...why not, Trudy? I know how much this land means to you. I know you'd do just about anything—short of selling kisses—to keep it."

Trudy bowed her head, brushing her cheek against Dulcie's soft curls. True, she'd saved Regret's life, and maybe in some bizarre sense he owed her for that. Whether he owed her seventy thousand dollars' worth of gratitude was still open to dispute. But, then, he'd rescued Dulcie from those vicious dogs and that had upset the balance. Now she owed him. It didn't matter what debts had gone before. They were all insignificant compared with the unmarred skin of her little girl. She could no longer expect or even wish for Regret to bail her out of her financial mire. How could she? She'd asked him to give up flying for her. And he'd answered her ultimatum with a look of utter betrayal. No, she was on her own again.

"Buck, I know I have no right to ask it, but please, just a few days more."

The loan officer sighed audibly, wiped the perspiration from his forehead and finally nodded. "Okay. Okay, a few more days. But we've got to settle this before the auditors get here. Trudy, it's my job on the line. God knows, I think the world of your family, but I can't cover for you and your grandfather any longer."

One way or the other, Buck wouldn't have to. She would get an answer from Regret—either a yes or a "Hell, no!"— as soon as she returned from the woods. Returned from capturing unwanted wildlife on film.

For hours Trudy had been hearing a new noise from the bowels of the woods. A steady drone, like that of an irrigation pump, had replaced the hammering blows and sputtering chain saws. Regret had taught her to use his camera, and if Sheriff Jim Clayton wouldn't believe Regret's eyewitness account of trespassers on her land, how could he possibly doubt photographic evidence taken by Trudy herself? She might lose her land in the end, but she had a score to settle with the local good ol' boys.

In the three days that had passed since she'd killed Wayne and Claude Tabor's mangy mutts, she'd seen neither hide nor hair of the brothers or of Rooster Reed. Or Jordy, for that matter. Although she knew that they knew there'd be no more hunting expeditions with the German shepherd or the pit bull, she hadn't heard a word of displeasure from the Tabors. In the back of her mind, she feared more strange dogs might even await her in the woods. This time her rifle was ready, and Dulcie was safely out of harm's way at Miss Naomi's.

Unlike the day Regret had spied on Rooster and his accomplices, Trudy wasn't concerned about the steady hum of the four-wheeler's motor as she putted along the wooded path in her bike helmet. The drone of equipment near Alligator Pond overwhelmed any noise she might make. The ground itself was hardly damp after several weeks without rain, and Trudy was able to press the four-wheeler deeper into the woods than usual.

When the woods became thick enough that she could see mosquitoes swarming in clouds near the swampy landscape of Alligator Pond, she pulled the four-wheeler into a muddy clearing, turned off the engine and left the key in the ignition.

The camera still hanging at her neck, Trudy carried the rifle tightly in her grip. She peered through the cypress trees and mayhaw bushes. The drone was louder, but the crinkle of something under her footfalls startled her.

Beer cans! Someone—probably Rooster and the Tabors—had been in the clearing before them. The footprints in the mud and soft leaves were cleated and deep—and fresh. Aluminum foil, plastic sandwich bags and several crumpled paper sacks lay scattered in the underbrush.

Something shiny and silver in the leaves caught her attention. Trudy snatched it up, then wiped away the grit from the mirrored lenses of a pair of man's sunglasses. She'd seen glasses like those before, but not on Rooster or the Tabor brothers. Someone else then had been in the Dugan woods.

Trudy inched closer to the droning, tugging down on one thorny limb to aim the camera through the brush. At the edge of the pond a dredge was poised, siphoning water from the bottom of Alligator Pond and spitting muck onto the grassy bank. Three dingy motorcycles leaned against cypress trees on a drier bank. Propping the rifle against her hip, Trudy snapped pictures furiously.

Abruptly the droning stopped.

Something stung her arm. She frowned down at it. A mosquito the size of a hummingbird! She slapped it away.

She raised the camera again to her eye and clicked off another round of pictures as Wayne and Claude waded through the mud in their gray, rubber boots toward Rooster, who was climbing down from the dredge.

"Any luck yet?" Rooster asked the brothers.

"Not the least damned bit."

"Nothing?" Rooster exclaimed incredulously. "Then you're not lookin' hard enough! Our metal detectors went haywire!"

"Man, I know that," whined Claude. "But all we've found so far has been old fence wire and a tractor muffler. There ain't no gold out here."

Rooster lifted the camouflage cap off his forehead and fanned his reddened face. "You're jes' not lookin' hard enough."

"Maybe that boyfriend of Trudy's got to it before we did," suggested Wayne.

"I don't know what Trudy sees in him," the other brother said nervously, obviously afraid that Wayne had overstepped the bounds with Rooster. "She's such a feisty little thang. You'd think she'd go for a real man like—"

"Leave Trudy out of this." Rooster's voice crackled with warning.

"Aw, Rooster! Man, you're still sweet on her, ain't you?"

Trudy zoomed in close with the telephoto lens as Rooster glared back at Claude. It wouldn't do for them to see her now, she thought.

Whap! She slapped at another mosquito. The sound resounded through the clearing, louder than she'd expected. She rubbed at the welt rising on her bare arm.

Through the camera lens, Trudy saw the three men look up in surprise at the same instant she whirled on one foot. Dangling by the thick strap, the heavy camera thudded against her chest.

Too late! The three men had seen the flash of Trudy's dress in the clearing. They knew they'd been discovered.

She could still outrun them on the four-wheeler, she told herself. Trudy lifted the camera to her face for yet another round of pictures. She'd expected to see the three men struggling through the grass toward her, but they were headed in the opposite direction, toward the motorcycles.

Straightening her helmet, she bounded onto the four-wheeler and carefully tucked the stray tresses at her neck underneath the protection of the helmet. She'd have to make it down the path fast, and she couldn't risk tangling her hair in the thorny mayhaw branches that overhung much of the shaded trail through the woods. She heard the first cough of a motorcycle as she cranked the four-wheeler.

Trudy seized the steering wheel with both hands. The tires spun. The four-wheeler lurched forward. She left a flurry of leaves behind her.

By the time she passed the mayhaw thicket where she and Regret had picked the two buckets of berries, she could hear the rumble of motorcycles faintly over the hum of the four-wheeler. She dared not turn to look behind her. The path was too dark, too winding and often too narrow to navigate safely. The wind whipped at her face and dress, and her skirt flew out behind her like a flag to be followed.

She pressed the accelerator to the floor. The machine spurred forward under her command. She couldn't go much faster. Already the shadows blurred ahead of her. She fought to stay between the low-hanging trees.

The snarl behind her grew louder. The motorcycles were more maneuverable on the narrow trail than her clumsy all-terrain vehicle. At least without the cart she could move faster. If only she could reach the open field on the outskirts of the woods...

Ahead, sunshine drenched the end of the shaded tunnel where the trail opened onto the incline above the turpentine well and the spot where the errant banker had been lynched in 1907. Trudy shot out of the woods and toward Johnson's Creek.

Out of the corner of her right eye, she watched with sinking dread as one of the motorcycles overtook her with a disturbing agility. A second biker closed in from the left side. Neither man wore a helmet. The determined faces of the Tabor brothers angrily defied her. She heard the third motorcycle behind her and knew it must be Rooster.

Wayne veered in front of her, cutting her off, and she kicked at her brakes, squalling to a jerky halt halfway between the old well and the edge of the woods. Fury coursed through her veins. How dared Wayne Tabor put her life in danger with such a stupid stunt! And how dared the three of them chase Trudy on her own land, hunt her down like a fleeing rabbit!

Trudy stayed on the seat of the four-wheeler while the three cyclists dismounted. The engine still putted stubbornly. She was boxed in, but maybe there'd be a chance to jab at the accelerator again, knock a motorcycle out of the way—maybe a grown man—and head to the house as fast as she could before they knew what hit them. Stealthily she reached behind her for her rifle. They'd be sorry when she made them carry their damned motorcycles over the fence and off her land with a little persuasion from a smoking barrel!

The rifle!

Trudy angled in her seat and seized empty space where the rifle had been. A sinking dread swelling in her stomach reminded her that she'd dropped the rifle in the clearing by Alligator Pond where she'd snapped pictures and slapped mosquitoes.

"Lose somethin', Trudy?" asked Rooster as he pranced up next to her.

His T-shirt and khakis were caked with smelly swamp mud. She drew back in repulsion. The sweat-drenched ringlets of hair clinging to his forehead under his camouflage cap did nothing to improve his appeal.

"I told you before to stay off my land." Her voice was steady, confident. He couldn't see her knees trembling under her skirt. She was cornered, trapped.

"And I told you," he said, reaching past her to yank the keys out of the ignition, "that if you want me off your land, you'll have to throw me off yourself." He grinned at her rebelliously. His eyes reminded her of dirty ice. "You think you're strong enough to pick me up and throw me over that fence?" He didn't wait for an answer. "I didn't think so. Not without your rifle. Not without your dog."

Trudy clenched her jaws. "Get off my land."

"Where's that boyfriend of yours? Not much of a man to let you go wanderin' around the woods by yourself. A girl could git hurt."

The Tabor brothers snickered behind her.

"Get off my land. Now."

"Aw, Trudy. You're not much fun anymore. Maybe you should go back to the kitchen and bake somethin'." He glanced down at her bare feet. "Too bad you can't be barefoot and pregnant in the kitchen."

Trudy drew in her breath sharply. She hated Rooster for that. Enough to kill him.

"Yep, Trudy. Some men might say you're not worth much 'cause you can't produce a whole passel of young'uns." He slipped one sweaty arm around her shoulders in mock intimacy. "But I'm a real forgivin' sort if you ever want to—"

"Go to hell."

"Tsk, tsk. You shouldn't talk that way. People are liable to think you're not a fit mama."

"You leave my little girl out of this."

"You know, Trudy, we don't have to fight. If there's ever anything I can do for you—"

"You can get off my land." Trudy shrugged off Rooster's clumsy embrace.

"Not yours for much longer. Where you gonna go then? I got a place of my own, you know." He wove his arm around her back and wrested her against his massive, muddy chest. "You and your little girl would be welcome to stay with me for a while." He winked at his accomplices. "Of course, you'd have to *earn* your keep."

"Jordy!"

The dark-haired deputy flashed the revolving light on top of the county car. He'd parked in the yellow grass of the neighboring property. Fingering his revolver, he climbed over the boundary fence with an air of authority.

"Trudy? That you, girl? Are these lowlifes bothering you?"

Her sister-in-law's husband. She breathed a relieved sigh. *He'll help me. He has to. He's the law.*

Striding toward Trudy, Jordy rubbed the revolver like a teenager itchily caressing his first lover. A hint of swamp mud dulled his normally shiny shoes.

"I'm so glad to see you, Jordy!" Trudy said when he was within earshot. "Rooster and his...his *friends* are trespassing again. Just like I told your daddy. They chased me on their motorcycles. I want them off my land, Jordy. I want them to leave me alone. And I want you to do something about it."

"Oh, I intend to." He glanced angrily at the three men. They looked away sheepishly.

"Jordy, they *are* dredging for gold in Alligator Pond. Just like R.J. said. Just like we told you and your daddy."

The deputy laid a reassuring hand on Trudy's shoulder. "Trudy, Trudy, Trudy. You've got to be careful about these accusations. You know what people around here will say about you."

"I can prove it." She held up the camera that hung around her neck. "I've got it on film."

He lifted the camera from her neck. "I suppose I'll have to take this in as evidence," he said, hanging the thick, black strap around his own neck. A smirk played at the corner of his mouth.

Then she remembered. Jordy wasn't wearing his sunglasses. He'd always preferred mirrored sunglasses—like the ones she'd found in the clearing. As a teenager, they'd enhanced his machismo. As an adult, they'd been a standard part of his uniform, enforcing his aura of command. But if Jordy had lost his favorite fashion accessory in her woods, then Regret was right. Jordy had known all along. He'd been trespassing on her land from the very start. Right through her back door—and with Louisa coming to her front door with promises of buying land and letting her keep the house.

He must have seen the realization in her eyes. "Trudy, think you should be a good girl and forget everything you've come across here today. Go on back to the house and bake some muffins or sumpin'. Call Weezer and go shoppin'."

She shook off his hand. "Don't patronize me, Jordy Clayton. You're no better than the rest of them." She nar rowed her eyes in disgust. "No, you're worse. Hiding behind that uniform to break the law."

"Breakin' the law, Trudy?" Jordy grinned down at her. "I told you not to be spreadin' rumors. My reputation doesn't need that sort of thang. Everybody knows Daddy's retirin', and I'm gonna be the next sheriff of this here county. So you watch your pretty little mouth, sugar. I'm here to protect you."

"Protect me? No, thanks, Jordy. I'd be safer with the wolves. You and Louisa try to buy me out for a little of nothing, knowing what kind of pressure I'm under from the bank. I thought you were being nice, offering to take care of me the way family takes care of family. But all this time the only thing you wanted was the chance to upturn every acre of woods to find a bag of gold that doesn't exist."

"Oh, it exists, Trudy. It's just a matter of time until we sift it out of Alligator Pond."

Rooster coughed and scratched his head through the camouflage cap. "Um, Clayton, I'm not so sure. We haven't turned up anything yet—"

"You'd better," Jordy warned, his voice tight. "It's costin' me an arm and a leg to finance this operation. You three better git back to the pond and find sumpin', you hear? That dredge's only rented till tomorrow."

Trudy watched in surprise as Rooster cowered and nodded. Since he'd flunked out of college, Rooster had been the town bully, giving orders to local yokels like Wayne and Claude Tabor. But now he plainly took his orders from the deputy. Maybe he'd been acting on Jordy's instructions all along.

"As for you—" Jordy turned back to Trudy "—you be a good girl and go on back to your house. You might as well start packin' your things, 'cause you know you won't be livin' there much longer. I know Buck Witherspoon has been to see you again. Not hard to figure out why he'd be visitin' the young widow Sandlin. Certainly not for pleasure. You should've taken Weezer up on her offer when you had the chance."

Trudy shot daggers through him with her angry glare. "I'm not going to lose my land. I'll hang on to it somehow.

But you're going to lose your job. I'll see to that. Just wait till your daddy finds out—''

Jordy seized her hard by the fleshy part of her arm and wrenched her around to look at him. "You'll keep your mouth shut!"

"Let go! You're hurting me!" She was suddenly afraid of the rage in his dark eyes. He was uncle to her child. Surely he wouldn't hurt her, and yet . . .

"Clayton."

There was something fearful in Rooster's expression. Trudy hadn't seen it since their early courtship in high school. Rooster stepped forward, then backed up when Jordy glared at him.

"You'll keep your mouth shut, Trudy."

"I will not. What you're doing is wrong, and you know it. I won't let you treat me like a doormat, and I won't keep my mouth shut so you can get your daddy's job next election."

Grabbing her by both arms, Jordy shook her hard, jolting her neck. "No one will believe you, sugar."

Some people had told her that all her life. She knew now it wasn't true, though. Cornerstone was a small town, with its share of gossips and good ol' boys, but most of the people were good country folks who'd known her family for decades, sympathized with Trudy's financial plight and wouldn't easily dismiss her claims. "Oh, they'll believe me all right."

Jordy lifted the camera—Regret's expensive camera— from his neck, and with all the accuracy of tossing a foot ball when he'd been star of the Cornerstone Cougars, he aimed the molded plastic and delicate lenses at the open well twenty feet away. The camera thudded into the muddy round wall of the well and splashed far below. Horrified Trudy stared at him.

"Now it's your word against mine," he told her. "So go home and forget you ever saw us here."

"We'll see what your daddy says about it when he shows up here and finds you—"

He spun toward her, his fist clenched and ready. Without thinking, Trudy shut her eyes, bracing herself, expecting th blow to land on her cheek. Instead Jordy dragged her off the seat of the four-wheeler, holding her captive by her arm and the strands of loose curls that had fallen from under her helmet. He unbuckled her helmet strap and threw it on the ground, then pulled her up to his face by her neck. His large palm was hot and bruising against her jugular. She held her breath, unable to exhale. Then he shoved her backward, hard enough that she lost her balance and fell at the feet of the Tabor brothers. Trudy looked up at Wayne and Claude, expecting to find them pleased with her posture on the ground. Instead they exchanged uneasy glances.

His hands on his hips, Jordy appraised her from above. "By the time Daddy gets here, we'll be long gone. And everybody will think your accusations are a petty attempt at revenge against Rooster Reed, your old boyfriend." He pointed to Rooster. "Put her down the well. We'll haul her out at the end of the day." Jordy turned and started toward the sheriff's car.

"Down the well?" sputtered Rooster. On the day Regret's plane had crashed, Rooster and the Tabors had terrorized Trudy with the same threat—but Jordy's threat wasn't an empty one.

"No, Jordy!" Trudy's heart skipped a beat as she scrambled to her feet. "I'll go home. If Rooster will give me the keys to the four-wheeler."

Jordy shook his head. "You'll go home and call Daddy. Can't risk that."

"No, I won't. I promise."

"I can't trust you, Trudy." He nodded to the three men. "Put her down the well," he ordered.

"N-now?" questioned Wayne.

"Yeah, of course now. You got wax in your ears, boy?"

Trudy's throat closed, her jaw working uselessly. She could run, maybe even get away from the men. But all four were stronger, faster. They'd catch her. Maybe kill her trying to catch her.

"You're crazy, Jordy! You can't do that to me! I'm your wife's sister-in-law!"

Shrugging, Jordy walked away, not bothering to look over his shoulder at her. "You should've thought of that before you crossed me . . . bitch."

Trudy fired a pleading glance toward Rooster. He looked away quickly, ashamed. "Don't let him do it," she whispered.

"You boys better git back to work," Jordy shouted back as he climbed the fence and headed toward his car. "I don't want to have to rent that dredge for another day. And I'm sure Trudy doesn't want to spend the night in that well."

"Give me the keys," Trudy said calmly to Rooster when Jordy had driven off.

"I can't do that. You heard what Jordy said."

Her cheeks burned. The Tabor brothers reluctantly seized her by either arm and held her firmly while they waited for Rooster's instructions.

"Since when do you follow anybody's orders, Rooster?" Trudy demanded.

For the first time as far as she could remember, Rooster's eyes had the look of a beaten puppy's. "Me and Jordy go back a long way."

"So do we. Or have you forgotten?"

"I haven't forgotten. You're the one who ran out on me."

"You have a short memory, Rooster. You know that's not true."

"You could at least have given me a second chance."

"I don't feel that same way about you." She knew he was uncomfortable hearing her argument in front of Wayne and Claude, but she didn't let it stop her. "It can't be that way between us again. I'm sorry, Rooster. Too much has happened."

"I'm willin' to try."

Rooster's eyes met hers. They were suddenly deep with long-hidden emotion, but the only feelings she could summon were fear and pity.

"I'm not," she whispered.

Rooster's face turned to stone. "Put her down the well," he told the brothers.

Trudy jerked against them, trying to free herself. She stumbled as Claude shoved her toward the open hole. B fore she could fall to the ground, he lifted her by the elbow and dragged her along.

"No, Rooster! You can't do this! You can't! My grandfather will come after you with his gun! You know he will. He's an old man—he won't care if he kills you or not if you do anything to hurt me!"

"Shut up! Just shut up!" Rooster yelled back at her. "It's your word against ours, and there are four of us who'll say you're lyin'."

"Rooster!" She clutched at Wayne's shirtsleeve as he tried to pry her away from him. Her legs dangled over the well, and she heard the soft plunking of loose rocks as they struck the water below. "Rooster!" Falling halfway over the rim, she grabbed for Claude's ankles, pulling him to the ground with her, until he slid feet first into the outer rim of the well. Trudy plunged downward, into the damp darkness. Digging her bare feet into the muddy walls, she held on to Claude's rubber boots. The well wasn't deep, but it wasn't pleasant, either, and Trudy had no intention of being deposited there without a fight.

"Gently," she heard Rooster say from somewhere above. "I don't want her hurt."

"Damn it, man!" Claude shrieked back at him. "She's takin' me down with her!"

One of Trudy's feet slipped, and she went down a few more inches. She dug back into the wall with her bare toes, her legs open to the bottom of the well in a most unladylike position. She seized the man's pants leg, near his knee, as she tried to climb his body toward the light above.

"Let go of him," Rooster stoically ordered her from above.

She looked up at his silhouette against the sky. "You can't leave me down here! Rooster, why are you doing this? You're not a bad person!"

"Of course I'm a bad person, Trudy. That's why I know better than to go against Jordy."

She grasped Claude's belt from behind and hung on. "What's Jordy got on you, Rooster?"

"Does it matter? I'd rather have you mad at me than him."

"Mad at you? Rooster, I'll *kill* you if you leave me down here! How could you do this to me?" Her voice broke. "You loved me once." Still clinging to Claude with one hand, she raised the other to Rooster for him to help her out of the pit.

Rooster sighed and shook his head. He stepped back from the rim. "I'm sorry. You have to go down there. Won't be for long. Just till we finish up. I'll come back for you myself."

"Rooster—"

"Let go of Claude. That's your choice, Trudy. You go down the well of your own free will or I'll put you down there myself. Be a good girl and I'll come back for you. Otherwise, if Jordy has his way, your grandfather may never find you." He wasn't joking anymore. It wasn't even a threat. He was pleading with her.

She stared up at Rooster Reed, not knowing if she could trust him to keep his word just once. Dulcie, the most important thing in her life, was safe with Miss Naomi. For now. Miss Naomi would be worried by nightfall. She might even send Mr. Horace to look for her. But that was hours away.

She could scream, she knew, but who would hear her? Papa was in the field on his tractor, and Regret was at the house, faraway and asleep and angry with her. Maybe she could escape on her own, digging and clawing her way up the muddy pit. But she certainly couldn't do it if they hung around to watch her. Or if they hurt her forcing her down that damp hole.

"Okay," she agreed finally.

At Rooster's prompting, Wayne bent over the opening and helped her as she slowly descended into the darkness, using Claude's body as a ladder into hell. By the time she was holding on by Claude's boots, her toes skimmed the cold water in the well. She couldn't tell how deep it was or whether it was over her head, and the thought of having to stay afloat for the next five or six hours chilled her spine.

She took a deep breath and let go.

Chapter 15

Who's making all that noise? Regret wondered, then pulled the pillow over his head to muffle the banging that had interrupted his sleep for the past twenty minutes. The hammering began again, after a few seconds' respite. Regret groggily pulled himself upright and squinted at the clock on the bureau.

Four o'clock!

Against his will, he'd slept away the afternoon. Trudy had fed him sweet-potato pie, fried chicken and the freshest produce from her garden, then she'd changed his bandages and ordered him to rest. He didn't want to stay in the hospital any longer than necessary, and Trudy had agreed to let him come home—provided he took care of his injuries and allowed himself to heal properly.

Regret swung his legs over the edge of the mattress and shook himself awake. His arms were still sore and starting to itch, and the medicine Trudy had fed him to stave off infection had left him drowsy and unproductive. As soon as his antibiotics stopped making him woozy, he'd be on his way home. Away from Trudy and her ultimatums. Forever.

Hammering rattled the house again. No, it wasn't hammering after all. It was someone at the kitchen door, knocking relentlessly. Had Trudy locked herself out? If it wasn't Trudy, what could be so all-fired important? Maybe it was a very determined door-to-door salesman. Regret was tempted to drop his weary head back to the pillow and wait for him to go away. But he hadn't gone away yet, and he suspected that the person didn't intend to.

"Coming, coming," he mumbled as he stood and stretched. He pulled on one of Johnny's shirts over his newly taped ribs and then a pair of freshly laundered but wrinkled jeans. Barefoot, he limped out to the kitchen.

"Louisa," he said, pulling open the door as the frantic knocking stopped abruptly. "What can I do for you?"

"You can let me in," she said smoothly, trying unsuccessfully to disguise the contempt in her eyes.

She sashayed past him in her gray designer suit tailored to her slim figure. In one cool move, she flipped the blond hair off her collar, exposing the gold bangles at her jawline. By the time Regret closed the door, she'd already settled herself—partially reclining—on the living-room sofa. She pulled her gray-heeled feet up under her. Her skirt snaked up her thighs to a disconcertingly revealing station.

"Uh, Trudy's not here," he informed her, but from the not-so-subtle come-hither in her smile, Louisa already knew her sister-in-law wasn't home.

"Really? Where did she go?"

"I, uh, don't know. She was going to take Dulcie to the Meltons'. I'm not sure where she was going after that. She left hours ago."

Louisa patted the cushion beside her. "Why don't you come sit down?" she suggested.

Raking one hand through his tousled hair, Regret sat instead in the chair opposite the sofa. Louisa was up to something. Why else would she be paying a visit to Trudy during her office hours? "I don't know how long Trudy will be gone."

"That's okay. I really didn't come here to see Trudy."

"Mr. Dugan's working this afternoon. He's not expected home until suppertime."

"I didn't come to see him, either." Louisa rearranged herself on the sofa. This time she bent forward just enough that he could see the curves within the neckline of her pink blouse.

"Oh? Then why are you here?"

Her newly painted lips pouted. "You don't have to sound so...so inhospitable."

"Cut the crap, Slick. You know I have no use for you. Why are you here?"

"I came to see you."

"Why?"

"To talk."

"You took care of getting Trudy's insurance reinstated. We have nothing else to talk about."

With all the grace she could muster, Louisa glided from her seat on the sofa to the easy chair where Regret sat straight backed and tense. "We have plenty to talk about," she purred as she settled on his lap and encircled his neck with her arms.

"We have *nothing* to talk about," he repeated, breaking her loose embrace.

She chained her arms around his neck again. "We have Trudy to talk about. I want to know your intentions toward my sister-in-law."

"Really?" Regret smiled at her. "Didn't I tell you?"

She shook her head.

"Then it must not be any of your business."

She narrowed her eyes at him briefly, then laughed unconvincingly. "R.J., I think you should leave town and go back to wherever you came from."

"You think I care what you think?"

"No, I suppose you don't. But if you really care about Trudy and Dulcie—"

"I do."

"Then you'll do what's best for them and leave here before they get hurt."

"I told you last time we talked that I have no intention of hurting Trudy. Or Dulcie."

Louisa scraped one long fingernail down Regret's throat. "No intention, yes. They say the road to hell is paved with good intentions. And I think you'll end up unintentionally hurting them."

"And how do you propose that to happen? Do you expect Trudy to come home and find you rubbing up against me like a dog in heat while I salivate? It's not working, Slick. I won't hurt Trudy that way."

"Whatever." She pressed her mouth against his cheek, hard enough for the stain of her lipstick to remain. Irritated, he rubbed at it, not knowing if she'd left evidence of her visit on his skin. She had aroused him once before, but this time she left him cold.

"You don't want to be here, Slick. I can feel it. You don't like me any more than I like you."

She kissed his forehead, then his hairline as she lifted the curls off his face. "You don't have to like me. And I don't have to like you. But if that's what it takes to convince you that Trudy's not the woman for you, just give the word—" her tongue flicked across his brow "—and I'll do it."

He reacted without thinking, shoving her away too fast. Her eyes widened in surprise as she lost her balance and fell onto the floor at his feet. Scowling, she rubbed her bruised thigh.

"What's your story, Slick? You march in here so concerned about Trudy's feelings, yet so ready to seduce me into leaving. A few days ago, you told me how devoted you were to your husband. What am I supposed to believe? What kind of game are you playing?"

"It's not a game!"

"Then what is it?" he demanded, grabbing her wrists and pulling her onto her knees in front of him. She glared back in hatred. "Why the cold passion, Slick?"

"Don't you understand?" All the husky seduction of her voice had changed to a desperate squeal. "Trudy is going to get hurt because of you!"

"I told you, I am *not* going to hurt her!"

"Not you, stupid! Jordy! Rooster! Their friends!"

His grip relaxed. "Are you telling me that somebody's going to hurt Trudy because of my relationship with her?"

"Nobody gives a damn about your relationship with Trudy Sandlin! Marry her if it'll make her happy, but get her out of here if you do. You stay here, and you're gonna get somebody killed." Tears welled in Louisa's eyes.

"Louisa? What's wrong? Spill it. Is Trudy in trouble?"

"All I know is that she wouldn't be interfering with what Jordy and Rooster are working on if it weren't for you. Damn you, R.J.! You go running to Jim Clayton with a story about Jordy and then give the girl your camera to prove—"

"Whoa! What are you talking about? I didn't run to your father-in-law about Jordy. I saw Rooster Reed on Trudy's land. And those two friends of his—Wayne and Claude or something like that. I never saw Jordy. I never told the sheriff I did. You're telling me Jordy is the mastermind behind this scheme to dig up gold on the Dugan land, aren't you? Just like I thought!"

Louisa chewed her lips as she looked up at him. Under the tear trails on her cheeks, her face had turned pale.

"I know you and Jordy have talked to Trudy about buying her land. I know you're both interested in finding this gold that some people think was buried in the woods. But there's a difference in offering to buy land and in stealing it out from under her." He remembered what he'd overheard during the few long hours he'd spent in the Cornerstone county jail. "Jordy's been operating on the edge of the law all along, hasn't he? Having Rooster do his dirty work for him so he could keep his political hands clean."

"Does Trudy know?"

"She knows. She just doesn't want to believe it. For some reason—God knows why—Trudy cares about you, Slick." He noted with satisfaction that Louisa winced. "And until lately, she believed in your power-hungry, juvenile husband who can't seem to reconcile the glory days of his high-school popularity with the trivial chores of his present career as a uniformed flunky. She's lived for years with that illusion—that you and your husband are wonderful people who care about her and her little girl. But she doesn't believe it anymore."

He released her wrists and pushed, making her fall back onto the living-room floor. Timidly, not moving except to rub the bruises of his handprints on her skin, she watched him.

"You're wrong," she said quietly. "I do care about Trudy and her kid. I'm not the horrible person you paint me to be."

"Then prove it."

"I am proving it! I'm trying to get you out of here!"

Regret stood up. He'd had enough of Louisa and her paradoxes. "Go back to your office, Slick. Go back to your husband. Better yet, why don't you get professional counseling?"

Tilting her face upward to him, Louisa caught the legs of his jeans. Her eyes begged for understanding. "Please, R.J. You and Trudy will only get in his way."

"Whose way?"

"Jordy's. I don't know what he'll do if he doesn't find that gold. He's small-time. Strictly small-time. But I'm afraid of what he'll do if he gets mad. He's already spent just about everything we've got so he can get rich quick."

Regret stared down at the woman pleading on her knees. She no longer looked glamorous in her silk suit, with her expensive hairstyle. Sympathy tugged unexpectedly at his heart. He bent and lifted her by her elbows so that her eyes were inches from his.

"What are you doing here, Louisa? The truth, this time. How did you know Trudy wouldn't be home? Do you know where she is?"

"N-no. Not exactly."

Worry swept over him. "Is she okay?"

"I . . . don't know."

He shook her hard, whipping her neck back and forth. "I asked you a question, Louisa!"

"I don't know! I don't! Honest, R.J.! Jordy showed up at my office and told me I'd better get out here to the farm and make sure you were gone by the end of the day. No matter how I did it."

"Why? Why does he want me gone so bad?"

"He said . . . he said Trudy was going to ruin everything. He said he could handle Trudy if you weren't here to egg her on. We could always handle her before you showed up."

Regret almost laughed. Trudy could be one stubborn lady, and she didn't need the likes of him to incite her to action.

"I would've been out of here weeks ago if your husband and his friends hadn't vandalized my airplane."

"They couldn't risk your flying out of here. You would've seen the trees they were cutting in the woods. You would've seen the construction at Alligator Pond. You would've told Trudy. And the law."

Heated blood rose in his cheeks. "They damned near destroyed my bird to keep me from seeing that they were building a bridge to bring in a dredge?"

"Trudy wasn't to know. They were going to go in and find the gold and that would be the end of it. They've been working night and day to find the gold before Trudy loses the farm. They came out here under the pretense of doing a little bird hunting, but they were really looking for gold all along. Once the farm changes owners, it won't be so easy to come on the land."

"That's why you and Jordy wanted to buy the farm?"

Louisa nodded. "It would've been easier that way, but she wouldn't sell it to us."

"And that's why everyone has been pushing her to reconcile with Rooster Reed? So he could marry her and have access to the land."

"One reason. He does want her back."

An image flashed through his mind. Her dark curtain of hair falling on his cheek while she'd made love to him. He missed her.

"I want her back, too. But I'm not willing to use her like the rest of you."

"You love her?" Louisa sat down uncomfortably on the sofa and chipped at the polish on her nails.

"I—" He sighed and plopped down in the easy chair. "I've never loved anybody."

"Well, I love Jordy. He's not an easy man to make happy, but I try. I'd do anything for him." She glanced up meaningfully. *"Anything."*

"Even betray your sister-in-law?"

Frowning, she started to say something, then thought better of it. "I'm trying to help Trudy. And I'm trying to keep Jordy happy. What's so wrong with that?"

He laughed before he could stop himself. "Other than your methods?" Sobering, he added, "What if Trudy's grandfather is right? What if the gold is just story? Jordy won't find any gold. What then?"

"There's gold on the Dugan property. It's not a myth."

"What makes you so sure?"

"Jordy's great-grandfather was one of the men who lynched that banker."

Regret had heard the story from Lester Dugan at least twenty times already. "The man died without telling where he'd hidden the gold."

"Doesn't matter," Louisa contended. "He had the gold when he reached the Dugan woods. He didn't have it when he died. Where else could he have hidden it?"

"Too many people are getting hurt because of this treasure hunt. If any of you would simply ask Trudy to let you look for the gold, she'd probably let you and wouldn't care if you found it or not. Instead you're talking about Trudy getting hurt if she doesn't let Jordy and Rooster walk all over her. And you're willing to prostitute yourself to keep peace in your marriage. That's got to be one miserable marriage, Slick. If he makes you that unhappy why don't you leave *him*? Surely you're not afraid of a small-town scandal."

She shrugged. "I like being married to Jordy. I always wanted to be married to him. Ever since he was captain of the football team and I was a cheerleader. I can't imagine not being married to him. It's not that bad really. And...and I love him."

"So you'll do anything for him. No matter who gets hurt. Louisa, is it really worth all this?"

"Almost a hundred thousand dollars? Yeah, Jordy thinks it's worth it. In a small town like this, we'd be set for life with that kind of money. Plus my salary, of course."

Regret leaned forward in his chair. "According to Mr. Dugan, people around here have been talking about that gold for years. Looking for it for almost as long. Why the sudden resurgence of interest?"

Louisa bit into one of her long fingernails, tearing it at the quick. "It's my fault."

For a change, Louisa Clayton was taking responsibility for something. Maybe he'd gotten through to her.

"Back in February, I was at an insurance agents' convention. One of the agents was into numismatics. You know, coin collecting. He gave a presentation on making sure our clients with coin collections were properly insured. He even showed his own collection as part of his speech. That got me to thinking about the gold buried here on Trudy's land, so I talked to this agent for about an hour after his speech and he showed me what kinds of coins the banker may have had on him when he got himself lynched."

Trying to compose herself, Louisa dried her tears with a tissue. She wadded the tissue in her palm and leaned back against the sofa.

Regret regarded her suspiciously. "Don't even bother to lie to me and tell me you were planning to insure Trudy's coin collection. We both know what happened when you took it on yourself to insure her four-wheeler."

"I...was going to mention it to her. But I told Jordy first. The guy at the convention said the coins could be worth a few thousand or maybe as much as a hundred thousand, depending on what kind of coins they were. There was a new type of coin that came out that year—1907. It was known as a Walking Liberty because that's what the woman on the coin was doing. It's a very famous coin designed by a guy named Saint Gaudens. If that banker was carrying freshly minted coins, they would've been Saint Gaudens Walking Liberties. Probably twenty-dollar gold pieces."

"And those are worth a lot more?"

"About five thousand dollars a coin if they're in good condition."

Regret whistled. That would be enough to save Trudy's farm without touching the cold inheritance he'd been given. Without her worrying about how to pay back her debt to him. "I can see why your husband found the idea so appealing. I still think it's downright dirty of him to try to take it out from under Trudy—if it's really buried on Trudy's land, that is."

"Oh, it is. They've found it."

Regret frowned at the woman, now dry eyed and calm. "Are you positive?"

"Well, they think they've found it. At Alligator Pond. It's just a matter of hours till they bring it up."

"The dredge. When were they going to start?"

"They've been dredging since early morning. That's what Jordy told me when he came by my office. Everything was going great till Trudy showed up with your camera."

"She *what?*" He glanced at the table where he'd left his camera. Gone! His knees weakened at the thought of Trudy in danger. What if there were more dogs? Bolting to his feet, he grabbed Louisa's collar and pulled her to her feet. "Slick, where's Trudy?"

She blushed and pulled away. "I told you. I don't know. Jordy said he'd keep her out of the way until they found the gold and that I was to get rid of you any way I could. He doesn't want Trudy running to Sheriff Clayton until it's all over with. It's real easy to intimidate Trudy, and if you're gone, it'll be even easier."

"If he hurts her, I'll..." Regret didn't finish the sentence. He let the threat hang in the air for Louisa's benefit. He ran to the back door. The four-wheeler was gone.

Regret tore barefoot into the backyard. The screen door slammed behind him, with Louisa catching it as it bounced open again. She was several feet behind him, running puffing after him and managing to keep up in her high-heeled pumps.

"Where are you going?" she called, catching up with him at the rusty gate that opened to the grassy pasture between the farmhouse and the Dugan woods.

Regret didn't answer. Louisa grasped his elbow as she stared out over the fields. "Wait! I'll come with you!"

"Call your father-in-law," Regret commanded, jerking open the gate.

"But—"

He turned back to glare at her once before he was out of earshot. "Now, damn you!"

Chapter 16

*W*here was she?

Gasping for breath, he reached the edge of the woods. Jordy said he'd keep her out of the way until they found the gold. But out of the way *where?* Jordy wouldn't really kill her, would he?

Sickness rose in his throat. *What if they've actually killed Trudy over that damned gold or left her for dead somewhere in the woods?*

His hands clenched into fists. Who would take care of his little angel now? And Trudy—his jaw ached with sudden tightness—what if she'd died before he could tell her how desperately he wanted to stay with her? Before he could tell her that if he could ever love a woman, then it would be her. Before he could tell her that if he ever put down roots anywhere, it would be on Dugan land.

If they've hurt a hair on her head, he would kill them, he silently swore.

Chest empty and aching, he trudged toward the woods. He wanted to run, to find Trudy as fast as he could, but he couldn't run very fast or very far. He was too tired, too woozy from the medicine.

"Trudy!" he called when he reached the woods' edge. His voice came out hoarse and desperate.

"R.J.?"

Trudy's voice—her living, breathing voice—echoed thinly back at him.

"Thank you, God," he murmured. Then, more loudly, he called out, "Trudy, where are you?"

"I'm down here."

He glanced around the grassy incline where they'd put up bluebird houses the day he'd fended off the two dogs. Only the ancient oaks and pines stood before him. His gaze swept over the pond at the bottom of the hill. No sign of Trudy. Then he saw the four-wheeler near the fence. And Trudy's helmet.

"Down here," Trudy repeated in the seemingly long silence. "In the well."

"Trudy!" He raced toward the open pit. "Trudy, are you okay?"

He skidded on his knees at the rim of the well and peered down into the dimness. Standing knee-deep in water, she peered up at him with grateful eyes. She was standing on something—something large enough to keep her out of the deeper water—and she kept shifting her weight from foot to foot to keep from losing her balance. Her dress, wet and muddy, clung to her body. She shivered in the damp, earthy heat of the well. A splattering of muck dotted her cheeks, forming droplets in her hair.

"Are you okay?" he whispered.

"I will be as soon as you get me out of here," she said, the quiver in her voice betraying her brave facade. Her tone might have been angry earlier. Now it was distressed.

"Get me out of here, R.J. I—" Her voice cracked. "I feel like I'm in a grave."

Her words wrenched at his heart. Trudy Sandlin was probably the strongest human being he knew. She'd faced the death of her husband, the birth of a premature child, a brush with cancer, the death of her mother, bankruptcy. Too, too much for a woman so young and beautiful! Yet, for all her strength, she'd reached her breaking point.

She was beyond his reach. He'd need rope or a chain. And he had neither.

"I'll have to go back to the house and—"

"Don't leave me, R.J."

"I've got to, Trudy. I can't reach you." He bent over the dark hole as far as he dared and stretched his dog-bitten right arm down to her to prove he couldn't span the distance. "Damn that Jordy!"

"Jordy? How did you know he was here? Did you see him?"

"Louisa told me."

"Louisa?" Trudy stared up at him, disbelief in her eyes. "Louisa would never say a bad thing about Jordy. She—"

"She told me everything. Trudy, he intends to get that gold, and it doesn't matter who gets hurt. Louisa's been in on it, too."

He heard the sigh that rose from the well.

"I didn't want to believe you," Trudy said.

"I know."

"Get me out of here, R.J."

Summoning hope, he glanced around for anything that might help him get to her. "I'll move the four-wheeler over here. It should fit over the well without falling in. I could hold on to the underside and—"

"That won't work. You can't move it without cranking it, and Rooster took the keys."

"Oh. I told Louisa to call Sheriff Clayton. He'll be here soon. He can help get you out."

"No. Please, R.J. We can't wait. I don't trust her to make the call. It'll be dark in a few hours, and Jordy and Rooster will be back. There's no telling what they'll do if they find you here. And if Jim Clayton's going to catch them on my property, he'll have to do it before then."

Her thirst for justice was coming back, overpowering her fear of the dark well. As he looked down into the dimness, his eyes adjusted to the fading light in the hole. He could see where she'd dug footholds into the dirt wall of the well, halfway up, and where her bare feet had slipped more than once in a futile attempt at escape. She must've tried again and again to climb out of that god-forsaken pit where her grandfather's mule had fallen and died in the 1930s.

"R.J., please. You have to get me out."

If only his arms were stronger, unscarred. Or his ribs completely healed. How could he fail her now!

"Hold on," he called. "I'm coming down after you."

"What? No! We could both be trapped down here when they come back."

"We won't both be trapped down there," he argued. "You can stand on my shoulders and climb out."

Trudy shook her head. "It won't work. The drop's too far. We'll both be trapped."

"But—"

"No! I'd rather stay here than risk both of us being trapped here when Rooster and Jordy come back. Go! Just go and get help."

"I won't leave you, Trudy Sandlin. I will never leave you. Not here. Not ever." He had to find a way to get her out.

He glanced back at the four-wheeler. As the late-afternoon sun's rays caught a glimmer of cobalt blue in the sky, a bluebird fluttered to the rusty fence behind the ATV. The idea flitted across his photographer's brain that a photo of the bluebird on the half-fallen fence would sell easily to any number of magazines. Then the idea solidified.

"I'll be right back," he whispered to Trudy, and ran toward the fence before she could protest.

The fence between the woods and the grassy pasture had fallen almost to the ground in several places where the fence posts had been partially burned or had rotted away even with the ground. In a few places the posts had been severed completely and the rusty fence lay on the ground between the sturdier posts.

With a running start, Regret slammed both feet against the first fence post that separated the woods from the pasture—the cornerstone—and both he and charred post fell with a thud to the hard ground. Picking himself up, he attacked the second post twice before it, too, toppled. The next two posts were already leaning on the ground.

"R.J.?" Trudy's voice echoed from the well.

Did she think he'd abandoned her?

"I'm still here." He tugged unsuccessfully at the first fallen post, the largest of the four. "Hang in there, Trudy. I'm coming." He hoisted the log, his chest screaming under the strain of its weight and his ribs and arms protesting.

By the time he alternately rolled and carried the post across the incline to the well, the sun was fast sinking on the horizon. Perspiration stained the back of his shirt and dripped from his brow. He hadn't lifted weights since before he'd crash-landed in Trudy's cow pasture. Now his body, damaged temporarily by the crash and the Tabor brothers' dogs, rebelled against what should have been a simple task.

"Stand back against the wall," he instructed Trudy as he slowly lowered the post down the well, hanging on to the rusty wire to guide the log as it went down. Trudy grabbed the log when it was within her reach and steered it downward until it splashed beneath her. Smiling, she looked up at Regret and the wire ladder he'd lowered to her and started to climb up toward him.

"R.J.!" She wrapped her arms around him as he sat cross-legged and weak-kneed on the ground beside the well. "I don't want you to stop flying. I was just scared. I couldn't stand it if something happened to you."

"I know, Trudy. It's going to be okay."

She was as dirty as a street urchin, he thought happily, but still the most beautiful woman he'd ever known.

He returned her hug, kissing her on the cheek, the side of her neck, her hair. He lost himself in the sweetness of her caress.

Sobering, Regret stood sluggishly. His back ached from pulling at the fence. Sheriff Clayton should have been there by now, he thought, suddenly realizing that Louisa probably hadn't followed his instructions to call for help. Had he really expected her to? Was the smidgen of ethics she still had stronger than her fear and love of her husband? Even if she had called Sheriff Jim Clayton, Regret couldn't realistically expect Jim Clayton to arrest his own son. The sheriff had been faced with Jordy's and Rooster's bullying tactics before and had never done anything about it. Jordy had thrown Regret in jail with little or no cause, invoking

Rooster to pummel the prisoner at his convenience. Jim Clayton had issued a simple reprimand and nothing more, warning the boys to stop playing childish games with Jordy's authority as a deputy. Then, when Trudy had asked Jim Clayton for help in getting Rooster and the Tabors off her land, the sheriff had brushed her off, exhorting her as he would a first grader to resolve her problems with her playmates. No, Regret decided, Sheriff Clayton couldn't be counted on for help.

"Come on, Trudy," Regret urged, loosely embracing her. "Let's get you home where you'll be safe."

"Too late," she whispered, looking past Regret.

He whirled on one foot, expecting to find Jordy Clayton behind him. Regret was ready to deliver a lethal punch if necessary. Instead he saw the flashing lights of a sheriff's car on the other side of the property-line fence.

Louisa came through after all, he thought, a pleased smile twitching at the corners of his mouth. He started for the sheriff's car.

"R.J., where are you going?"

Glancing over his shoulder, he motioned for his frowning companion to join him. "Hurry up, Trudy. We're going to tell Jim Clayton—" He stopped in midstride. The driver of the car, a man in a tan uniform, unfolded his tall frame from behind the steering wheel and surveyed the man and woman who stood entranced. The man resembled Jim Clayton but was too tall, too young, to be the sheriff.

"Jordy," Regret heard Trudy behind him growl with distrust.

The lone passenger, who wasn't wearing a deputy's uniform, exited the car next. Regret could tell by the man's loping gait that he was Rooster Reed. As the two men climbed over the perimeter fence, Regret took a step backward and eased one arm around Trudy. His back straightening to his full height, Regret tried to look his most menacing, in spite of his bandaged arms and ribs.

Jordy squared his jaw as he and Rooster swaggered through the tall grass. Hands on his belt, fingers fondling his revolver, Jordy hesitated to spit tobacco juice at one of the old oaks. Rooster lingered behind, seemingly less eager for a confrontation. He was carrying Trudy's rifle. Protectively Regret stepped in front of her to shield her from Jordy's wrath.

"Git up here, Reed." Jordy addressed Rooster, even though his steely eyes were focused on Regret. Without the mirrored sunglasses, Jordy had only his uniform and his revolver to hide behind, and Regret could read the bitterness of bygone glory days in the deputy's eyes. Regret knew the type. Without the popularity of his youth, Jordy was a bully at heart but a coward when it came to delegating the deed.

"Reed!"

Rooster startled at the harsh ring of his name. He nearly leaped to Jordy's side. "Right here," he choked out.

Jordy never broke his gaze from Regret's, and neither of them surrendered to the urge to blink. "Reed, I thought I told you to put that little whore down the well for safekeepin'."

Whore! Regret flexed his fists. *How dared that mongrel call Trudy that!*

"I did put her down the well," Rooster answered nervously. Then he pointed to the ladder of fence posts and wire descending into the murky depths of the hole where he'd discharged Trudy hours earlier. "That fly-boy must've gotten her out."

Jordy squinted at Regret. "My wife tells me you been botherin' her. Comin' on to her. I oughta kill you for that."

Mentally Regret calculated Jordy's size and the damage the deputy could inflict on a slightly smaller man with bandaged ribs and arms. The hint of cowardice in the larger man's eyes told him that Jordy would use his size and position to intimidate. But Jordy himself would never lay a hand on Regret.

"I came on to her? She told you that?"

Regret wanted to glance at Trudy. He wanted to see her reaction to Jordy's claims, yet he wouldn't be the first to break the death grip of their locked gazes. From Trudy's stoic silence, he guessed that Jordy hadn't elicited the response he'd wanted. Jordy and Louisa had lost their power over Trudy, and neither of them could turn her against him. Not now. Not ever.

"She didn't have to tell you anything because you sent her to the farm to seduce me." Trudy gasped behind him, and Regret realized that in spite of what she'd learned about Jordy, the extent of his actions could still surprise her. "You're the one who told her to come on to me if that's what it took to get me away from Trudy."

Jordy took one threatening step forward, bearing down on Regret, leaning into his face. "Are you callin' my wife a—"

"No, but I'm calling you a pimp."

Jordy turned dark red. Out of the corner of Regret's eye, Rooster fidgeted and fixed a stare at the ground.

"What did you say, boy?"

"Your wife loves you. Although why, I can't begin to guess. Do you think so little of Louisa that you'd resort to such low-life tactics to get rid of me?"

Jordy's grip tensed around the revolver. "I *will* git rid of you," he snarled. "But first, you're gonna tell me what you've done with the gold."

"Gold? What gold?" His voice lilted an octave higher. All his life, Regret had had a tendency to push people to the edge, and in spite of the growing undertone of danger, he couldn't resist giving Jordy a good verbal shove.

"I'll tell you what gold." Jordy grabbed him by the collar and dragged him up on his toes. "We've been dredgin' all day. We haven't turned up one danged piece!"

Trudy edged in between them. With the gentle blue eyes of a peacemaker, she smiled up at the deputy. "Jordy, I told you, it's only a story. There is no gold."

"Shut up," Jordy barked at her despite an uneasy glare from Rooster. "I'll bet your lover boy here stole it right out from under you, you dumb little country hick. I know for a fact there was gold in that pond. Our metal detectors went crazy down there."

"Well, of course they did," she said quietly. "That's where Papa dumped a bunch of old fence wire."

Jordy's fist unclenched, and he dropped Regret flat on his feet with a rush of breath. He turned to Trudy then, standing over her with definable resentment. His entire body tensed under the effect of the new knowledge. "Then where is it?"

Trudy shrugged. "How would I know? I told you, it's just a story."

"It's okay, man," Rooster offered uneasily. "It just means we've been looking in the wrong place."

Jordy glanced over his shoulder. "Now's a hell of a time to decide you've been looking in the wrong place! I spent all Weezer's savings for you to look in the wrong place!"

"Maybe—I don't know, Clayton—maybe Trudy's right. Maybe it is just a story."

"She's not right, damn it! That gold is here—somewhere—and we're gonna find it!"

"Clayton, if Buck Witherspoon forecloses before—"

"Shut up!" Jordy turned toward Rooster and shook his fist. "Did I ask your opinion on the subject, Reed? Huh? Did I ask you to open your mouth?"

"N-no."

"Then shut up! When I want your opinion, I'll beat it out of you." Jordy turned back to Trudy. "You," he said, stabbing his index finger into the bare skin of Trudy's throat, "git back to the house."

Trudy didn't question his change of heart. She slipped her hand into Regret's, entwining her fingers with his, and started to lead him toward the house.

"Not you, fly-boy." Jordy shoved Trudy hard, breaking the bond of their clasped hands.

Trudy stepped between them. "No, Jordy. He goes with me."

Jordy shoved her out of the way before she could finish her sentence. "Cain't you do like you're told for once? Now git on back to the house."

"It's okay." Regret nodded to Trudy, trying to reassure her. "Go on back. You'll be safe there."

"No, R.J. Either you come back with me or I'll stay here with you." She shifted on her bare feet. If this was a last-ditch effort to convince Jordy to let him go, it wasn't working.

"Suit yourself," Jordy growled at her, still glowering at Regret. "We don't have many more days to find that gold. And I can't afford any more interruptions. Rooster?"

The man behind him lifted his chin, dazed. "Yeah?"

"Git rid of 'im."

Rooster frowned. "What?"

"Git rid of 'im."

Regret braced himself as Rooster laid the rifle on the grass and cracked his knuckles. "You want me to beat 'im up, Clayton?"

Impatiently Jordy picked up the rifle and thrust it back into Rooster's hands. "No, you idiot! I want you to git rid of him!"

"You mean, shoot 'im?"

"If that's what it takes, do it! Throw 'im down the well when you're done and fill it in. Nobody will ever find him there."

Regret didn't move. He barely heard Trudy gasp, "You can't, Jordy! Are you crazy?"

Rooster handled the rifle with sweaty palms. He lifted it to his shoulder and then lowered it. "But what about Trudy? You can't expect me to shoot Trudy."

"Trudy will be a good girl and not say a word. Won't you, Trudy?" Then Jordy grinned, his cheeks rising into his eyes. "We all know that if something were to happen to Trudy, Weezer and me would be the best choice to raise our little niece."

A chill settled down Regret's back. He couldn't let that happen. He couldn't let Dulcie grow up calling Jordy Clayton "Daddy."

"Go back to the house, Trudy," Regret ordered through clenched jaws.

"I'm not leaving you."

Jordy slapped Rooster on the back. "Git rid of 'im, Reed. I'll be back in a few hours."

Regret watched Jordy's back as the deputy started back toward the car. "What's the matter, Jordy?" he taunted. "You have to get someone else to do your dirty work? Can't do it yourself? Or are you making sure Rooster takes the fall so you can run for sheriff with clean hands?"

Jordy stopped and turned slowly. He surveyed Regret first, then his gaze moved to Trudy. One corner of his mouth curled upward. "Git rid of 'im, Reed."

Rooster swallowed hard, his Adam's apple bobbing up and down. "In front of Trudy?"

"That's up to her," Jordy said, without looking back. He stalked toward the boundary fence. "She can look the other way if she wants to."

Rooster's complexion, normally ruddy from the abuse of alcohol for so long, drained to an ashen white. He lifted the rifle to his shoulder, the barrel aimed point-blank at Regret's heart.

Chapter 17

The pilot didn't flinch.

"Stop, Rooster! You can't!" Hot tears scalded Trudy's cheeks. "You can't do this, Rooster! You can't shoot a man in cold blood!"

"Shut up, Trudy," Rooster said under his breath. The rifle trembled in his grip.

"What are you waitin' for?" Jordy called from where he straddled the fence.

"Yeah," Regret chimed in, "what are you waiting for?"

Oh, God, R.J.! Trudy thought. *What are you doing? Don't you know Rooster's capable of anything? Especially of killing his ex-girlfriend's lover!*

Beads of sweat glistened on Rooster's broad forehead. As the sweat ran into his eyes, he blinked out the saltiness and tried harder to focus on Regret.

"Well?" Regret urged. "Aren't you going to carry out your boss's orders?"

"He ain't my boss."

"Looks like it from here, Rooster. Jordy says 'frog,' and you jump. He says 'Jump,' and you say 'How high, boss?'"

"I do not."

A flash of color to her far right caught Trudy's eye. Across the pasture, beyond Johnson's Creek, through the gate behind the farmhouse, she saw another sheriff's car racing toward them, leaving Papa's tractor moving tortoiselike in its dust.

Sheriff Clayton!

Jordy swung his leg over the fence. He was now completely off her property. "Reed!" he yelled.

Rooster didn't respond. His arm muscles quivered with tension.

Regret smiled dangerously at the man. Something sparked in his eyes. "You think you can win Trudy's heart by getting rid of me?"

"It's a start."

"Look at her, Rooster. Look at her."

Rooster glanced sideways at Trudy and then back to Regret. He bit his bottom lip. He glanced again at Trudy, this time for a second longer. Then he frowned at Regret.

"She's beautiful, isn't she, Rooster? Even after everything you've done to her, she's still beautiful. And you know what else, Rooster? You can never have her. And you know it."

"Shut up, fly-boy."

"Do you really think you can win her heart by killing me? Or don't you think you'd lock yourself out of her heart forever?"

The siren wailed as Sheriff Clayton's car reached the creek and slowed to cross the dry bed.

"I told you to shut up." Rooster's fingers had turned ivory white where they clamped down on the rifle. The red button glinted on the weapon. The safety was off, and the .22-gauge was ready to fire.

Rooster peered over the rifle at Trudy with the expression of one of his trapped animals. "Trudy, I—"

"Reed!" Jordy nearly screamed over the approaching siren. Standing beside his car, Jordy could see his father's vehicle as it crawled up the closer bank of Johnson's Creek. "What are you waitin' for, Reed? Do it, you coward!"

Trudy held her breath. How could she have been so wrong? Although no one but a one-horse lawyer in Cornerstone knew, she had even listed Jordy and Louisa in her will as Dulcie's guardians. She'd always thought—until a few days ago—that Louisa could provide a stable, loving environment for the child. Louisa had always wanted a baby, and on her commissions, she and Jordy could certainly afford a family. Papa, at his age, wasn't able to run after a two-year-old. Funny, but if anything should happen to Trudy, the Dugan land would go to Dulcie, under the guardianship of the man who was willing to kill to get to buried treasure on the Dugan land. Jordy had been right about Louisa and him being a logical choice for Dulcie's guardians, but he hadn't known what was in her will. And if he had, would he have left her in the well to die—to get her land through Dulcie?

As much as she hated to admit it, she was a poor judge of character. Always had been. She didn't have Papa's gift for reading people. She simply trusted. She'd misjudged Louisa and Jordy. She'd misjudged Rooster. And if she had been a fair judge of character, she never would have brought an injured stranger into her home.

Lowering the rifle, Rooster tilted his head toward Trudy in an almost affectionate way. "I don't want you to hate me, Trudy. Not any more than you already do."

"Reed!" bellowed Jordy. "What are you waitin' for? Frost?"

"I can't, man." Rooster's arms relaxed, and he cradled the rifle in his loose arms.

"What do you mean, you can't? Shoot 'im!"

"I mean, I can't. I won't. I won't shoot a man for you, Clayton."

"You want me to run you in, Rooster? 'Cause you know I got enough on you to have your mail forwarded to the Cornerstone county jail for the next six months if I had a mind to do it."

Jim Clayton's car was close enough for Trudy to see two people in the front seat, a man in a white hat and a woman. Papa's tractor was barely halfway between the house and Johnson's Creek.

Rooster turned his back on Regret and glared across the field at Jordy. "I'd git a hell of a lot longer than six months for killin' a man!"

"Not if you do it right and git rid of 'im!"

"No way, Clayton. I'm not your flunky."

"Flunky!" Jordy yelled back. "You and me were partners, Reed. We were gonna split the gold fifty-fifty. Well, I'll be plenty happy to take your share, too, if you're gonna forfeit our partnership because you've still got it bad for your high-school sweetheart." He pointed to the sheriff's car bumping across the pasture toward the Dugan woods. "I'll jes' let you explain to Daddy why you're holdin' a gun on these fine folks."

Jordy opened the car door and had one foot inside, when Rooster raised the rifle and fired a shot into the front tire. "I'm not goin' to be the only one doin' the explainin'," Rooster grumbled, firing a second shot into a back tire.

Trudy extended one hand toward Regret. He took it, squeezed it, then slipped his arm around Trudy. They were a family, the two of them plus Dulcie. Trudy leaned against his shoulder, curling her arm through his in a claiming gesture.

Jim Clayton jumped out of the car before it rolled to a stop. Louisa, in a stylish gray suit, took her time, stepping gracefully out of the passenger's seat and shielding herself behind the open car door.

"Drop the rifle, Rooster!" the sheriff ordered as the siren died. Rooster obeyed, raising his hands in surrender without having to be told. Then the sheriff turned to his son. "Jordy, git out of that car." A minute of silence passed while Jordy sat pouting behind the steering wheel. "Now, boy!"

Slowly Jordy withdrew from the car. He put his elbows on the roof and waited.

"Git over here, Jordy!" his father yelled, all patience gone.

"Daddy, you'll never believe what I caught Rooster—"

"Shut your mouth, son, before you make a bigger fool of yourself than you already have."

"But, Daddy—"

"Come here, boy."

"But, Daddy—"

"Son, it would kill your mama if I had to shoot you. Now, git over here."

"Yes, Daddy."

Jordy crawled over the fence and sauntered up to his father, giving Louisa a blistering glare. "Okay, Daddy," he said when he reached Jim Clayton. "What do you want?"

The man held out his hand. "Your revolver."

"Why?"

"Louisa's been tellin' me some interesting stories about you and your friends and what you've been doin' on Trudy's land."

Jordy glared even more intensely at Louisa. "I don't know what Weezer's been sayin', but rest assured, Daddy, it ain't nothin' but lies. I just found out the woman came out to the farm today to bed her own sister-in-law's boyfriend. You can't depend on a word she says."

He might as well have struck Louisa with both fists. She paled and leaned heavily against the car. "I love you, Jordy, but I can't let you hurt Trudy. Not anymore."

"Son? Give me your revolver."

Jordy tore his gaze of daggers away from Louisa and squinted at his father. "But I need it, Daddy. I'm a deputy. I've got to—"

"Not anymore you're not."

Jordy stamped his foot like a little boy. "You can't do that, Daddy!"

"It's within my authority to fire a deputy."

"But I'm your only son—"

"And my only disappointment. Your revolver, boy."

Reluctantly Jordy pried the revolver off his hip and slapped it into his father's open palm. "I hope you're happy," he growled at Louisa. "Now we'll never find that gold."

"It's gone too far, Jordy," she said, her eyes watery. "I won't steal from Trudy."

"Nothin' to steal no how," Jim Clayton declared. "Everybody knows that gold is just a story. If people want to believe in buried treasure, that's fine, but you can't go diggin' up somebody else's land whenever you want to. You have to respect other people's property."

"Aw, Daddy. Come on. Give me my gun back. How's this gonna look when I run for sheriff next year? How am I gonna follow in your footsteps when you retire if you fire me now?"

Jim Clayton merely shook his head.

"Daddy?"

"Son, I've been groomin' you to be sheriff for several years now. But I see by what's happened here today that you're not ready for it. Probably never will be. I've decided not to resign from my post. One Clayton in law enforcement is enough for this county."

Watching his dreams evaporate, Jordy stared at his father. "But, Daddy—"

"Git in the car, son."

Jordy obediently stumbled to Louisa's open door.

"Not in the front seat, son. Git in the back. I'm taking you down to the station. You, too, Rooster."

Rooster lowered his hands and turned back to Trudy. With two fingers, he reached into his shirt pocket and extracted the four-wheeler key ring. He tossed it on the ground at her feet and winked at her. "I don't want you to hate me, Trudy." He almost smiled. The ghost of the boy she'd loved in high school still haunted his older, rounder face.

"I don't hate you." She meant it. If she felt anything for him at all, it was pity. He walked toward the sheriff's car.

Louisa stared back at her, and their eyes met briefly. Trudy had never before seen the vulnerability in the violet eyes. In fact, she realized, she'd never seen past the silk suits and expensive hairstyles and glamorous earrings. Whether or not Louisa stood by Jordy, she would need a friend, a friend like Trudy.

"Trudy?" Sheriff Clayton laid an apologetic hand on her shoulder, then nodded to Regret. "R.J.? I'm gonna need you two to come down to the station so we can get the boys properly charged." He hesitated, seemingly uncertain how to phrase his next sentence. "You can wait until after...after you've had a chance to git cleaned up."

Trudy smiled back at him. She knew she must look a mess in her muddy dress and dirty hair. "Thanks, Sheriff. I could really use a hot bath right now."

The sheriff nodded his acknowledgment to Papa as the old man descended from the tractor. The sheriff steadied him, stopping to explain in hushed tones what had happened. With a frown on his dusty forehead, Papa watched Jim Clayton drive away with Jordy, Louisa and Rooster. Jordy's car continued to flash from where it remained on the other side of the fence, the driver's door still open.

"Trudy," wailed Lester Dugan, hobbling toward her. "Are you all right, girl?"

"I am now, Papa."

He hadn't heard her. "'Cause if those boys touched you, I swear I'll git my gun and put 'em in the ground." Papa's pale eyes watered. He feebly pulled Trudy to him in an awkward embrace. "Dulcie. Where's my great-grandbaby?"

"She's with Miss Naomi."

"Did they hurt you, girl?"

"I'm fine, Papa," she assured him again, knowing he was concerned about her muddy dress and the dirt on her face. She returned his hug, not letting him go when he pulled away. "And I've got R.J. to thank for that. He got me out of the well. And I think he would've taken a bullet for me if it had come down to it."

Skeptical, Papa squinted at Regret. "You did that for my grandbaby?"

Regret backed away sheepishly. "I'd do just about anything for Trudy." He hesitated, glancing at her. "For a chance to stay with her, I'd even give up flying."

Papa broke free of Trudy's affectionate embrace and dug his hands into his khaki pants. "I saw the commotion from the field. I knew something was wrong when I saw all them police lights. I thought...I thought you might've gotten hurt. I don't know...." His voice trailed off as he fought to keep it even. "I don't know what I would've done if sumpin' had happened to you."

"Shh, Papa." Trudy put her arms around him, mothering the old man the way she mothered everybody. She suddenly felt tall against his frame, felt strong and young. "Everything's okay, Papa. Jordy and Rooster won't be coming back to look for the gold."

"Gold!" he sputtered, turning away to curse under his breath. "Damn fool boys! How many times do I have to tell all you young'uns that there ain't no gold on this land? Damn bank's gonna take it away from us soon enough anyway. Then I guess they can come out here and dig up every gopher hole they can find just like that Clayton boy did. Well, they ain't gonna find nary a thang."

"Uh, Papa?" Trudy glanced around to make sure the three of them were alone. "I think there might be some truth to that old story after all."

"Huh?" Both the old man and Regret shared the same dumbfounded look.

"There's a box in the well. A little trunk or something. I was standing on it to stay as far out of the water as I could."

Papa ambled over to the hole and peered into it. "Lots of stuff's fallen down there over the years. But if there's a trunk, then somebody put it there on purpose."

"You stay there, Mr. Lester." Regret patted the old man on the back. "I'll take care of it."

The sun was little more than a deep red ball in the western sky when Regret ascended from the murky depths of the well with his broken camera and a muddy, rusty box in his wet-sleeved arms. The little trunk was obviously heavy by the way he carried it, and Trudy fretted over whether he might reopen his old wounds hauling it out. He'd insisted Trudy not go down into the well again. That had left the task to either a trembling old man or an injured pilot.

Papa made himself useful by retrieving a ball-ping hammer from the toolbox on his tractor. While Regret dumped the camera and the box onto the grass beside the well, Papa bent over the box and swiped at the hinges and latch with the hammer. Sheaths of mud and rust fell into the grass. He struck at the box again, but the latch held.

"Here. Let me try," offered Regret, taking the hammer from Papa. He pounded the latch and the hinges several times, then dug his fingers into the lid and pulled up on it. The trunk opened by a slit and fell shut, after exhaling a musty perfume from decades gone by. Regret lifted the lid again, this time wedging the hammer into the crack and prying the lid upward.

Papa stood fidgeting, looking downward in expectation as the crack widened. Trudy, her heart thrashing with excitement, crouched on the ground beside Regret. Then Trudy gasped as the lid fell backward, exposing nothing but water and sediment.

"It's empty!" she cried, glancing up at Regret for an explanation. "There's nothing in it but mud!"

"I told you so," Papa said with a nod. "I told you all. 'Tweren't nothin' but a story."

Regret scooped up the clear water in one hand and let it dribble through his fingers. Below the water was a layer of mud. Cautiously he stirred the muck with his index finger and left clouds of mud where he'd touched the sludge. Then he frowned.

"What's wrong, R.J.?"

"Paper," he whispered.

He dug into the sediment and drew out a fistful of crumbling black mud, like leaves settled on the bottom of a pond. It might have been paper once, but now it disintegrated under his touch. Some of the corners still carried a design, enough of an etching to distinguish what the paper had once represented.

"Money!" Trudy gasped. "There's no gold, just paper money. And lots of it."

Regret dropped the handful of deteriorating paper into the grass. "Lots of it, all right. But it won't do you much good in this condition. The trunk's worth more than the money." He smiled at Trudy and her grandfather. "Maybe we could give it to Jordy and Rooster."

She grinned back. "Would serve them right." Trudy shrugged and stood up. "I never expected to find it. At least now we know what happened to the money the banker was carrying before he was lynched." She inclined her head toward the hanging tree. "They lynched him within sight of where he'd hidden the trunk."

Papa stood up and plowed his hands into his pants pockets. "We sure could've used that money if it'd been an good." He sighed, and Trudy felt the nagging guilt return. Buck Witherspoon wouldn't accept a trunk filled with mud for the next payment on Johnny's debts. Papa would never say aloud that it was her fault the Dugan land would be lost forever, but she knew he thought it.

"There really was buried treasure here," she said, pressing her lips together in resignation. "At least it makes a nice story to tell the grandchildren."

Rising to his feet, Regret shook his head in disbelief. "You still think the story is more important than the gold?"

For a moment, Trudy considered it. Maybe she was losing her land and maybe she'd lost faith in people like Louisa and Jordy, but she still had Papa and Dulcie. And maybe she had Regret James. "I suppose it doesn't matter anymore." Then she mustered the strength for a smile. "Let's go home. I really want that hot bath."

Regret's eyes sparkled in a subtle invitation that seemed to request the pleasure of her company in warmer waters than the well had offered. He motioned for Trudy to move back while he tilted the trunk with his foot to dump out the water and muddy ruin. The water swished over the side of the trunk, streaming into the grass. The muddy paper tumbled over the side and plopped onto the ground. Then something jingled. Something metallic.

Frowning, her green-eyed lover dropped back to his knees. With his bare hands, he burrowed into the thick sludge and drew out a double handful of muddy circles. He selected one circle and rubbed it hard against the leg of his jeans. Regret held up the clean side, catching the flash of sunlight on the mirrored gold surface.

"Well, I'll be damned," Papa said under his breath.

"Is it ... gold?" Trudy studied the coin. Regret quickly scrubbed two more coins against his jeans and handed one to Trudy and the other to Papa.

"Twenty dollars," Papa noted, squinting at his coin. He wiped at the dirt on his forehead and fondled the coin loosely. "Well, girl, I s'pose every little bit helps."

"It's worth more than twenty dollars, Mr. Dugan. A lot more."

Trudy rubbed at a patch of mud on the coin she held. "How much more?"

"Oh," he stated nonchalantly, "about five thousand dollars more."

"What?" Papa almost dropped his coin. The old man's hands started to tremble. He tightened his grip on the gold piece.

Her pulse quickening, Trudy clenched her coin. She dared not drop it in the grass and risk losing it.

Regret looked up at the two of them and laughed, his voice echoing in the darkening woods. "Don't worry. There's plenty more." He raked his fingers through the muck and scooped it up with both hands, letting the coins clink back into the trunk.

Spellbound, Trudy stared at the box. "H-how much more, R.J.?"

"About a hundred thousand dollars' worth, I'd guess."

Trudy sank to the ground. "That's . . . impossible."

"Look," he said, pointing to the coin in Trudy's quivering palm. "It's a very special coin. A 1907 Saint Gaudens Walking Liberty."

"Oh." Trudy ran her finger over the surface of the coin, along the outline of a striking woman on the mirrored gold. "I didn't know you knew anything about coins."

"I don't." He grinned. "No more than I know about *Beowulf* and fine literature. I only know what I've been told, and your sister-in-law told me what it was worth."

"Worth putting me down a well for," she mumbled, bitterness resonating in her voice.

Regret brushed his hand against hers. "Worth a fortune. You could sell it to a coin dealer and have enough money to travel anywhere in the world you could ever want to go."

"I've never cared to travel the world, R.J. All I ever wanted was to stay right here in Cornerstone on my own land."

"But you could do anything you wanted with the money. You and Dulcie would be set for life with that kind of nest egg."

Her gaze flitted over the muddy treasure and then up at Papa. "I could pay off Johnny's debts."

"And have a small fortune left over," noted Regret.

"I wouldn't have to borrow money from you, R.J. You wouldn't have to touch your father's money. We wouldn't lose the land, Papa. Dulcie can grow up running barefoot through the fields just like I did. She can pick blackberries in springtime just like I did. She can eat boiled peanuts grown right here and—" Trudy froze when her eyes met Regret's. For one brief moment, she'd forgotten. She was forever tied to the Dugan lands and the rural community of Cornerstone, Georgia. And Regret James was tied to nothing and no one. Just the sky.

"What's wrong, Trudy?" Regret asked. "Why the tears?" With a dirty thumb, he skimmed a teardrop from her cheek.

"I don't want you to give up flying. You'd be miserable without it." She swallowed the lump in her throat.

"I'd be miserable without you."

"Flying can be dangerous. I'm just scared of losing you, R.J."

"Not nearly as scared as I was of losing you. I love you, Trudy. My place is with you." He wove his fingers through hers. "I've never had a place to settle down and sink my roots into. I've never had a place that meant anything to me. Until now. If I'm going to put down roots, I think this is the best place to do it."

Trudy looked down at their clasped hands, at the hand that had worn Johnny's ring and then at the masculine hand that had never worn a ring. "What if the skies aren't good to you? What if we don't have a future together?"

"We can spend the rest of our lives alone and safe or we can take a chance on loving each other. We have a present together, Trudy. And as for the future, we'll have to find that out together. That is, if you don't mind facing the future with me."

Trudy sniffed back the tears. "I don't mind."

Papa coughed, more for emphasis than for need. "You hang around here much more, boy, and you're gonna have to marry my granddaughter."

Regret winked at Trudy. "That's kinda what I had in mind. That is, if Trudy wouldn't mind having me for a husband."

She sniffed and laid her head against his chest. "I wouldn't mind at all."

Papa coughed again. "Well, you'd better hurry it up, boy. It's gonna be you and my grandbabies out here all by yourselves for all the town to talk about when I marry Clarice and move to her house in town."

"When you *what?*" Trudy stared at her grandfather. She knew he'd asked Clarice to marry him, but she'd expected to find herself and Dulcie living under the reign of a new mistress of the house. "You're moving to Miss Clarice's house?"

"Well, Clarice has got her own place, and I've already given you this here land. I ain't gonna take it back from you just 'cause I'm an old man needin' a little company. This here land is yours. Yours and Dulcie's. You don't need a new stepgrandma to fight with, and you don't need an old man to look after. And I sure would feel better if you had an able-bodied young man around the farm."

Trudy's heart skipped a beat as Papa and Regret eyed each other.

"Boy," he said, extending a hand to Regret, "you take care of my girls."

"You can count on it, sir."

Papa shook Regret's hand and squeezed it. "You know, boy, when I first saw you, I felt it in my bones that you were a man I couldn't trust."

Regret nodded slowly. "Trudy tells me your bones are never wrong."

"Much as I hate to admit it, boy, I think my bones were wrong about you."

Regret smiled broadly, both at Papa and at Trudy. "Well, I'm glad to be the first."

"You ain't the first, boy. My bones have been wrong only one other time."

"Really, Papa?" Trudy had never heard her grandfather admit his judgment could be wrong. He certainly hadn't been wrong about Rooster or Johnny, or even her own father, for that matter. "Who was it, Papa?"

The old man hesitated. Gradually the look of agitation on his face turned to a pleasant memory. "Your grandma. I knew she was trouble from the minute I laid eyes on her. But I loved Gertie for almost fifty years." He turned before Trudy could get a good look at the tears in his eyes, and he headed back toward the tractor.

Trudy rubbed her cheek against Regret's chest, and he kissed her furrowed brow. "I hope you're still in my life in fifty years," she whispered, too low for Papa to hear.

Regret kissed her dirty knuckles and tilted her head. "I will be, Trudy. I will be."

* * * * *

Rugged and lean...and the best-looking,
sweetest-talking men to be found in the
entire Lone Star state!

In July 1994, Silhouette is very proud to bring you
Diana Palmer's first three LONG, TALL TEXANS.
CALHOUN, JUSTIN and TYLER—the three cowboys
who started the legend. Now they're back by popular
demand in one classic volume—and they're ready to
lasso your heart! Beautifully repackaged for this
special event, this collection is sure to be a
longtime keepsake!

"Diana Palmer makes a reader want to find a Texan
of her own to love!"   —*Affaire de Coeur*

**LONG, TALL TEXANS—the first three—
reunited in this special roundup!**

**Available in July,
wherever Silhouette books are sold.**

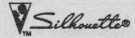

Take 4 bestselling love stories FREE

Plus get a FREE surprise gift!

Don't miss the newest miniseries from
Silhouette Intimate Moments

Southern
Knights

by Marilyn Pappano

A police detective. An FBI agent. A government
prosecutor. Three men for whom friendship and
the law mean everything. Three men for whom
true love has remained elusive—until now. Join
award-winning author Marilyn Pappano as she
brings her **Southern Knights** series to you, starting
in August 1994 with MICHAEL'S GIFT, IM #583.

The visions were back. And detective
Michael Bennett knew well the danger they
prophesied. Yet he couldn't refuse to help
beautiful fugitive Valery Navarre, not after her
image had been branded on his mind—and
his heart.

Then look for Remy's story in December, as
Southern Knights continues, only in...

INTIMATE MOMENTS®
™ *Silhouette*®